'THE LAST SCRAMBLE'

RONALD SCOTT THORN

'THE LAST SCRAMBLE'

SEVERN HOUSE

This title first published in Great Britain 1990 by
SEVERN HOUSE PUBLISHERS LTD of
35 Manor Road, Wallington, Surrey SM6 0BW.

First published in the U.S.A. 1991 by
SEVERN HOUSE PUBLISHERS INC of
271 Madison Avenue, New York, NY 10016

British Library Cataloguing in Publication Data
Thorn, Ronald Scott *1920–*
The last scramble.
I. Title
813.54 [F]

ISBN 0–7278–4116–5

Printed and bound in Great Britain
by Bookcraft (Bath) Ltd.

In memory of my school-friends in Churchill's House at Shrewsbury

Christopher Andreae
John Bone
Norman Bowring
Paul Davies-Cooke
and
Richard Hillary

who were killed serving in the RAF.

And in dedication to

Desmond Edyvean-Walker
George Nelson-Edwards
William Pritchard
John Rhys
Ewen Robertson
and
Philip Whitfield

who also flew, but happily are not all yet ghosts in the sky.

'scramble, v.i & t., & n.
1 . . . (of aircraft) take off;
2 . . . eager struggle or competition. . .'

Concise Oxford Dictionary.

Acknowledgements

I wish to thank all the people who have been kind enough to give me technical details about aircraft construction and recovery, and other information about fighter-planes of the RAF and Luftwaffe used in World War II; and the flying experiences of British and German pilots. I am also indebted to the publishers of numerous books and works on the subject of the Battle of Britain, and flying tactics, the authors of which are too numerous to list. In particular I would like to mention the publications of Francis K. Mason, Len Deighton, Bryan Philpott, Bruce Robertson, Alfred Price, Dizzy Allen, Richard Collier, and Winston G. Ramsay, and Hugh Falkus and the help of the staff at the RAF Museum, Hendon.

For records of prisoners of war, both British and German I am indebted to the work of Matthew Barry Sullivan, and the personal reminiscences of Siegfried Taubenheim. Certain mechanical details I have discussed with Colin Cawsey of British Airways and the comments of James Lazenby, Ivan Avery and Don Everson have been most helpful.

For their efficient secretarial help and research throughout I am grateful to Claire Postles and Angela Smith and my daughter, Vanessa Fergusson; and to my wife Muriel for editorial assistance.

I wish to thank Macmillan & Co for permission to quote from The Last Enemy, and Methuen & Co for the verse quotations from the anthology 'The Terrible Rain' and the respective authors Richard Hillary, Donald Bain, and John Pudney, and Wing-Commander George Nelson-Edwards RAF (Rtd) D.F.C. for reading and commenting on the book. (One of the remaining 'Few'.)

CONTENTS

PART ONE

GHOSTS IN THE SKY

'Shall I live for a ghost?'
'The Last Enemy'
Richard Hillary.

CHAPTER ONE

'All I want, Doc, is a general check-up.' Peeb endeavoured to convey the impression of prudent interest, casual concern. Anxiety he tried to leave out, but the young doctor picked it up.

'Nothing particular you're worried about?'

'No, no. No. . . .'

The shake of the head, like the word, was repeated once too often, belying the sense. Well, it would come out in the end, the real reason for the visit. Brian Bayliss looked across his desk in the sunlit village surgery at the man sitting on the other side of him. Late sixties, stocky, old-fashioned well-trimmed moustache, brisk manner. Scarred face left side, burns, plastic surgery, Brian pulled the trolley towards him, a mobile filing cabinet carrying envelopes and card notes. He checked the name from his secretary's typed appointment list on the desk.

'It's Mr White, isn't it?'

'Peebles-White,' said Peeb, faintly irritated.

Brian found the card under 'W'. As far as the National Health Service was concerned the name was 'M.P. White'.

'I'm afraid you've been filed under "W", said Brian. 'Which probably explains why I haven't had the notes from your last doctor.'

'Didn't go to my last doctor. No need,' said Peeb. 'Is my daughter filed under "W" as well.'

Brian found her card next to the other one.

'Yes.'

'At least that's consistent.'

'Apologies again.'

'It was my daughter who badgered me into coming along,' said Peeb. 'She thought it'd be a good idea if someone, er. . . .'

'Ran the rule over you?'

'Absolutely,' agreed Peeb.

Brian remembered then a dark-haired beauty who'd called to be put on his list some five months ago on the 10th March 1989. She and her father had bought Bluff Cottage at the top of Barrow Lane. Susan Peebles-White. She'd never been into the surgery again, but he'd seen her once or twice on his rounds driving a bright blue Metro. He took her father's envelope and altered the heading to 'Peebles-White, Michael'. He read what he had entered previously. 'Group Captain, RAF (Ret'd), DFC and Bar' and recalled the affectionate pride with which the daughter had given this information. Hero-worship of Daddy. There was a small 'w' signifying 'widower'. That tallied.

'I don't appear to have your date of birth, Group Captain,' he said.

'September the 15th, 1920.'

'Thank you.'

He wrote the date on the card. The man suddenly spoke gruffly.

'I suppose that date doesn't mean much to you . . . to your generation?'

Brian looked up.

'1920?'

'September the 15th.'

'September? . . . the 15th. . . ? The Ides of September?' he tried.

'Battle of Britain Day.'

'Ah . . . yes, of course.'

'All the fuss this year about anniversaries . . . the Froggie's Revolution 1789; outbreak of World War II 1939 . . . but for us the war really started in 1940.' Peeb suddenly looked belligerent. 'Let me tell you, Doc, the really important memorial is next year. September the 15th 1990. That's when we stopped the Hun. Alone. That's when we saved the world.' Peeb was riding his hobby-horse, indulging his life-long fantasies.

'You may be right, but Group Captain. . . .' Brian

interrupted the flow, flicking his eyes at his wrist-watch, 'If I'm going to. . . .'

But there was no stopping Peeb now. He gestured upwards jerkily.

'Quite a lot of it went on in the sky over here . . . over Bishop's Felix – here over the Isle of Sheppey. Did you know that?'

'Yes,' said Brian. 'I've heard this place was in the thick of it. So you're one of "The Few"?'

'Fewer still now. We're almost down to single figures,' said Peeb quietly, failing as always to repress the excitement in his voice at the far away, but still vivid memories. 'I shot a Hun down near here. Messerschmitt BF 109E. My fifth kill actually.' He shook his head sadly. 'My last too. But it was my third that day.' He gazed upwards as if he could see through the roof to the sky. 'Heinkels. Dorniers. Bags of them. Coming across Kent heading for the Thames estuary. And above them, the fighters, dozens of the bastards. . . .'

'Group Captain Peebles-White,' interrupted Brian again wearily.

Peeb stopped talking.

'Quite right,' he said. 'Tell you some other time.'

He still found it hard to realise, though Susan kept reminding him, that it was so long ago. Long before she was born. He looked at the doctor. Before *he* was born too. In his early thirties, he guessed. These kids were only mildly interested. It wasn't right. It had all been for them. Their new world. Their generation's heritage. They should show some respect for their own history. Never mind about Tianenman Square, the Czecks, the Polskies, the magyars and the rest . . .' Peeb tried hard to give the young man an encouraging smile, but it came out as a sour grimace. 'Carry on, Doc,' he said, reaching for some common ground, 'the ball's in your court.'

'When did you retire?' Brian asked.

'Over twenty-five years ago. Compulsory, of course. Never felt fitter. But that's the RAF. Nothing one can do about it. Except resent it.' Peeb smiled again. More successfully this time. For a moment their glances met, then the doctor's slid away unpointedly, purveying, for all his relative youth, professional competence. Neither of them was fooling. Mutual respect was being established.

Brian quickly covered the ground of his patient's medical history. There was nothing of importance except for the war injuries in 1940. The cosmetic result was not bad – Peeb had been one of McIndoe's monkeys at East Grinstead. The scarring was unilateral, which was unusual in a fighter pilot. The unlucky ones had been burnt in their cockpits before they could bail out. But the Group Captain's injuries had not been sustained in his plane.

'After I'd sent my Hun and his Messerschmitt down into the drink, I pressed on back to refuel at Eastchurch. I'd just enough juice to taxi to a standstill when I heard the first crump as two Heinkels came in low from the south-east dropping sticks across the airfield. Couldn't take off again so I jumped down and ran for it. Almost reached the perimeter when a petrol-bowser went up and set me alight. A few bomb splinters hit my head. Don't remember any more. Apparently the blast lobbed me up in the air like a hand-grenade and dropped me in a slit-trench on top of a lot of chaps. Not awfully popular, but they put my flames out. After the raid I was whisked off to hospital.'

'How long were you unconscious?'

'Not long enough,' Peeb smiled. 'Only a couple of days . . . those endless dressings . . . and the smell. . . !'

Brian wanted to know one important fact. Was there any brain damage? He doubted it or the Group Captain would have been invalided out of the RAF before the end of the war. He asked the question obliquely.

'Fractured skull?'

'Fissure. Left parietal, but no brain damage if that's what you're after, Doc. No fits, nothing like that. Damn it. I was passed OK for flying again in less than two years.' Peeb looked away at the corner of the room, where the sight-test chart was hanging. Odd. All the letters were back to front. Very odd. Yes, he'd have to ask the fellow to test his eyes. That might be the best way round it; not telling him exactly what was worrying him; at least the full information about what was worrying him. He appreciated the illogicality of his attitude. Wanting to find out what was wrong, yet not wanting to learn the worst. These modern medics could be pretty alarming.

'Never managed any more combat,' he said. 'Wouldn't let me back on ops, God knows why. So I did a tour as an instructor. After the war, of course, I was given one of the latest supersonic desks to fly.'

Brian wrote down, *No intracranial damage*. He got up and asked the Group Captain to undress behind the screen. Then he went over all the routine tests system by system, collected a urine specimen and dipstick tested it. Normal. Heart, lungs, CNS, normal. Ten pounds overweight but very fit and trim for a man near on seventy. Blood pressure 150/100. Not enough raised for anti-hypertensives, at his age.

'Smoke?'

'Fifteen . . . well, more or less.'

'Cut it down or better cut it out. Drink?'

'Two pints a night. Never more,' Peeb laughed, 'except for the odd glass of claret with a meal.'

'Try not to have both. Get seven pounds off your weight. Thank you, Group Captain, you can get dressed.' Brian went back to his desk and entered the findings in shorthand form on Peeb's card.

The usual publicised advice, thought Peeb.

'Have I passed?' The clipped voice came from behind the screen.

'Oh yes,' said Brian and then added, unable to resist the temptation, 'with flying colours.'

Peeb fastened his trousers and pulled the polo-neck sweater over his head. He was in half a mind to leave it at that. But then what had he come for? This was the time to mention it, or not at all. Besides, Susan would certainly want to know what the doc had said about his problem.

'Do you think, Doc, you ought to . . . er. . . ?' he faltered.

'Get a chest x-ray, blood count, electrocardiogram?' Brian cut in. 'One could, but honestly, it's a lot of unnecessary expense. And I'm against unnecessary investigations. I don't have to tell you that statistically you're right for a coronary. But you look well. You feel well?'

'Yes. . . .'

'Which means in nine nine nine cases out of a thousand, you *are* well.'

Peeb came round from behind the screen, putting on his jacket.

'I was going to ask you, Doc,' he said almost apologetically, 'if you ought to check my eyes?'

So that was it, thought Brian. He knew the reason would surface in the end. All this fussing around and all the man wanted was an eye-test. Obviously he'd been too proud to admit his sight was falling off, like everyone's does in time, and too vain to wear glasses.

'All right,' said Brian, failing to keep the tang of irritation out of his voice. 'Stand over here and look in the mirror.'

Peeb obeyed. He could see the test-type. The letters seemed much smaller, but now they were the right way round. The doctor moved the card disclosing it to be a rotating box-cylinder. Another set of random letters appeared. Peeb turned round and checked the test card. Of course. They were back-to-front making the mirror-images normal in appearance. Brian had observed Peeb's actions.

'Just a simple device for enlarging the size of my surgery,' he said and switched on a light which illuminated the cylinder brightly.

Peeb laughed nervously.

'Clever chaps, these Chinese,' he said.

These old RAF types never lost their old jargon, their old jokes.

'Cover your left eye. Don't press on it. Now read from the top.'

Peeb read all the lines without difficulty except the last one, where he had to make two corrections.

'Now your right eye.'

Peeb repeated the procedure. This time he read the smallest line without a hitch.

'Remarkable', said Brian. 'For your age. There's nothing wrong with your sight for distance.' He put a printed folder into his hand. 'Have a go at that with both eyes. Read out from the smallest print you can focus clearly. Hold the card where you like.'

Peeb pushed the card a little way from him. He tried the very smallest type at the top on the left.

'The place of our retreat . . .' he began.

Brian took the card.

'Remarkable. J1. You don't need any reading-glasses, either.'

Peeb grinned with satisfaction.

'I can also identify the quotation,' he said. '"The place of our retreat was in a little neighbourhood consisting of farmers who tilled their own ground and were equal strangers to opulence or poverty." Oliver Goldsmith. *The Vicar of Wakefield*.'

Brian was genuinely impressed. 'I didn't know that.' He folded the card and put it in his desk drawer. He glanced at Peeb. 'Remarkable,' he repeated for the third time.

'Like most people, Doc,' said Peeb, 'I expect you think flying bods are an illiterate philistine bunch. Especially the old ones.'

'Well, I didn't really. . . .'

'Quite wrong', said Peeb. 'It's the sky, you know. The clouds. Make anyone feel he can write poetry.' He glanced through the window. He could tell by the light there was a spectacular sunset building up, over London. 'A lot of pilots wrote verse,' he said. 'At the time of course.'

'With your exceptionally good vision,' asked Brian, 'why did you ask me to test your sight, Group Captain?'

'I didn't', said Peeb. 'I asked you to check my eyes.'

Brian absorbed the reply and then said, 'What do you notice wrong?'

'Well, Doc', began Peeb. 'Since we came to Bishop's Felix . . . the last five months or so . . . I don't know if it's anything to worry about or not. . . .'

'You're here,' said Brian.

'Yes . . . well . . . it's difficult to describe exactly. . . .'

'Try.'

'I keep seeing something moving . . .' Peeb stopped. It sounded ridiculous.

'Where,' Brian nudged him gently.

'Across the sky.'

'Always the sky?'

Peeb considered the question carefully.

'Once it was over the water. Along the coast towards Whitstable.'

'Ever seen it when you're inside?'

'Only through the window.'

Brian smiled. The diagnosis was a near certainty.

'In other words it's something moving across your field of vision – when you're looking at a bright background, like the sky?'

'Yes . . . that could be so.'

But the doc was jumping to conclusions. Peeb had mostly seen the thing at night.

'What size is the object . . . roughly?'

'Small. A bit variable.'

'Shape?'

'Irregular.'

'Always from left to right or right to left?'

'Either.'

'Which eye do you see it with?'

'Both.'

'What . . . ! Haven't you tested it by covering one eye?'

'No.'

Brian relaxed again.

'Look at that wall.' He shone his desk-light on it. 'Can you see your shape there?'

'No.'

Brian switched off the light a little irritably.

'But when you do see it Group Captain it moves as you follow it with your eyes.'

'It moves all right – bloody fast sometimes.'

'You mean it's like a flash?'

'No it's not like a flash.'

Brian began to eliminate remote possibilities as a clinical precaution.

'Any migraine?'
'No.'
'In the family?'
'No.'
'No headaches?'
'No.'

Brian took out his ophthalmoscope, drew the curtains and scanned the retina of each of Peeb's eyes. They were quite normal. Discs clear. Vessels OK. No exudates. He tested the peripheral fields with a large white-headed pin. The near-perfect acuity and absence of other symptoms ruled out a number of conditions such as a temporal lobe tumour. He could hear the dry voice of his first clinical teacher, 'The commonest diseases occur most frequently'. It was a floater of course. And you rarely saw one with an ophthalmoscope unless it was huge. Needed a slit-lamp which as a GP he didn't possess. He drew back the curtains.

'Simple floater,' he said. 'Small opacity in the vitreous of the eye – moves about inside the eye, as you move the eye. Quite harmless. Most people collect one at some time or another. You have to learn to look 'through' it, so to speak. It's always there, but you may only see it in certain conditions. Or if you're worried about it. Then you see it more often. No treatment. No need for treatment. No need to worry. Forget about it.'

'I'll try', said Peeb.

He didn't look as convinced as Brian would have wished. Then the Group Captain said something which destroyed Brian's facile, soothing, diagnosis.

'The trouble is this . . . floater thing . . . looks exactly like a plane . . . a Messerschmitt . . . a BF 109E actually.'

'I see,' said Brian, after a pause. They were in different country altogether now. Delusional psychosis? Depressive episode? Yet the man's mood wasn't right. He tried a smile, and spoke slowly.

'But there isn't any Messerschmitt, is there, Group Captain?'

'Shouldn't think so', Peeb laughed uneasily. 'I expect I'm just going a bit bonkers, eh Doc?'

'Not at all,' said Brian. Sometimes patients had startling insight. Or he, the doctor, was on the wrong tack. He'd have to keep a watch on developments. In the meantime he took out an EC10 prescription form and wrote a script for fifty, two-milligram Diazepam tablets. 'Take one of these night and morning. See how you get on.'

Peeb looked at the prescription.

'What's this stuff, Doc?'

'Simple tranquilliser. Tamps down tension, fatigue. That's all that's wrong.' Brian was trying to convince himself as much as the patient. 'Call in again sometime. Any time. Tell my receptionist I said you could skip the queue.'

'OK.' Peeb folded the script and put it in his pocket. He hardly felt reassured, but he had no wish to prolong the interview. He stood up and gave a somewhat formal handshake. 'I'm much obliged. Evening, Doc.'

'Good evening, Group Captain.'

Peeb went out of the surgery, past the receptionist at the desk in the little waiting-room, which had filled up appreciably. Outside, he got into the old Lagonda, but sat a moment before he primed the Kigas. It was obvious what the doctor thought. Another neurotic wreck. He must see a lot of them. This time a retired Spitfire pilot who kept thinking he saw a Messerschmitt. Yet he hadn't been quite fair. He hadn't told the fellow everything. Such as that whenever he saw the bloody thing he heard it at the same time. On two occasions he'd just heard it alone. He looked at his watch.

'Christ', he muttered, 'They're open.'

He still hadn't got used to the new licensing laws. He touched the starter. The engine fired and died. The second time it let out a deep-throated roar. The village of Bishop's Felix had learnt to associate the sound with the regular early nocturnal visit of the Group Captain to the Three Crowns.

CHAPTER TWO

Susan Peebles-White drove along the motorway out of Canterbury. The Metro was a present from her father for obtaining her Articles as a solicitor. Her first job was with a law firm in the town. But they only gave her conveyancing, with which she was heartily bored; dull legal routines of the purchase and sale of property. She moved into the fast lane, overtaking the stream of local commuters.

Susan had aspirations to becoming a family lawyer. She was still young – in her thirties, but she looked years younger. She now felt confident enough to take on, single-handed, any problem of litigation as well as the more pedestrian matters of wills and torts and powers of attorney. She pulled down her sun-visor. Rays of gold and red burst out from behind a dramatic bank of cumulus over London. She left the motorway at Junction 5 and turned off to the north towards Sittingbourne. The light sparkled off the water of the Swale which separated the north coast of Kent from the Isle of Sheppey. Susan crossed the Kingsferry bridge to the island. Past the big filling-station Susan lost most of the traffic. She turned off to Eastchurch, where the wartime airfield used to be, and then followed a road through flat, fertile fields until she reached Bishop's Felix.

She opened the car window. There was a September bite in the air and the unmistakable smell of the sea or, as some said unkindly, the unmistakable stink of the Thames estuary mud, tickled her nose.

The village had avoided most of the ugly architecture of the nineteenth and twentieth centuries. Both sides of the high street had numerous white clapboard houses which gave a pleasing unity. The shops were not aggressively painted or signed; a butcher, a mini-supermarket, a tobacconist, confectioner and newsagent, a hair salon, a hi-fi and TV emporium, a chemist, a post-office and an antique shop. At the far end dividing the fork in the road was the church, the vicarage, the village hall and the war memorial. The old doctor's house and surgery were out of sight beyond the vicarage to the right. A property developer had converted the village school to a private dwelling, now occupied by a Yuppy from the city. The children went to the Eastchurch Comprehensive.

Her father's maroon Lagonda was conspicuous as usual at that time of day in the Three Crowns car park. Occasionally Susan would stop and go into the saloon bar and have a half with him, but more often, as today, she drove past and took the left-hand lane which twisted for perhaps half a mile rising all the time before it came out onto a grassy ridge of common land. Bluff Cottage, their new home, was barely a hundred feet above the village, but that was enough, in the billiard-table landscape, to command an impressive round-the-clock view over the marshes, to the Swale, the North Downs, the wide estuary of the Thames across to the distant Essex coast, and on out to the North Sea.

Susan parked the Metro on her side of the barn converted to a garage. As she crossed the cobbled forecourt to the cottage she flinched instinctively as two RAF Tornados on a training flight from Detling tore across the sky, it seemed only a few feet above the roof. The scream of the jets and the following thunder enveloped her. Almost before she had registered their appearance, they were gone. There were planes about in the sky above Bishop's Felix most of the time. Susan was mildly irritated by the noise.

Her father by contrast exulted in the whole vociferous display of power. He kept a pair of binoculars slung around his neck, when pottering in the garden or round the cottage, so that he could follow the planes. He would often shout to her, if she were at home, to come out and look, but invariably she could not reach a vantage point in time. Then he would shake his head and issue a sad accusation, 'You missed them again, Susan. Too slow, too slow, girl. That's how battles are lost.'

She had come to accept her father's obsessions and

prejudices. Even now, years after his retirement, a trip round the world, two dull directorships and late last year the loss of his wife, her mother. But planes and the men who flew them occupied his waking thoughts – and Susan suspected his sleeping thoughts too. Her mother had said to her just before she died, 'Your father's head is still in the clouds. Always has been. Look after him, Susan. Or he'll walk into something.'

Susan found the task full of problems and pitfalls. More recently she had detected a change in him, difficult to describe, which added to her anxiety. She hoped that today, he had actually kept the appointment he had made with the doctor, and not dodged the visit again, as he had characteristically done twice before.

She began to prepare the food she had bought for their evening meal. She worked with concentration, refusing to feel sorry for herself. She recognised she was in the classic unenviable situation of the only daughter of an ageing widowed father and still not married. Daddy was an angel but difficult and pigheaded, though transparently warm-hearted. She was aware too of his rapidly acquired local reputation, eccentric, with a bee in his bonnet about Germany and the last war and the relative merits of Spits and Hurricanes, both of which he had flown. Most of the locals now knew the stories of the Huns he had shot down. With minimal encouragement he would bore any willing listener in the bar at the Three Crowns. But then, he had paid for the privilege. Surely, she thought protectively, one of 'The Few' was entitled to some reminiscence in depth, if that was a way to keep his wings in trim.

'. . . So we dropped into line astern – one after another – nine Spits, beautiful sight – and came down from two o'clock high out of the sun onto these ruddy bandits heading for London – a hundred and fifty Heinkels at least – yes thanks old boy I'll have the other half – coming in over the coast near Dungeness. . . .'

Peeb was in full combat order at the end of the bar, using his hands to demonstrate the descent of the aircraft, his eyes bright and his voice filled with youthful enthusiasm. But it was also rough and hoarse from all the years of attrition of his vocal cords by gallons of gin and scotch and beer, and over a half a million cigarettes.

'Thanks, old boy. Cheers.' Peeb took a pull from the full pewter tankard. The tankard was his own, kept, in a near-forgotten tradition, on its own hook under the bar-ceiling, where he had persuaded the new landlord, Bill Mitcham, to hang it. It looked the anachronism it was, amongst all the glass tankards and the lighted refrigerated shelves below. The bar had been twice modernised since Peeb had frequented it during that summer of 1940. Then the beer was drawn up by wooden 'pulls' from wooden barrels stooped along the thralls in the cellar below. The ale was flat and clear, a potent brew with the full flavour of hops picked in the Kentish fields nearby; Mild and Bitter and Brown. Now the metal barrels gushed forth fizzy chemical-tasting ice-cold beverages from illuminated square boxes housing chromium taps; Keg and Special and Directors'. The pub was different in other ways from Peeb's heyday. One-armed bandits, instead of darts or shove-halfpenny. The present generation demanded the high decibel din of taped rock and pop to drown its talk. No longer came the glissandos of Glenn Miller from the bakelite radio on the counter. Jeans and leather jackets and brightly-coloured hair abounded, arctic boots and bizarre make-up, studded belts and strange insignia, the affluent freedom that Peeb's generation had unwittingly fought for. The present throng in the Three Crowns contrasted strangely with Peeb's memory of pale blue uniforms, and young faces, hoping the night's beer would not run out and the next day's scramble would not be the last. Wide as the generation gap was, Peeb was tolerated as a mildly interesting relic.

'Go on, Group,' urged a bearded lad of about eighteen. He had straight blond hair, and wore a T-shirt with the legend Michael Jackson across it. The lad's hand was round the waist of a vacant-looking girl who was chewing gum presumably to enhance the taste of her drink. The boy winked at her and said to Peeb, 'How many Krauts did you shoot down that day, then?'

Peeb put his tankard slowly down on the bar-top and lightly touched his moustache with the back of his index finger. What a slovenly-looking pair they were. And what the hell was he doing talking to them? He despised himself for it, but felt an irresistible compulsion to repeat the story of the most glorious and satisfying moments of his life. It didn't really matter to whom he told it. He lit a cigarette.

'We didn't call the Germans Krauts,' he said brusquely. 'We referred to them as "Huns". The Americans called them Krauts. Civilians called them Jerries. The French referred to them as Boches. Do you know any French or German?' he asked the young man.

'What me? No. What for?'

It was an unanswerable question. Peeb drank from his tankard taking the level down to the halfway mark.

'Go on. Tell us then. How many Huns did you get?' the boy persisted.

'Three,' said Peeb.

'I told you, Sal, didn't I?' he addressed the girl. 'Group shot down three planes in one day.' Suddenly his self-protective cheekiness dropped away and his manner changed to one of respectful enquiry. 'Did you get a medal, Group?'

It was irresistible. 'Er . . . yes, old boy,' Peeb replied. 'They gave me a gong or two.'

Sal giggled. 'What's a gong?'

'A medal, stupid.'

'I bet you'll never get a medal, Reg,' she retorted.

'I'll never get the chance, will I?' said Reg.

'I wouldn't be too sure,' replied Peeb. 'There are still plenty of Jerries about, West Jerries, East Jerries, They're still all Huns. Mark my words, as things are going there'll soon be a fourth Reich. Then, of course, there are all the Bolshies.'

'The what?'

'Russkies.' Peeb surveyed Reg sternly. 'In spite of all this glasnost nonsense, the Russkies and their satellites may give you a jolly opportunity, yet.' He smiled at the girl. She wasn't so bad really. Just the product of all this comprehensive bullshit. 'Can I freshen up your . . . sherry isn't it?' Peeb asked the girl with a charm he had never lost.

'I'm OK thanks,' she smiled. 'Go on, tell us what happened.'

'I'm not boring you, am I?'

'No,' she said. 'No. I haven't heard it, have I Reg?'

'No,' said Reg.

Peeb's voice dropped back into its discursive self-deprecatory tone, and the legend rolled out.

'We went down through the Heinkels like a knife through butter – broke up the whole formation. As the first one came into my gunsight, I put the button on "fire", closed to two-fifty yards, applied full deflection and gave a five-second burst. One engine exploded, the plane went into a steep dive, screaming down out of sight, black smoke streaming up from her. Bv then the whole sky was seething with aircraft. Vapour-trails, tracer bullets, smoke. I kicked the rudder over, put on full throttle and pulled the stick back, and shot up towards the Messerschmitts who were covering the bombers from above. As I levelled out, I looked into my mirror to make sure there was no-one on my tail. There was, a 109. He saw me and fired. I jinked about and slid away but several holes appeared in the old port-wing. We passed each other like a flash and there was another of the bastards coming straight at me on collision course. I waited, perhaps two seconds – he was doing the same – as we closed up – then I gave a three-second squirt straight into his yellow spinner. Something – the prop or the hood – flew off his machine. Glycol and oil streamed out. He turned on his back as I shot over him – about ten feet between us. He started to spin at first slowly and then like a top, and disappeared away down towards the earth.'

Peeb took a long pull at his beer. The conversation had stopped. It was the moment he always loved. Just sufficient pause – like the hold-back before you pushed the gun-button – making the whole skin tingle. His hand squeezed the tankard handle as he put it firmly on the bar-top. As he went on, he spoke quietly, adding to the tension which he had created around him. Bill Mitcham turned down the musak. Peeb's little shows were all good for business.

'Suddenly the battle seemed to have gone away and I was

alone in the sky. Blue . . . pale blue . . . with some distant vapour-trails at thirty-thousand feet. I checked the fuel gauge. I had just enough to get home to base at Hornchurch, the other side of the Thames. But the tracers at the end of my last burst told me I had perhaps a two-second shot left. I'd bagged two – a Heinkel and a Messerschmitt – it was no time now to seek out a third victim – mustn't be greedy. I turned north-west when I spied a BF 109 in my mirror. I heard the cannon shells whip over my head. I side-slipped, put on full throttle and shot upwards. Something thumped into the rear of the fuselage, but all the controls seemed to work. I made a tight turn and came back on the reciprocal. In response the Hun made off to the south. We were over the estuary but I was above him by then. I put the Spit into a dive, and came up under him. At a hundred and fifty yards I aimed and pressed the button. The last burst was barely a second but there were enough tracers to set things alight. The plane whipped over and went streaking away in flames down towards the water. It must have happened practically over this very pub. I just made it to the satellite field at Eastchurch.'

Peeb put out his cigarette. 'And that was the last plane I shot down.'

After a short pause, the girl asked, 'And the last person you killed?'

Peeb looked her in the eyes and smiled. 'Yes,' he said, 'As far as I know.'

'Didn't you fight any more, then?' Reg followed up the answer.

'No.'

'Did you crash. . . ? When you got back. . . ?' Sally made a gesture with her hand, pointing to the scarred side of his face.

Peeb drained his pint and smiled at her again.

'No,' he said.

'But. . . ?'

Peeb patted her playfully on the cheek. 'That's another story, old girl.' He turned round and put the precise money he owed for the drinks on the counter. 'Goodnight, Bill,' he said to the publican.

'Goodnight, Group,' replied Bill Mitcham. 'See you tomorrow.'

Peeb turned at the door and waved. 'Sure as hell old boy,' he said as he had said on thousands of occasions in hundreds of bars. Bill turned up the musak again. The show was over. Peeb went out and got into the Lagonda. After a few splutters, it throbbed into life.

Susan heard her father drive into the barn, precisely on time within a minute of half-seven. She put the steaks in the microwave. As Peeb came in through the front door, the bracket clock in the hall struck its single silvery note. She smiled at his thing about time, and remembered some of the maxims he had instilled into her upbringing. His familiar voice called from the hall the voice that used to make her heart jump with the promise of exciting expeditions on childhood Saturday afternoons.

'Hello, Susan. It's me.'

'Daddy. . . .'

He entered the kitchen, hugged her, and kissed her hard on the cheek.

'Not late am I?'

'That'll be the day.'

'Good show. What's for tiffin?'

'*Filet mignon a la* Fran*caise*,' she said.

'Ah. You mean steak, underdone, British style.'

She laughed at his xenophobia, which in fact was more a pose than a conviction.

'Well, it's definitely French dressing on the salad.'

'*Magnifique*,' said Peëb. He opened a door and disappeared down some steps into the cellar, returning with a half-bottle of St. Emilion. Nothing special but chateau-bottled and a tolerable year. He uncorked it, poured half a glass and swallowed some wine. She watched his ritual expression and the sage nod of his head. He half filled the glass again and began nosing around behind her as she stood at the stove.

'No spuds?' he enquired.

'No. You're chubby enough as it is.'

'Only by a few pounds according to the doc.'

'You did actually go then?'

'Of course. Nice young fellow. Good looking.'

'That's what I thought.'

Peeb raised his eyebrows in mock surprise.

'Oh? When have you been. . . ?'

'I've seen him about.'

'Ah-ha.'

'And what does that mean?'

'It means "Ah-ha". Never thought of a doctor in the family. Could be useful.'

'Really, Daddy,' said Susan. 'How many conclusions can you jump to at the same time? Now do sit down.'

'Yes ma'am,' said Peeb, smiling.

He poured her a glass of wine. Susan served the steaks and put the salad-bowl between them.

There was silence for a second and then Peeb pronounced on the steak.

'Bang on,' he said.

'*A point*,' replied Susan.

They didn't speak for a time. Peeb watched his daughter covertly. Half-closing his eyes he could see her mother when she was the same age and they were stationed in Germany after the war. It was not so much the eyes and mouth which had been inherited, but the set of the head on the long neck, the precise elegant movement of the hands. He missed Barbara. God he missed her more than he ever thought he could. Peeb swallowed some claret and jerked himself out of a temporary cloud of melancholy.

'Good day at the office, darling?' said Peeb, imitating a wifely falsetto.

'Don't be ridiculous,' Susan retorted in a rather better contrived stentorian tone.

She knew the perverse streak in her father's nature – knew the same one in her own – which would only let him elaborate on his visit to the doctor in his own good time. She was anxious in an unwarranted way about his health – perhaps because her mother had seemed robustly well until there were tell-tale signs of illness which they all seemed to pretend weren't there. Then last year she was dead from a carcinoma of the uterus. She didn't want the same experience with her father. She wanted to ask him direct the simple questions, 'What did the doctor say? Did he find anything wrong?' But she remained patient listening to her father's day, the day of a retired man, a man who had not even now, touching seventy, come to terms with that status, a superannuated man, who had never found the exhausting satisfaction of vigorous inactivity.

She learnt that the two front shock-absorbers on the Lagonda needed replacing and the brakes on one wheel were binding badly. There was also a pin-hole leak in the radiator which Peeb had temporarily stopped with eccentric expediency by emptying a packet of greenpea soup powder into the water circulation. 'When she gets warmed up, the smell of a meal being cooked wafting back from the bonnet jollies up the old gastric juices no end!' He'd cleared ten more yards of the back coppice where an assorted root crop would eventually grow. He'd read the *Telegraph* eschewing her *Guardian*, but not done the crossword, had a snooze and at long last written a letter to his younger married sister, who'd settled in Edmonton, Alberta with a Professor of Social Ecology, whatever that was.

'Quite a constructive day,' commented Susan.

'Financially unrewarding,' said Peeb. 'Not unenjoyable however.' He drained his glass. She took the used plates away and brought back the fruit bowl.

'I'm sorry I didn't get any fresh cheese,' she said.

Peeb put his hand across the table-cloth and closed it over Susan's.

'Don't apologise for anything like that – ever. I'm very well looked after.'

'Of course you are.' She didn't draw her hand away. 'I like looking after everything here far more than doing a Search on some dreary property.'

'Well, give it up, darling,' said Peeb magnanimously.

She smiled affectionately knowing her income was a useful part of their joint budget. His pension had just not kept up with inflation.

'I shan't do that, but I shan't stay with Mortimer, Mortimer and Spink indefinitely, that's for sure.'

'What *would* you like to do, Susan?'

She looked at him seriously.

'My own legal practice. Marriage. Children. Nothing very original I'm afraid.'

'Unless it's in the reverse order,' he observed.

Peeb took his hand from hers, and finished the claret.

'Go in the other room, Daddy. I'll bring the coffee in there.'

'Fine,' he said. He rose and took his glass to the draining board. 'Damn good dinner.' He pecked her on the cheek. 'As always.'

'Come again, sir,' she smiled.

In the living-room he sat in his comfortable old armchair, brought from the old house. He turned to take in the view through the sliding double-glazed windows he'd put into the cottage. They were half-open. He lit a cigarette, inhaled and gazed through the open windows at the Naples-yellow glow on the water of the estuary over five miles away. Some house-martins dived and swooped round the outbuildings to his left. A copper beech tree stood black and inpenetrable to the other side. It was a scene of peace and gentle solitude.

Then he saw it. The small black shape to the extreme right of his visual field. The doc's floater; the thing he didn't have to worry about. He flicked his eyes to the left and back again. It was larger now and right in the centre of his gaze. He blinked hard and looked again. It was like a little T-shaped black shadow moving fast above the water of the estuary, he estimated no more than a hundred and fifty feet. Suddenly it appeared to be heading inland. And all this was inside his own eye? Bloody hell! As the distance closed up, there was no mistaking what it was. Already he could make out the bulges of the ducted radiators under the wings on each side of the fuselage. Further back the struts supporting the tail-unit were dark against the evening light.

The sound caught up with the image then. Instinctively Peeb braced himself sinking back deeper into his chair. He threw his cigarette away and brought his clenched hands together in front of him as he watched the familiar silhouette diving straight at him. He flinched as if cannon shells were zipping past him through the living-room. The plane banked slightly and waggled its wings over the beech tree. He heard the crackle of the Daimler Benz engine. With a roar it was gone over the roof of the house. For a second Peeb froze, sweat making his face shine in the dim light. Then he was on his feet yelling 'Susan! . . . Susan . . . Susan!'

Peeb shot out through the open windows into the garden and forecourt. He spun round a couple of times, trying to locate the fading sound and orientate his search over the western sky where the plane must have gone. He picked it up banking round and heading back towards the estuary.

'There!' he shouted. 'There!'

'Daddy, what's wrong? What's the matter?'

Susan came hurrying out through the front door.

'Look girl, look!' Peeb grabbed her arm and pointed vehemently with his finger. 'Can't you see it?'

'See what?'

'A bleeding Messerschmitt 109 for Christ's sake! Look. There it goes. . . .'

Susan followed the direction he was pointing and as she did so, Peeb saw the plane become obscured behind a low ridge of pine trees a couple of miles to the north-west.

'I can't see anything, Daddy,' she said quietly.

'Well, didn't you hear it. . . ?' he shouted.

'No . . . but. . . .'

'But what. . . ?'

'I had the dishwasher on in the kitchen, and. . . .

Peeb's hands dropped to his side. He looked shrunken, bewildered. Susan took his arm gently.

'Come in, Daddy. Come inside.'

'Oh, my God,' said Peeb and allowed himself to be led back into the house.

CHAPTER THREE

The church at Bishop's Felix, where Thomas-a-Beckett is said to have stopped to give a dispensation on his way to Canterbury, was a mixture of styles: Saxon, Norman, Early English. It had a tower without a spire, an eccentrically placed clock, and eight bells which were seldom all rung. Beside the church was an eighteenth-century vicarage in mellowed brick. A short drive ran up between two handsome cedars to a porticoed front door. The scene was the essence of that Britain for which the Battle had been fought.

The vicar came out of the house with the doctor. John Siddons, like many young Church of England clergymen was feebly left-wing. He had just learned that his wife had contracted a right-wing disease.

'On the contrary,' Brian Bayliss demolished the assumption, 'gout affects all classes.' He flung his medical bag into the back of the Mini and got in the driving-seat. 'Get your wife to take the Naprosen for three days – that should kill the attack,' he said and touched the starter.

'Thank you,' replied the clergyman.

Brian accelerated down the drive and pulled up at the gate to let some rucksacked cyclists go by. While waiting, he noticed Susan come out of the mini-market on the opposite side of the street. She was wearing narrow yellow trousers and a matching sweater. She shook her head in the light morning breeze. Her hair swung and settled in shape like a TV shampoo advertisement. She walked away with short steps, each buttock alternately tightening the material of her pants. Brian drove across the road and drew up beside her.

'Miss Peebles-White, isn't it?' he smiled.

Susan stopped and peered at him.

'Doctor Bayliss,' she said. 'Good morning.'

'I wondered if I could give you a lift? I'm going right past your cottage,' he lied.

'Thank you, but being stuck in an office most of the week, the idea is that Saturday morning shopping on foot will give me some exercise.'

'Very commendable,' he said. 'But you shouldn't be lugging a loaded carrier-bag like that. Two bags but not one. Distorts the cervical spine you know.'

'Thanks, Doctor. I'll remember next time.'

She turned and took the left-hand fork, past the church. He inched the car up beside her again.

'Much healthier to dump the bag in the car. Then I'll drive slowly while you jog along beside me,' he proposed.

'Or why don't *I* drive the car, and *you* jog along? For *your* health, Doctor Bayliss.'

'I would gladly,' he grinned, 'but I've got terrible corns, hammer-toes and bunions, to say nothing of a calcaneal spur and metatarsalgia.'

'No Athlete's Foot?' asked Susan.

'Only get that in the Spring,' he confessed.

She laughed, so he opened the door, took her shopping bag and placed it on the back seat. As she got in beside him Susan was acutely aware of his slender fingers, firm and delicate on the steering-wheel. Brian drove very, very slowly.

'I assume you're not on an emergency call, Doctor?' Susan remarked.

He stopped the car and switched off the engine.

'No,' he said. 'Something more important.'

'Professionally, that's difficult to imagine,' she said.

'But not socially.' He held her gaze.

'Would you care to have dinner with me?'

'Yes,' she said.

The immediate directness of her reply nonplussed him.

'Good,' he managed and switched on the engine.

'Where?' asked Susan.

He switched the engine off again.

'We could have a bite at a little place I know in Canterbury. It's quite good food and you can dance. Do you know Peter & Paul's?'

'It's only five minutes' walk from my office.'

'Good,' he repeated. 'That's all settled then.'

His hand reached for the ignition key.

'Except for the time?'

'Oh yes. Well . . . You're coming to see me on Tuesday evening, aren't you?'

'Professionally. About my father.' Her expression clouded perceptibly.

'Then afterwards we could. . . ?'

'I'm very worried,' she said. 'Could . . . could you spare a few moments *now*, Doctor Bayliss? Daddy came to see you at the surgery a few days ago. . . ?'

'That's right.'

'. . . And you found nothing wrong with him?'

'That's what he told you?'

'Eventually.' She gazed into Brian's eyes unflinchingly. 'But it's not true is it?'

'Yes . . . basically,' said Brian. 'He's a bit overweight. Seven to ten pounds off and his BP would drop to normal. He should stop smoking, and cut down on the booze. Then I'd pass him for first-class life insurance.'

'What about this thing he sees?'

'A "floater". Absolutely harmless and unimportant. That's what he's seeing.'

'And hearing it too?'

'He didn't tell me that,' said Brian.

'Does that change your diagnosis?' asked Susan.

Brian noticed that her eyes, without losing anything of their size, could appear quite coldly analytical. A little frightening. But exciting at the same time.

'It doesn't change it,' he replied, 'in a way it confirms it. Your father is building an auditory neurotic symptom – overlaying we call it – on a small organic visual defect. He didn't mention hearing anything when he saw me but he laughingly suggested that the shape he sees in his eye looked like a little Messerschmitt.

'Well two nights ago,' Susan began 'that little Messerschmitt in his eye, according to my father, flew at the rooftop over our cottage and sent him into a state of total agitation.

I've never seen him like it before.'

'I'm sorry to hear that,' said Brian. 'It sounds as though he's going to need some help.'

'What sort of help?'

'Psychiatric.'

'You'll never get him to see a shrink. Daddy'd shoot him down in flames at fifty yards.'

'I know a really sensible one – no Freudian poppycock – a practical, pragmatic doctor – he taught me at Barts. Peter Fergusson. One visit to Harley Street might do the whole trick.'

Susan shook her head.

'Not a hope.'

'He'll have to talk to someone.'

Susan paused, weighing up the impression Doctor Bayliss made on her, trying to keep it impersonal. She had checked his qualifications in the Medical Directory in the Public Library in Canterbury. He had much more in the way of post-graduate qualifications than most GP's including an M.R.C. Psych. Apart from his physical attraction – which in the context was irrelevant – he dispensed an air, not only of competence, but compassionate concern.

'Can't you . . . handle my father, yourself?' she asked.

Brian registered the compliment with an inner glow. Unprofessionally, he wondered how long it would be before he actually kissed her lips which formed such a wide generous mouth.

'I'll try,' he said. 'If that's what you want. And what he wants'.

'If he's to cooperate it's all-important that Daddy likes a person. And he likes you.'

'Oh. . . ?' said Brian.

'He's already referred to you as "My quack,"' she smiled.

'I'll accept that,' laughed Brian.

'He's afraid. Ought I to be afraid too?'

'Of what?'

'That he's got something . . .' she steadied her voice. 'Something malignant somewhere. It's not yet a year since my mother died of cancer.'

Brian gave her hand a brief reassuring pressure.

'There's nothing whatever of that sort. He's a retired fighter pilot who's started seeing and hearing enemy planes. There are only three answers. *One*, he *is* seeing and hearing enemy planes. Impossible. Two, he is suffering from delusions . . . hallucinations if you like. Out there in the outside world, he sees and believes there is something which does not exist. *Thirdly*, there *is* something out there in the outside world, which he sees and hears, but he misinterprets. Put another way, certain objects give him an illusion of something else.'

With stunning impact the sound of a jet fighter aircraft in low level flight swept over them. They watched the plane, already a mile away, streaking to the north with a fuzz of exhaust smoke.

'Like imagining that that was a Messerschmitt and not a Lightning,' finished Brian.

'Tornado,' corrected Susan. 'Two Turbo-Union RB 199 engines.'

Brian bestowed on her a long look of appraisal.

'I should be surprised if you had any illusions about anything.'

Brian started the engine and they continued up the lane.

'Stop before you get to the cottage,' Susan warned. 'I don't want to alert Daddy about any collusion between us. I'll get you together fairly soon.'

He pulled up a hundred yards short of the building. Susan got out, picked up her shopping-bag and shut the door.

'Thanks for the lift, Doctor. I'll meet you at Peter and Paul's at seven-thirty on Tuesday, OK?'

'OK.'

She walked away without looking round. She heard him reverse and go back the way he had come. She smiled. So much for his earlier statement that he was going past the cottage.

Through the open barn doors she saw Peeb's feet protruding from under the jacked-up Lagonda as he worked on something underneath the chassis. He was whistling contentedly.

To make up a convivial number for their annual reunion dinner, Peeb's squadron, No. 063 joined forces with 54, 65 and 74, all Spitfire squadrons from the Sector Airfield at Hornchurch, and 613, a Hurricane squadron from Kenley. From year to year, the date and venue varied, but the function was always in early September, and comfortably before the Battle of Britain air displays opened to the public at various RAF airfields around the country. In 1989, Peeb's dinner was held in the Members' Dining-room of the House of Commons, because ex-Squadron Leader Billy Battley, MP for Nutley North East had invited his old flying chums and some younger ones to share the view of the Thames and Westminster Bridge.

'Do you want me to tie your tie, Daddy?' Susan called upstairs.

Peeb pulled tight the black bow in front of the mirror. Susan's voice was identical to her mother's. For a second he let himself remember the same night a year ago in the house in Chelsea and the same question. It was almost Barbara's last day there. And she knew, and he knew and still he went to the dinner. She had insisted. And she had waved goodbye with the same smile she had used so confidently, all through the war and the years after. So now he gave the same answer to Susan.

'No thanks, darling,' he called. 'Always could do this for myself.'

Peeb set the tie straight and put on his dinner-jacket. He clipped his medal ribbon-strip to his left breast pocket and trotted down the stairs. Susan gave him an approving check-over.

'Now please stop drinking at *least* four hours before you leave for home. Promise?'

'Promise.'

'And drive carefully. Especially as it's my car,' she smiled.

'Very kind of you to lend it to me, sweetie. I've got two more day's work on the Lag. All the shocks need doing.' He kissed her on the cheek. 'Bye, Susan. And for heaven's sake don't wait up for me.'

''Bye, Daddy,' she said. 'Enjoy yourself.' She watched him back the Metro out of the barn and tear away down towards the village. 'And please, please come back safely,' she whispered to herself, and shut the cottage door.

Peeb was stopped at the entrance to the car-park of the House of Commons. Peeb's invitation card and driving licence were taken, studied and returned to him. There were two policemen. They asked him to get out. One searched the interior and under the bonnet while the other inspected the chassis and passed a reflector under the vehicle and looked in the boot. Amongst other things they found a pair of women's tennis shoes, size four, a gaudy towel and a bikini rolled up inside it, and a lipstick case.

'Is this your car, sir?' the sergeant asked.

'No, it's my daughter's,' said Peeb.

The sergeant closed the boot. He pointed towards the main archway.

'Would you mind parking over there, sir, in the right-hand corner? Then go through the arch, fifty yards, and up the steps on your right.'

Peeb got in the car and started the engine.

When he stopped inside the entrance to the dining-room he could see and hear that the bar-table at the other end was being heavily patronised. He listened to the official announcement of his arrival 'Group-Captain Michael Peebles-White, D.F.C. and Bar, Number 063 Squadron'. A chorus of cheers rose up, with welcoming cries of 'Good old, Peeb'. Peeb raised his hand in acknowledgement and walked between the set tables down the elegant room. No curtains had been drawn so that the impressive view was available for enjoyment. Peeb gave more than a passing glance over the famous terrace. How long will it all last, he thought? Old enemies, new enemies. Enemies without, enemies within.

At the bar was 'Blinks' Needham, Pip Arrowsmith, 'Baby' Foreman and Dickie Oldfield. Other faces were familiar and names too, and suddenly Peeb was surrounded by the old men he had known as young men. They were all of a kind. When the first gin and tonic was thrust into his hand, Peeb began to feel a calm and confidence, a peacefulness which flowed from past common dangers, shared fears and the intense comradeship of times of war. Another arrival appeared at the door. Shorty Bunton. It couldn't be. Yes, it was. Bald as a coot. Another cheer went up. And the gin flowed and the Scotch flowed. And under the influence of these magic fluids, the years were spuriously shed. When eventually they stood at their labelled places, they were silent and obedient during the Grace. Then they sat down with all the noisy anticipation of schoolboys at an end-of-term feast.

Peeb didn't remember any particular item of food that he ate, nor did he remark on the wine which he drank. The formal speeches were mercifully short, and consisted of jokes which seemed hilariously funny at the time, but later could not be recalled. As he returned to the bar-table afterwards, the sensation of a tilting floor rang a bell of warning, but it was faintly heard. He paid token heed to Susan's request by filling a glass tankard to the top with Perrier and ice, thereby drowning, he surmised, the single Scotch at the bottom. The conversation became more and more repetitive.

'Good to see you looking so "bang-on", Peeb.'

'One side of his face anyway,' said someone without malice.

'Don't see any difference myself . . .'

'Always was a bloody ugly bastard, if you ask me. . . .'

'Nobody did, old boy.'

'Still it's good to see you.'

'Peeb's round, chaps.'

They ordered the drinks and Peeb paid for the round.

'Aren't you having anything, Peeb?'

He put his hand over his tankard.

'I'm OK, thanks.'

'Not like you.'

'As a matter of fact my quack told me I should cut down.'

'What quack doesn't?'

Peeb thought he saw a shape flash past the long windows. He looked again. Above the Thames two swifts dived and soared against the evening sky. Reassured he wondered if he should mention it. The problem stayed in his mind and wouldn't go away.

'Been having a spot of bother with the old optics, actually,' Peeb announced abruptly.

'Alcoholic neuritis,' observed a bleary voice.

'Don't want to worry about that, old boy. Just change to champers and brandy. See anything then.'

'That's the trouble,' went on Peeb. 'I keep seeing something.'

'An old pink elephant perhaps. . . ?'

There were general guffaws.

'No,' said Peeb. 'A bloody great Messerschmitt BF 109E. And I see it when I'm cold sober.'

Peeb's voice was unexpectedly sharp and forceful. He found himself in the centre of a circle of silence and unnervingly discerning gazes. A nervous laugh broke the little spell.

'I'm not joking,' snapped Peeb and restored the tension. 'I tell you, it's bloody frightening.'

After a short pause, Pip Arrowsmith said, 'I still get awful dreams. A Heinkel blows up in front of me and I go slap into it. Then I wake up shouting. The wife doesn't care for it at all.'

'They say the bomber boys have the worst nightmares.'

'But I see this thing when I'm wide awake,' said Peeb.

'You're being haunted old boy, that's all,' said Dickie Oldfield.

'By a plane?'

'A ghost plane.'

'With a Jerry ghost-pilot in the cockpit, I suppose?'

'Why not? Ghosts don't have to be housebound. The sky must be full of dead bods like us.'

'Didn't know you were a spiritualist, Dickie,' remarked Shorty Bunton.

'I'm not, old boy, but I know a bloke from 604 Squadron who every time he flies to Hamburg, a barrage-balloon chases him all along the Reeperbahn.'

The resultant laughter enveloped the now dwindling crowd round Peeb at the bar-table. Of course the chaps had the right attitude. They took his unsettling experience in the light-hearted spirit they had taken much worse realities nearly fifty years ago. Someone was talking now about Gremlins. The little people who lived on every airfield. Gremlins could sabotage parts of an aircraft and play all sorts of tricks. Perhaps his Messerschmitt was a Jerry Gremlin playing tricks on an old enemy. Peeb was suddenly ashamed of the fuss he'd made; annoyed he'd upset Susan and seen the doc about it. He felt aggreeably woozy. He was very glad he'd mentioned the problem to the chaps.

The mood of confidence stayed with him on the way home along the M2. He drove carefully and slowly nevertheless. He didn't feel drunk and he wasn't drunk. He wasn't quite sober either and waves of drowsiness kept assailing him. He opened the windows of the car to keep himself awake. Abruptly the engine spluttered, back-fired, coughed twice and was then silent. Vaguely, Peeb switched off and twisted the key again. The starter turned the engine, but it did not fire. The petrol-gauge needle was flat on the bottom. Automatically he switched off the ignition. A faint breeze sniffed round the car like a spaniel. Very unusual for him to run out of gas. Never mind, he'd use the emergency can he always carried. He was out of the car before he remembered it was Susan's Metro and not the Lagonda. He opened the boot on the off-chance that she kept a spare supply. Unfairly perhaps, he cursed the irresponsibility of youth.

Peeb tried to recall the last garage he had passed, not that one would be open after midnight. Then he tried to recollect the last half-hour of the journey. But in both cases his memory failed him. He must have been driving automatically and somewhere had taken a wrong turning. He surveyed his surroundings. The road stretched away dimly in each direction between flat fields, without any relieving feature. The landscape had a desolate anonymity. Peeb was lost.

He turned up his jacket-collar and thrust his hands into his pockets against the chill. He began to walk in the direction from which he had come, an incongruous dinner-jacketed figure trudging he thought, like Christian, through the Slough of Despond. After about five hundred yards, the road took a bend. He saw reflection on water. The mud-beach of the estuary was barely fifty yards away. A narrow creek dived under the road through a culvert. There was the sibilant sound of reeds shaken by the wind. Ahead, was a collection of buildings. Way at the back were two Dutch barns. A farmhouse adjoined garage workshops, and to Peeb's relief he saw two petrol-pumps. An upstairs window was lit up.

William Household stood at the bedroom window. As on every night he adjusted the gap of the top sash to a precise six inches. This was necessary to give his wife the requisite amount of air for her night's sleep, disturbed as it would inevitably be by her asthma and bronchitis. He glanced at her propped up on her three pillows and saw she had already dozed off.

Household had seen the car go by, the headlights swinging from side to side, the engine coughing and spluttering. Then it cut out abruptly. A short time later the lights were extinguished. He knew it wouldn't be long before the driver would come to the farm and garage for assistance. Sure enough Household saw a figure approaching. He drew the curtains and walked quietly downstairs, picking up his torch from the hall-stand.

Peeb walked down a short path to the farmhouse and rang the bell. The door opened immediately and a torch shone in his eyes, then rapidly moved off taking in his dress-shirt, trousers and shoes, before flicking back to his face. The torch wandered again to the ribbon-strips on Peeb's breast-pocket, held a second and then snapped off. In the dim illumination from the sky Peeb gradually picked up the man in the doorway. He wore a dark sweater and his trousers were tucked into knee-boots. Peeb couldn't make out his features which were in deep shadow, but he had a shock of grey-white hair.

'Can I help you?'

'I hope so,' Peeb said. 'I've run out of petrol about a quarter of a mile away. I've no spare can. Damned annoying. You see it's my daughter's car. . . .' He felt the man surveying him silently, critically. 'I've a vintage Lagonda myself. . . .'

'What year?' The other showed sudden interest.

'1937.'

'An L.G. 45 Rapide?'

'That's right. Picked it up for a couple of hundred way back during the war.'

'Nice jobs.'

'Yes. Unfortunately it's temporarily laid up. All the shocks need. . . .'

'Listen,' the man said agreeably enough. 'It's a bit late for chatting about shock-absorbers. Do you want some petrol or not?'

'Er . . . yes,' said Peeb. 'That's why I'm here, old boy.' The condescension in the tone shot through Household's memory through all the years irritating him as it had always done.

'Follow me,' he said brusquely.

The man shut the front door and flipped on the torch again. Peeb followed him through to a remarkably tidy garage office. The man took out a pair of cotton gloves from the desk drawer before searching amongst a stack of objects in a corner. He eventually brought out an empty two-litre oil-tin with a screw cap.

'This will be enough to get the car back here. Then you can fill up your tank from the pump.'

Peeb found both the helpfulness and the civility refreshingly welcome.

'That's damned decent of you,' he said. 'I didn't expect. . . .'

'You should have stopped when you passed here a few minutes ago.'

'Yes, I should,' agreed Peeb, 'but I hadn't realised. . . .'

'You backfired a couple of times. You were weaving down the road all over the place,' the man chuckled, obviously finding the situation amusing. 'I thought you might be back.'

He had unlocked the four-star pump. Peeb swayed slightly when he smelt the gasolene as it gushed into the oil-tin. When full, the garage-owner screwed on the cap and handed the tin to Peeb.

'Four pounds give or take. . . . How far are you going?'

'Not sure . . . can't be far though . . . Bishop's Felix.'

'That's the other way.' The man pointed past the garage. 'Down there, about six miles. You come out onto the main road. Turn left. It's signposted. You can't miss it. Two litres in a Metro will get you there easily. No need to call back after all.' Peeb fumbled in his pocket. He found a five-pound note and handed it to the garage proprietor.

'Thank you, sir,' he said. 'No charge for the can.'

'Thank you,' said Peeb. 'Sorry to bother you like this, at this time of night, Mister . . . er. . . ?'

'Don't drop off to sleep while you're driving.' The man spoke as if he were giving an order, then coughed and walked away briskly, returning to the house.

Household put out the hall light. He kept the door ajar listening to the irregular footsteps fade away as his visitor made his way down the road to the marshes. The familiar smell of the mud from the estuary wafted towards him on the gentle breeze.

Then abruptly Household clenched his hands as the never-to-be-forgotten events of the last days of the war nearly fifty years ago tumbled back across his brain and body as if they had happened only yesterday. He opened his hands again realising they were sweating profusely. The memory was fixed in his mind forever.

CHAPTER FOUR

London District Cage had a dreaded reputation. It was the high-powered interrogation centre for prisoners of war, though the processing was quick in 1945, because information was so rapidly out of date as the allied armies rolled across the north German plain towards the German surrender on Luneberg Heath. It was the second time Willi had been taken to the Cage.

From Bow Street police-station he had been transferred to Kempton Park racecourse where he was quite unnecessarily deloused under the old stands, and sprayed with DDT. He had slept on straw in a loose-box. At the camp Willi learnt that the English intended to keep him and his compatriots in captivity until all those bad German ideas to do with Nazi-ism and Hitler, were expunged from his character. Then perhaps, but only then, would he be allowed back to his own country, a 'good' German at last.

Just before dawn the van stopped with a jerk in the deserted street outside the large dilapidated mansion a stone's throw from the Kensington Odeon. Willi tramped the echoing corridor to the room where he sat awaiting his call. At the former interrogation he had correctly refused to give more than his name, rank and number. He had stuck to this through several hours of bullying talk, cajoling and ridicule. He was not touched physically but as he waited for the second round, he wondered what tricks the British had in store for him this time. Like every prisoner he was afraid his breaking point would inevitably come when he would tell all. His mind kept jumping to imaginary police cars arriving to pick up Anna and take her away to unmentionable degradations. Grimly he stiffened his resolve to protect her from such an outcome whatever his own provocation.

'Greifswald!' shouted the sergeant, and Willi followed him up the stairs to the same bare paint-peeling room. This interrogation was different. In place of little Major Feather, '*Der Skorpion*' as he was known to his victims, this time a forty-year old uniformed RAF Wing-Commander offered Willi a cigarette and a cup of tea. So this was to be the soft, friendly approach, the man to man contact, the 'We're all in this together' ruse, the father-figure-you-can-trust-me ploy, which could, if pursued to unbearable tedium, often get surprising results.

'By the way, good news,' was the opening gambit. 'Your *Fuhrer*'s done the decent thing at last. Committed suicide yesterday. The Russians have over-run Berlin.'

What faint remaining glimmers of hope Willi had entertained about the effect of pilotless planes or V2 rockets dissolved. So it was unconditional surrender. Abject defeat. Total humiliation.

'No comment, *Öberleutnant?*' asked Wing-Commander Benson.

'If that's true. . . .'

'It's true.'

'The war is over. . . .'

'Bar the shouting. . . .'

'And Germany is finished,' said Willi.

'Not for ever, old boy. People like you will be needed to put it back on the map with a decent democratic government – that is if you're the sort of person I think you are.'

'You mean a "good" German?'

'A democratic German.'

'How do you know?'

'Von Greifswald. That's a place in Pomerania isn't it?'

'Yes.'

'Family estate?'

Willi hesitated.

'Don't worry. We don't take reprisals of that sort. I might be able to get a message through to your wife . . . parents . . . anybody. Just to say you're OK, that sort of thing, if. . . ?'

'If. . . ?'

'Well you haven't told us very much have you?'

'I don't have to tell you anything. Under the Geneva . . .'

'Oh, come off it, Willi . . . we're Fighter pilots. . . .'

'How do you know I was a Fighter pilot. . . ?' he blurted out and then cursed himself for seeing the trap too late . . . the lucky probe that scored the bull.

Benson smiled and made a mark on a piece of paper.

'Good,' he commented. 'I said to the others you weren't a secret agent – "spy" to me and you. Which was your squadron?'

'You can guess that one,' said Willi, still angry at his own admission.

'Look, old man. What's the point in holding out now? It doesn't really matter. I just want to get the record straight. Then off you can go to a decent POW camp until you're ready to go home. . . .'

'I'm ready now. . . .'

Benson tapped with the unsharpened end of the pencil on the desk in front of him. It went on for a long time. Willi put out his cigarette. He wasn't offered another one.

'If my colleagues convince themselves . . . they'll get you shot. They can't explain otherwise how you can turn up in civilian clothes in the centre of London, well-fed, in a first-class restaurant, unless . . . where did you get the money incidentally?'

'I saved it.'

Benson shook his head.

'You know, Greifswald, I shall have to hand you over to the Special Branch – rather like your Gestapo but a bit nastier if anything – unless you cooperate more . . . How many planes did you shoot down?'

'Seven.'

'Hurricanes or Spits?'

'Two Hurricanes, five Spitfires.'

'Bloody good plane the Messerschmitt.'

'The BF 109E is the best fighter in the world,' said Willi.

'Haven't seen too many over here recently. When did you cop it?'

Willi realised he was starting to talk. A wave of exhaustion hit him. Perhaps some of the truth was the safest way. To give something near the truth. Something that would confuse and lead them away from Anna.

'Some months ago now. I can't remember exactly.'

'Where was it?'

'Near Southampton.' As a town it seemed a plausible reply.

'Baled out?'

'Yes.' It was his first real lie.

'Plane?'

'In the sea.' Well that was true.

'And you were wounded?'

'Nothing much.'

Benson looked at Willi's left hand and made a wrong deduction.

'Nasty enough. The leg too?'

'What. . . ?'

'You limp.'

'A little.'

'Swam ashore?'

'Yes.'

'Crawled up the shingle?'

An obvious catch. Willi didn't know if the beaches there were sand or shingle, cliffs or mud-flats.

'Can't remember,' he said.

'You went to ground?'

'No. I got a job.'

'Without any papers?'

'It can be done.'

'Where?'

'Near Southampton.'

'Come on, man. What sort of a job? Who employed you?'

'A farmer.'

'Name?'

'He was very good to me. I don't want him to get into trouble.'

'He won't.'

'Why not?'

'I don't expect he thought you were German. Your English is very good – did your secret agent training give you that?'

'So you *do* think I'm a spy?'

'Not really,' smiled Benson. 'Not me. Just checking. Why is your English so good? Educated over here? Oxford?'

'No. Family governess.'

'Where was the farm?'

'Somewhere in England', is the phrase your radio often uses.'

'So you listen to our radio?'

'Of course.'

'What were you doing in Town?'

'Town?'

'London.'

'Eating. A theatre.'

'Oh yes. You had two tickets. Gave one away. And in the restaurant there was a girl. Who was she?'

'I don't know.'

'Come on now. . . .'

'I picked her up.'

'Where?'

'In the Savoy.'

'The Savoy!'

'The best hotels have the best whores.'

'Not in England. Try again.'

'I don't know where it was. Some street or other.'

'What street?'

'I don't know.'

'Was she your control?'

'For what?'

'You know very well what I mean. What wavelength did you use?'

'I didn't break radio silence.'

'What. . . ?'

'In the plane. . . .'

'Look, Greifswald. Are you a Nazi?'

'I told you. I'm a German.'

'And we need Germans in the various camps to re-educate. . . .'

'The bad Germans. . . .'

'I think you're a good German.'

'A good German spy.'

'Don't be ridiculous. . . .'

'Exactly, I don't even have any papers. The first thing a spy would need is papers.'

'What have you done with your papers?'

'Very careless.'

'For a spy – ridiculous. It is also ridiculous for a German spy to say in English he is a German in a public place in England.'

'Almost as if you wanted to be arrested. . . .'

'I was somewhat drunk. . . .'

'Why. . . ?'

'Because I was celebrating. . . .'

'What?'

'My last day in this country.'

'I see. And how were you going to leave England the next day?'

'By flying back to Germany.'

'In what?'

'My Messerschmitt.'

'Your 109E?'

'Yes.'

'Which came down in the drink.'

'Oh I salvaged it and serviced it.'

'Stop the funny act, Greifswald . . . You'll find being here in England may not be the joke you think it is.'

Willi said very seriously. 'You should know, Wing-Commander, that Germans are not good at making jokes.'

Benson pressed the buzzer on his desk. The sergeant came in.

'Escort the prisoner back to the waiting-room, Sergeant.'

'Sir!'

Willi followed the thick-soled nailed boots as they stamped along the corridor.

They gave him no food or drink for six hours. His mouth was dry and his throat sore. His eyes were red-rimmed and his voice was hoarse. This time they shone a light in his face and there were two men behind the desk. One was '*Der Skorpion*'. He knew the voice. The other said nothing. He heard the ice chinking in their glasses. He smelt their cigarette smoke. Willi sat in the chair.

'Stand up, *Oberleutnant*,' ordered the Scorpion.

Willi stood up.

'Take your clothes off. Jump to it.'

'I am not obliged . . .' began Willi.

'Get everything off! How can Doctor Gillibrand examine you with your things on. Move!'

Willi undressed except for his underpants.

'I said everything!'

Willi stepped out of his pants.

'Christ! Look at his bush. It's blond!' The Scorpion rasped at Willi. 'Why have you dyed your hair and your beard?'

In the nude Willi felt totally vulnerable, but he summoned up all his spirit of defiance. The attitude which seemed to annoy these uncharming Englishmen most was disdain, mockery. Willi looked into the light, half bent one knee, put a hand on one hip and affected a lisp.

'I rather fancied a change,' he said. 'Do you like it?'

To Willi's satisfaction, the Scorpion seethed with anger.

'Christ!' he shouted. 'What a second-rate lot of degenerate bastards you Germans are! Carry on, Doc.'

'Turn round. Show me your arse,' said Dr Gillibrand.

Willi obeyed. He heard the man get up. He flinched as something touched his buttock.

'What's the matter, tender?'

'No I thought. . . .'

'We don't torture people here, like you bastards do,' the Scorpion snapped. 'Well, Doc?'

'Scar's several years old. Bullet wound.'

'How did you collect that?'

'The day I ditched my plane.'

There was a rustle of papers.

'I said "how"?'

'A Spitfire. Through the seat of the cockpit.'

'And through your parachute?'

'Yes.'

'So how could you bale out?'
'I . . . I didn't.'
'You said you did.'
'Did I?' Willi shrugged. 'Well I ditched my plane.'
'An BF 109E?'
'Yes.'
'Near Southampton.'
'Yes.'
'Some months ago.'
'Sit down . . . No! Without your things!'

Willi sat on the cold seat of the hard wooden chair. He was shivering now, and wanted to pee.

'*Oberleutnant*. No BF 109E's have been shot down. . . .'

'I wasn't shot down!' Willi suddenly shouted. 'I ran out of fuel.' The fact that he had not lost one air-combat was still and perhaps always would be, of extreme importance to him.

'No BF 109E's have been over Britain for years. The 109F, G and H's have long since superseded them. You're talking about the Battle of Britain?'

'Of course.'

'That's not months ago! That's years.'

'If you measure in months, it's months,' said Willi wearily.

'So you're asking me to believe, you hopeless liar, that you ditched an BF 109E in the sea, salvaged it, re-serviced it, and for four and a half years you've been at large in this country without detection, and the day after we arrested you, you were going to fly the plane back to Germany?'

'Yes.'

'Where's the plane?'

Willi trembled visibly with the cold and suddenly there did seem a real blank in his mind. He tried to see Anna's face and he couldn't.

'Where's the plane?' repeated the Scorpion.

'It won't be there any longer,' Willi sobbed hoarsely and fell forwards off the chair.

Two orderlies dragged him to his feet. Willi came round. They helped him dress. The Scorpion and the doctor had departed. In the next room they deliberated.

'What do you think?'

'I think he's genuine. Completely cuckoo of course.'

'He was shot down in the Battle of Britain all right. We captured the fighter squadron he belonged to in Normandy. There's an actual record of his being missing, believed killed since September the 15th 1940.'

'But where's he been all the time?'

'I don't know. You don't know. But somebody knows. Hell of a job to find them though.'

'Does it matter now?'

'No. Strictly yes. But no. Not really.'

'All that about salvaging the plane. . . ?'

'Impossible of course. Plane's in the sea.'

'Simple case of traumatic neurosis with delusions. The dream that kept him going.'

'Odd. That hair.'

'Didn't want to look too Aryan, I suppose.'

The Scorpion sighed.

'Well, he's obviously not a spy. He's obviously no danger to anybody. But better keep the tabs on him. Letters in, letters out etc.'

The Scorpion smacked a rubber stamp on Willi's file. It left a letter 'A'. This stood for White Camp. The other grades were Grey and Black. 'A' meant Willi would cooperate. Willi would need the least amount of de-Nazification.

'Just another poor bugger of a POW. I'm afraid we're going to have these ruddy people on our hands for a hell of a time.'

'Willi. . . ? Willi, what are you doing?' Anna's voice came from upstairs.

'Coming now,' said Household and shut the farm door and locked it.

'Anything wrong?'

'No. Just some silly bugger ran out of petrol,' he said.

He went upstairs to the bedroom, quickly undressed, put out the lights, and got into bed beside her. He put his arms gently round her waist. She took a couple of inhalations from her puffer.

'*Gute nacht, liebchen*,' said Willi.

She didn't reply. She was already dozing off again.

When he got back to Susan's car, Peeb emptied the oil-tin into the tank and then tossed the tin onto the back seat. He got in, realising he had carelessly left the ignition key in its place. He switched on and waited a full ten seconds. Then he twisted the key. At the third go, the engine came to life. With two reverse arcs he turned the car round and drove down the road. He looked at his watch. Two-thirty. Peeb slowed down as he came back to the farm and garage. The upstairs windows were now dark. The headlights lit up a notice-board which declared 'Marsh Farm Garage. Specialist Repairs'. Underneath was 'William Household. Motor Engineer'. He drove on, but fatigue began to overtake him again, and he had to jerk himself awake as the nearside wheels bumped along the grass verge. He pulled the car back onto the carriageway. He found the major road and the signpost and reached home without further incident.

The next morning was Sunday, and Peeb slept until midday. Susan brought him a cup of tea and the newspapers in bed.

'No need to ask if you had a good time,' she remarked.

'Oh? Why's that?'

'Well, the wheels of my car are covered in mud. Whatever happened?'

Peeb frowned and drank some tea.

'I must try and remember,' he said, but not with much conviction.

'There was an empty oil-tin on the back seat.'

'Ah,' said Peeb. 'Ran out of juice. Managed to come across a garage that was open.'

'Which one was that?'

Peeb smiled at her inanely.

'Haven't a clue old girl.'

'Daddy. . . !' said Susan.

CHAPTER FIVE

Peter and Paul's in Canterbury sported a bar, intimate tables, and a dance-floor. The trio, piano, guitar and drums arrived at eight. The guitar-player had an attractive voice.

'Cinzano bianco.'

'Tio Pepe.'

The barman departed. The waiter arrived and gave them each a *carte* and left them alone.

'Don't worry about the prices,' said Brian blandly.

'My menu doesn't have any,' smiled Susan, 'so *you* worry about the prices.'

The barman brought the drinks.

'Cheers.'

Brian raised his glass.

'Cheers,' said Susan.

They drank, ate olives and read in silence. After a very short study Susan put her menu down. The waiter reappeared.

'Mademoiselle?'

'Whitebait, coq au vin, courgettes.'

Brian was relieved by her moderately priced choice, and impressed by her lack of hesitation.

'I'll have the same,' he said.

'Coward,' said Susan and let another olive disappear between her lips.

The waiter proffered the wine-list.

'Monsieur?'

Brian decided to demonstrate his own brand of precision. After a glance he snapped the covers of the list together.

'A bottle of number seven please.'

The waiter bowed and melted away.

'That's plain extravagance,' remarked Susan.

'How do *you* know what I've ordered?'

'The single numbers are always the champagnes.'

Miss Peebles-White was not just a pretty face, decided Brian.

'Champagne is obligatory for special occasions,' he explained.

'Oh. . . .?'

'Our first date.'

'Ah. Then I'll overlook it.'

They both laughed gently.

During dinner, the pleasantries continued. Obvious clichés were studiously avoided. They exchanged potted biographies. Common experiences were aired, backgrounds sketched out. Susan had obtained a good 2:1 in Classics at Newnham before turning to Law in her third year at Cambridge. Brian had acquired an Honours Physiology degree at St Johns at Oxford before qualifying from St Barts Hospital. Brian had two generations of doctors behind him. Susan was an only child. Brian had an elder stockbroker brother. Susan liked Drabble; Brian's taste was science fiction. Both had grown out of earlier socialist dallyings and both had voted for Thatcher at the last election.

'One of the odd things about my father,' said Susan, 'is that he's still fighting the Germans madly.'

'"The only good German . . .", I know,' said Brian. 'My old man was a bit like that. How is Daddy?' Brian asked.

'Oh, he's . . .', she began. His glance picked up her hesitation. Then her lips pursed for a moment and she went on, 'You remember you mentioned three possibilities about Daddy's Messerschmitt – reality, delusion, illusion?'

'Yes . . .'

'Well, he came back – rather pickled by the way – from his annual Squadron Dinner with a fourth explanation. According to the 'chaps' he's being haunted by a ghost plane.'

'I see,' said Brian seriously. 'A ghost plane would fit in with his obsessions including the fact that he has finally chosen to retire to Bishop's Felix, where he fought his last battle, won his glorious victory. Now he's come there to lay a ghost.'

'We came to Bishop's Felix because the cottage enchanted us both. The old house was far too big, after Mummy died. And I had a job in nearby Canterbury. Why did *you* choose to do General Practice?'

'That's easy. Nostalgia. Before and after the war my father had a classic little country practice in the Midlands. I grew up in it. I had a wonderful childhood. He died before I was qualified.'

They danced non-stop for nearly an hour. The place became very crowded. The activity was hot and sticky, sexy and satisfying. Brian gave Susan a formal kiss as he put her in her car. Then he went to his own and followed her red rear lights all the way back to Bishop's Felix. Susan stopped in front of the church in the deserted village street. Brian pulled up beside her. She wound down her window.

'Thank you for a very enjoyable evening, Brian,' she said.

'How about dinner with us next Saturday? Just Daddy, you and me?' she asked.

'Love to,' he replied.

'Quarter to eight. 'Bye.'

Brian turned right and drove pleasantly slowly. Promising. Very promising, he thought with satisfaction.

Susan watched his car disappear into the distance. She couldn't deny her attraction to this new young doctor and was glad she had invited him to dinner. Slowly she drove the car home, feeling strangely elated by the prospect of seeing him again.

'But it's the Air Display at West Malling today,' said Peeb.

'I know, Daddy,' replied Susan. 'I'm sorry. I forgot.'

'But you come with me to a Battle of Britain show every year. . . .' Peeb turned the page of his newspaper noisily. 'You've let me down.'

'I didn't promise to come. How can I have let you down?'

'I feel let down,' said Peeb.

Susan switched on the dishwasher, took off her apron, went behind Peeb's chair, ruffled his white short hair.

'Stop being a spoilt boy. I can't come this afternoon and get back in time to prepare dinner for you and Brian, can I? And *you* make sure you're back in time.'

'You want to impress him, don't you?'

'Certainly I do.'

Peeb folded the *Telegraph* and put it on the table.

'Right, sweetie. For your sake, I'll try and impress him too.' He got up, kissed his daughter on the forehead and retied his dressing-gown cord.

'Don't try *too* hard, Daddy,' she pleaded.

'Roger. Willco,' he reassured her and went up the stairs to the bathroom two at a time.

Susan went out to do her Saturday shopping. She picked up the brace of grouse which had been well hung and prepared for her at the butcher's at the far end of the High Street. She reeled a little at the price but told herself it was all in a good cause.

When she came out of the shop she noticed an estate agent's van pulling away from the antique shop known as Anna's on the other side of the street. A 'For Sale' board had been fixed over the doorway. 'Freehold. Retail premises. Further details and viewing by appointment. Apply Wood & Wood, Maidstone or to the owner'.

Susan peered through the street-level window. The goods had been restored in a first-class manner. There was a Queen Anne bureau, some Hepplewhite chairs and an assortment of cottage furniture, stools and a variety of copper ware, some Majolica and two Chelsea dogs. But none of these objects were exercising Susan's mind. She was at that moment transposing the interior of the shop into a comfortably but simply furnished village solicitor's office.

Susan tried the shop door, but found it locked. She rang the bell and waited. She was about to ring again when an elderly woman wearing a neat nylon housecoat came to the glazed door. Susan gave a smile but it soon faded. The notice suspended on a string was turned from 'Open' to 'Closed'. The effect was softened by a bolt sliding back and a key turning and the door opening.

'I'm awfully sorry,' said the woman pleasantly, 'but I'm closed this morning. The notice should have been turned over.'

'I didn't want to buy anything,' announced Susan, 'I was enquiring about the property.'

The woman laughed and the laugh provoked a cough, and the cough was followed by some deep bubbling breaths.

'That's about the quickest I've ever known,' she said. 'The board's only been up five minutes.'

'Less,' smiled Susan. 'Are you the owner. . . .?'

'Call me Anna. Everyone does. Come in, Miss Peebles-White.'

She shut the door and locked it behind Susan.

'How did you know my name?'

Anna coughed and lit a cigarette. 'There's not much goes on around Bishop's Felx I don't know about. I've lived near the place since before the war. Like a coffee?'

Susan followed her thought to the back where there was a bright little kitchen which also served as office. A well-kept garden was visible through the open back door. Susan took in these details and began making an assessment of the condition of the walls and ceiling and floor. Her conveyancing experience had taught her to recognise the tell-tale appearance of rising damp, the smell of dry-rot and the depredations of any active beetle in the timbers. She also noted a man's jacket hanging on the back door. Anna put the cups of coffee on the table and motioned Susan to a chair. She produced a bottle of whisky from a cupboard.

'Like to make it Irish?'

'No thank you.'

'Very wise,' said Anna and added a generous double to her cup.

Susan observed her hostess. What an outstandingly beautiful girl Anna must have been, she thought, forty and fifty years ago. The eyes were wide-set and a little slanted. The nose had not thickened and the teeth had been carefully cared for. The expression too was still mischievously young enough to allow her grey hair to be worn straight, with a bun at the back, held by a decorative comb. Susan realised she was being studied in equal detail.

'You're thirty-four. Solicitor in Canterbury,' smiled Anna disconcertingly. 'Wouldn't mind starting up on your own. This place'd make good offices, right?'

'Very accurate,' said Susan, almost startled.

'Intuition plus a bit of quick deduction and some local intelligence. Don't live near to the Three Crowns for nothing. Upstairs there are a couple of rooms full of junk at the moment. Rates are commercial. Outside gutters and one floor need attention but the roof's OK. You'd have to put in a central heating. It's a schedule two building but a good buy at a hundred and thirty thousand. Of course I'm open to offers. Bishop's Felix needs a lawyer. Wills, litigation, conveyancing. A younger generation ought to settle in. We've got a nice young doctor now, but you know him. The padre's an awful wet. We need the right sort back in the village again.' Anna stubbed out her cigarette in her saucer. 'Anything else you want to know? If not, wander round, poke about. I've got some accounts to get straightened out.'

Susan felt dismissed.

'Thank you. And thanks for the coffee.'

She walked up the stairs and found two sizeable rooms crammed with furniture. The place had a dry wholesome smell to it. She came downstairs again.

'I'll be in touch', said Susan. 'What about the wiring?'

'Had it done three years ago. 13 amp ring main. It's all OK.'

They went through to the front of the shop.

'I hear your father's an old Battle of Britain pilot?'

'That's right,' said Susan. 'He flew a Spitfire.'

'I knew a Battle of Britain pilot,' said Anna. She opened the door to the street and looked up at the sky. 'It doesn't seem it was all those years ago,' she said. I could swear sometimes I can see the Spits and the Messerschmitts up there – battling it all out.' Her face suddenly looked sad and empty. 'As if they were not satisfied. As if they had to go on fighting forever.' She handed Susan a card. 'Ring me, darling,' she said.

Anna shut the door and disappeared into the room at the back. It seemed others besides her father saw ghosts in the sky over Bishop's Felix.

Shortly after Susan had left, Anna Household locked the shop and drove the six or so miles down the road which led past the old asylum to Marsh Farm and the garage. Willi was in the pit under a car working on the suspension.

'Lunch in about half an hour,' she called.

'OK,' said Willi cheerfully. 'I'm hungry.'

Anna parked her station-wagon and let herself into the farm. She paused a moment before she shut the hall door. The conversation with the young woman at the shop, her thoughts as she drove home, and the enveloping affectionate warmth which after so many years existed between she and Willi made her remember the moment in that glorious summer of 1940 when she had gone to the same door, her heart pounding as she opened it on the night of September 15th.

Anna switched off the hall light before she opened the front door because of the blackout. Her immediate instinct was to slam it again, and rush to the telephone, but the starlight caught the blue metal gleam of the gun in the man's hand. She backed into the hall. He followed her closely and shut the door behind him. Anna turned on the light. She had been right. It was Luftwaffe uniform. The intruder clicked his heels and gave a formal bow.

'*Oberleutnant* Wilhelm von Greifswald.'

Keeping her covered he used his free hand to find the door-key and turn it in the lock. He put the key in the pocket of his wet tunic under his muddied life-jacket. Anna had the impression that but for the support of the door behind him, his legs would have given way and he would have slid to the ground. He must have guessed her thoughts because with obvious effort he pulled himself upright and turned his head slightly, listening for warning sounds which could mean for him discovery. Anna found herself also picking out the familiar comforting noises of the house, the ponderous metronome of the grandfather clock at the end of the hall;

the cold tap in the kitchen left running when the front door-bell had dragged her away from peeling the potatoes; the radio upstairs where Joe Loss was just audible playing 'In the Mood'. Kim, Anna's Labrador began barking at the back of the house. She noticed the man looking at her hands. She controlled their trembling and lightly clasped them together.

'Besides you, *Fraulein*', he asked. 'Who else lives here?'

'My father.'

'Upstairs?'

'He's bedridden. He had a stroke.'

'Your mother?'

'She was killed.'

'I'm sorry . . .'

'Years ago. In a car.'

'Who runs the farm?'

'I do.'

'You? How old are you?'

'Sixteen – nearly seventeen.'

'And you run a farm alone?'

'No. With Arthur.'

'Your brother?'

'My brother's only twelve. He's been sent to California until we've defeated Germany.'

Willi put away his automatic.

'Bravo, *Fraulein*. But I have to know about Arthur. Where is he?'

'He lives in the cottage along the road. He won't be here again till morning. He's a very old man.'

'Old men have tongues.'

'You needn't be afraid of Arthur,' stated Anna audaciously. 'Nor me *Oberleutnant*.'

Willi smiled at her charmingly. He had wonderful even teeth. Anna smiled back.

'It would be a pleasure to be afraid of you Miss. . . .?'

'Household.'

'Miss Household,' he repeated. 'But a girl however attractive cannot run a farm with just an old man. It is not . . . er . . . *richtig*.'

'Two or three hands, as many as I need, come each day from the lunatic asylum.'

Willi stared at her. 'The lunatic asylum. Ah, so.' He spoke as if he was in a mad country where lunatic asylums would be necessary and numerous. He wondered who else might be upstairs.

'And your lover?'

'I don't have a . . . lover,' said Anna and then giggled.

'That is impossible to believe. Or are you trying to tell me you have many lovers?' asked Willi.

Blushing this time, Anna looked into his eyes, blue beneath the mass of blond hair. One of Hitler's young Aryan gods. His manner however, seemed to have escaped most of the reputed arrogance, the brutal callousness of the Nazi régime. But Nazi he must be, an enemy pilot who must be captured and sent to a prison camp. Yet, astonishingly, here she was, chatting to him as if they were flirting at a pony-club dance. Anna made a conscious effort to regularise her position; to put aside these traitorous feelings of attraction and act with swift resource and courage.

She had noticed that all his clothes were sodden. Caked mud covered his trousers and boots. He must have been hiding in the marshes until it got dark. The smell of the estuary was strong upon him. His face looked ashen and there was dried blood on his cheek where something had cut him. In no way now did she feel afraid.

'You realise,' said Anna, 'that I shall have to notify the authorities.'

The music upstairs stopped and her father's slurred voice called down.

'Who's that, Anna? Who are you talking to?'

Willi gripped her wrist and whispered, 'Has your father got a phone up there?'

Anna held Willi's eyes steadily. His grip increased until it was painful to her. She shook her head and indicated the instrument on the hall table.

'Anna . . .?' came the voice again.

'Yes, Father,' she called. 'It's only Arthur. I'll bring your supper up soon.' Why had she protected this Nazi airman in this way? As she looked into his clear blue eyes, she felt as if he had some strange power over her.

Almost straight away the radio went on again. The grip on her wrist relaxed.

'And I have eaten nothing since this morning,' whispered Willi.

'Well, thanks to your compatriots starting the war,' Anna whispered back, 'everything's rationed. All you'll get is spam and spuds.' Willi followed her into the kitchen. She shouted towards the back door. 'Quiet Kim. Quiet, boy. It's only a visitor.' The barking ceased. She didn't want Kim hurt. She had to get the pistol. She had not thought out how she was going to do it, but somehow, it had to be done.

'Sit down,' she said, turned off the cold tap and resumed peeling the potatoes. She heard him wince and curse as he slumped into a chair. He leaned forwards on the table, taking some of his weight on his hands.

'What is it?' she asked. 'Are you wounded?'

'Thanks to *your* compatriots', replied Willi. 'It is nothing.'

'I *am* sorry,' she said but he missed the sarcasm.

'Just a bullet.'

'Good,' said Anna. 'That'll teach you not to come dropping bombs here again.'

'I am not a bomber pilot. Do you English not yet understand?' he exclaimed. 'Today the German fighters have cleared the RAF from the sky. . . .'

'Which is why you were shot down. Was it a Hurricane or a Spitfire?'

'I was not shot down. I ran out of Benzene. A fighter plane has only enough fuel for thirty minutes over this country.'

'Hard cheese,' said Anna. 'Where have you hidden your parachute? They'll find it, you know.'

'They will not, because it is still in the plane, which crash-landed in the river.'

'Why didn't you bail out?'

'Because the bullet came up through the parachute while I was sitting on it, so I do not use a parachute with a hole in it, naturally.'

'Naturally,' Anna stifled a laugh and dried her hands. 'Well, *Oberleutnant*, if you've got a bullet in your bottom, it'll have to come out, won't it? I'll ring for Doctor Page.'

Willi sprang up and grabbed her like a flash. 'No doctors. I am determined not to be taken prisoner. In a few days it won't matter.'

'Why not?'

'The invasion. England will be occupied. You will then be part of the Greater German Reich.'

'Nonsense,' replied Anna. 'The Navy will sink all your army in the sea, and if a few of you do land or drop from the air, we shall. . . .'

'I know . . .', he smiled. 'We all hear Churchill. "We shall fight them on the beaches". After Dunkirk, with what *Fraulein!* With what?'

'Oh, do shut up,' said Anna and took the large pair of kitchen scissors out of the table drawer.

Willi shoved his chair backwards, and brought out the revolver again.

'Put that down.'

'What *is* the matter?' asked Anna. 'I'm only going to use these to cut your trousers. If you won't let me get a doctor, I'd better see what I can do about that bullet, if it's still there.' With the confidence and inconsequence of youth, she added, 'Don't worry. I did some nursing training last term at school.'

This reassuring remark made Willi feel sick and faint.

'Have you . . . have you any cognac?' he asked.

Anna went to the dresser cupboard and brought out a bottle.

'There's only scotch,' she said and handed him the bottle.

He put away the gun, unscrewed the bottle top and drank from it straight.

'*Danke*,' he said. '*Danke schon*.'

He took another long pull. Anna gently removed the bottle from him.

'Now,' she said, 'lean on the table on your elbows and kneel on the chair with your good leg and stretch your other leg out.'

To her surprise he obeved without argument.

'Ja, Fraulein Doktor,' said Willi, with almost a touch of humour.

Anna began to cut up the damp trouser-leg with the scissors. At the same time she told herself that on humanitarian grounds looking after a wounded man even if he was an enemy, absolved her from the guilt of collaboration, of being a traitor to her country.

The faint light which escaped round the edge of the blackout curtain told Willi it was past dawn. Holding his gaze was difficult and made his headache worse. The line of illumination wavered like a reflection in water. The smell of his shirt and the rugs under which he was lying proclaimed that he had been sweating, but now his skin was hot and dry again and he shivered fitfully with fever. He drew up his knees because the front-room couch was too short for him and tried to turn on his side away from the light. The effort escalated the dull ache in his buttock into throbbing stabs of pain. He gave up the endeavour readily. He found the glass of water Anna had put on the floor beside him, drained it and then shut his eyes.

Earlier his hand had explored behind the head-cushions where he had hidden the Luger and knew that she had taken it. Surprisingly he didn't care over much. He remembered Anna had visited him during the night, given him aspirin and water, and sponged his face. He guessed that was when she had removed the weapon and locked him in the room. Though he knew he could easily break the door, and overpower her, he admired the courage of this English schoolgirl, who so calmly had tended his wounds and then held her enemy prisoner in her own childish fashion.

Distantly he could hear a sewing-machine, long and short segments of sound separated by irregular intervals. Over it his youthful captor's voice sang some gay catchy tune. The English words enhanced the lilt which enchanted him. He closed his eyes. The air battles, the death-dealing and death-escaping combats of the long perfect summer slid away into a forgotten compartment of his mind. The conqueror's exhilaration and hard-won fatigue remained. War was war and now he had found an honourable respite. Drowsily he regretted missing the final victory which must be any day now.

A tapping on the ceiling above jerked him out of his half-sleeping state. The singing and the sewing-machine stopped. He heard the voices of father and daughter. The floor creaked over his head, indicating where she had gone. It was time to review his situation. He managed first to sit up. Then, by holding onto the couch and a chair, awkwardly he made his way to the window. Carefully he parted the curtains a few inches.

Instinctively he first looked at the sky. Grey slab-like wedges of stratus extended to an indeterminate horizon. The ceiling was barely two thousand metres. Small wonder he had not heard the unsynchronised throb of the Heinkels and Dorniers earlier, on their way to London. Damn the weather. The day would give the enemy time to lick and perhaps repair some of its wounds. Not that it would make much difference in the end.

The marshland fell away on either side of an old causeway down to the river Swale. The scene reminded Willi of school holidays spent on the family estate north of Greifswald on the Baltic. The road to the farm ran parallel to the river before it turned northwards. The other way it passed outbuildings and two Dutch barns in the distance. Dotted about the fields were obstructions to stop aircraft or gliders landing. Nearby there was a garage shed with a tractor and a lone Shell petrol pump. Painted red it was of the variety operated laboriously by a long cranking handle.

Willi found he could open the sash-window. So much for Anna's security. But he had no intention of climbing out yet. Not until his friends, the boys in the 109's and 110's screamed un-opposed by the last Spitfire over the same fields. Then he would stand and welcome the Panzer Pz Kw III's and IV's as they churned the road with their oiled tracks. Now he watched the three figures in loose blue coats and trousers, red kerchiefs round their necks, forking the harvest corn-stooks onto the horse-drawn wagon moving slowly towards the barns.

An old man, presumably Arthur, wearing a hat which seemed to have grown from his head, shepherded the men from the asylum. One of them danced a few steps now and again and another skipped playfully between sheaves dropped from the wain. It was a Breugel scene come to life. Through the window he could hear their unintelligible shouts to each other and Arthur's repetitive orders which mingled with the cries of the black-headed gulls. Eastwards towards the estuary he thought he saw a Redshank probing for his breakfast in the brackish lagoons. Willi knew if he waded amongst the reeds near the beach he would find the same sort of treasures he had done as a boy with such excitement on the coast of Pomerania; smooth newts and natterjack toads and earlier in the year the soil would throw up marsh orchids and buttercups.

A breakdown truck and a light lorry with about six men, appeared along the road. The vehicles turned down the causeway towards the water. Only one man was in uniform. He wore a tin hat and carried a standard rifle. The men jumped out and poked around the marshy area at the end of the causeway in a desultory fashion.

'You won't find it there, my friends,' Willi whispered to himself. 'I had to swim ashore at least fifty metres.'

As if they heard his remarks the aircraft recovery squad got back in its vehicles, returned along the causeway and drove away in the direction it had come. As it did so it passed an approaching open tourer. The car was a Bentley, Willi believed. He had seen such models in the motoring magazines he had studied so avidly at school, before his interest had been captured by gliding and flying.

In 1937 he terminated his engineering course at Berlin University which included practical work at the aircraft factory where Messerschmitts were built – the Bayerische Flugzeuwerke at Regensburg. Flying the planes seemed suddenly more attractive than making them. His father sighed and his mother cried but his sister Giselle kissed him on the cheek when he told them he had joined the Luftwaffe. His first solo flight in a Messerschmitt 109 was the most intensely satisfying day of his life, more so than the day he got his Iron Cross after Poland. Later, after France capitulated, he proudly collected his Knight's Cross of the Iron Cross with Oak Leaves.

The car stopped in front of the house and a man in his fifties, wearing a tweed suit got out. He carried a black, chunky attaché case and walked somewhat wearily up to the front door. Willi let the curtains close slowly. It did not need great powers of deduction to recognise the doctor, come to see Anna's father.

Willi heard her descend the stairs in answer to the bell.

'Come in, Doctor Page.'

'Has Nurse Knight been?' the doctor asked.

'Not yet. She doesn't get here till midday.'

'So you have to do all your father's morning toilet do you, child? Make his bed? Turn him over? Wash him? Empty the slops, eh?'

'It's nothing,' said Anna.

'It's everything, girl. Everything.'

Willi heard them mount the stairs. He eased himself over to the door. He turned the handle slowly. Yes, she had locked it. His head was leaden and painful. He allowed its weight to push him slowly down into a hard-backed chair. He sat there in the dim light of the room trying to ignore the pain in his leg and the bursting tension he now felt in his stomach. He had to get out soon and go down the passage. He listened to the noises above and eventually Anna and the doctor came down again.

'I'll write out that prescription,' said Doctor Page. Willi saw the handle turn.

'I keep it locked,' said Anna.

'Why?'

'Just an extra line of defence. In case a parachutist tries to get in,' she laughed nervously.

'Good girl,' said the doctor. 'Can't be too careful. But I think we've got 'em licked after yesterday.'

'Yesterday?'

'A hundred and seventy-five Huns shot down. Isn't it marvellous? Here. I'll write on my case.'

'Thank you, Doctor.'

'Those bedsores are badly infected. Perhaps these M & B 693 tablets will clear them up. I don't have to tell you, Anna how bad the outlook is, do I?'

'No, Doctor Page.'

'His blood pressure's still way up. What are you going to do when. . . .? Never mind. We'll all rally round. If I had a daughter, I'd like her to be just like you.'

Willi thought he heard some movement, some contact of comfort, and then the front door opened.

'They say they're working on something at Oxford . . . Some mould, the common green one – *Penicillium notatum* if my botany serves me right – which just kills every damn germ in sight. God knows when we civilians'll get it. Goodbye, my dear.'

The door closed. Willi knew Anna was standing in the hall. In imagination he saw her eyes red-rimmed with tears.

'Anna . . .?' he called. 'Anna. . . .?' Suddenly he felt an overpowering need to comfort this young woman.

After a pause he heard the key in the lock and she opened the door. Her eyes were a grey as he had imagined and her lips as perfectly shaped. She stood staring at him with an expressionless face and the tears poured silently down her cheeks.

'Daddy's. . . . Daddy's going to die,' she said.

Willi stood with difficulty and steadied himself by leaning against the wall. He pulled the lonely, lost child into his arms. Softly he pressed kisses on her hair as her yielding body moulded itself against his own. Not for the first time did he become aware of his growing attraction for Anna. Damn . . . damn . . . he cursed as instinctively she raised her head towards him, and fleetingly their lips touched.

Shocked by the realisation of what was happening his mind sharply returned to their present situation . . . and her dying father.

'Everything has to come to an end,' murmured Willi. '*Alles muss einmal zu* ende *sein . . . Alles. . . .*'

CHAPTER SIX

At the public Air Display, Peeb guarded his anonymity. He sported no medal ribbons here; not even an Air Force tie. Far less his old uniform or his flying-gear. The helmet with built in earphones and even his goggles he kept in a box in the loft unable somehow to discard them. He found it hard to accept he was a back-number, an old campaigner from a half-forgotten war. He mingled with the rest of the gawping crowd, as it gazed at the electronic intricacy of the exposed entrails of the aircraft on static display. These modern, unnervingly beautiful engines of destruction, the Phantoms and Jaguars gave him a feeling of awe, especially the Harrier of Falklands fame. But he felt no desire, no compulsion to fly them. He imagined that to become a pilot nowadays was to assume the role of an impersonal robot – the soft hundred-thousandth part inside a hard miracle machine of a hundred thousand electronic parts.

It was perfect weather. In the refreshment marquee he listened to the muffled sounds of the RAF Central Band playing nearby. Eventually the tannoy announced the first event of the flying programme. He went outside and saw the Falcons' parachutes, modern rectangular ungainly rigs weave and descend with coloured smoke-trails issuing from one of the heels of each suspended body. Before they had landed the second event had overlapped them. A Buccaneer Mark 2B skimmed beyond the crowd along the axis of the flying display. And then at five and ten minute intervals various other menacing shapes approached soundlessly, flashed across the airfield with deafening crescendo, to thunder upwards until they were dots in the pale space above.

Surely, inexorably, like an addict trying but failing to break the habit of a drug, Peeb wandered in a seemingly roundabout way towards his quarry at the far end of the spectator-barrier. There, not more than thirty yards beyond it were a Hurricane and Spitfire beside the Lancaster bomber waiting for the Battle of Britain Memorial Flight. He watched the familiar re-fuelling procedure from the bowser. Then the pilots, young nonchalant lads arrived, no older than Peeb was when he did his first solo. With the wheelchocks in place, they warmed up the Rolls Royce Merlins for a few minutes, keeping the cockpit hoods shoved back. Then they switched off and waited for their call from the controller. One pilot read a book. Another appeared to be dozing.

To Peeb, the sight of the eliptical wings of the Spitfire, the red, white, blue and the surrounding yellow of the roundel on the side of the fuselage, and the smell of the octane petrol, so different from the kerosene of the jets, set his hands sweating and his skin tingling. It was just like he used to feel, sitting in a deckchair, sunning himself outside the dispersal hut. He half closed his eyes and saw it all again. And the faces that he knew and the distant summer sounds and the old familiar phrases were all about him. A telephone rang and someone shouted 'Scramble!'

Peeb jumped visibly. The crowd came back with a rush of reality. There was laughter from the companions of a man who again shouted the talisman word. A surge of illogical anger gripped Peeb as he identified the humorist. He shoved aside a couple of people until he was face to face with him. He held his voice steady and hid his clenched hands.

'It wasn't a joke, old boy, at the time,' he said.

'What wasn't? What are you talking about?'

The fellow was about twenty-five, taller than Peeb, but he backed away a little, sensing the suppressed aggression in the old man.

'"Scramble", you called "Scramble", didn't you? Now don't lie. I heard you,' rasped Peeb.

'I'm not lying. And who do you think you are, anyway?'

Peeb suddenly felt ridiculous, impotent, sick. What did it matter? What was he trying to prove? This generation would never learn until they were fighting for their lives, like his lot had done.

'I happen to be an old Spitfire pilot, that's all,' said Peeb quietly, and angrily still, because his confession sounded like an apology. The crowd, now silent, made way for him back to his place by the barrier.

Peeb looked at the Spitfire again. He would forget there were others around him, blot out these ignorant yobs behind. He concentrated on the plane. An idea surfaced quirkily. What would it feel like to run out, jump on the wing and get into the cockpit? He lost himself completely in the thought of the action. He heard a voice say behind him.

'It would be a wonderful experience to fly a Spitfire again, wouldn't it?'

'Yes,' said Peeb, nodding his head as he watched the pilot shut his book, fasten his helmet and slide forward the canopy. 'Yes it would.'

Then he turned round to see who had spoken this time, but there was no familiar face. There was no one he knew. Faces, voices, the tourist hordes. But someone *had* spoken. He was sure someone had spoken. At least . . . a voice had spoken.

The Rolls Royce Merlin burst into life, drowning all other sounds. He watched the chocks being pulled away. The flaps did a practice 'up and down' and the rudder waggled. And then the Lancaster was trundling forward, and after it the Hurricane was speeding away. The Spit roared after it until they were right out on the runway. As soon as they were in the air, Peeb watched with nostalgia the wheels and undercarriage fold back into the wings. The Spitfire became a graceful beautiful bird climbing up to heaven. The Memorial Flight became lost from view temporarily behind the hangars and then you could hear them coming back – no supersonic approach this – diving down and levelling out at a hundred feet. The roar and the crackle of the exhausts was smooth and familiar. Peeb watched enchanted as glibly, effortlessly both the fighters did a victory roll and then roared away again into the distance, making separate arcs in the sky. Someone in the crowd cheered and Peeb discovered his eyes were hot and gritty and his throat dry.

Well, he'd seen what he had come to see; what he came to see every year. Unhurriedly Peeb walked back to the huge mass of cars parked on the grass. He watched the stunt flight of the Tiger Moth with the girl on the wing. He found the Lagonda, got in and dozed fitfully until at five o'clock the last item took place. The Red Arrows descended in tight formation and drew their spectacular geometry back and forth across the sky. He always waited for the Red Arrows. It would be a discourtesy not to, but Peeb was moving before they had gone. The Lagonda was one of the first hundred cars out onto the main road.

Because of the air display at West Malling, Peeb arrived later at the Three Crowns than usual. He wouldn't be able to stay long. He wanted to get home in good time for dinner with Susan and her doc. Besides, he had forgotten to open the Chateau Beychevelle before he left, to let it breathe. He noticed with unjustified irritation, that his usual place in the pub forecourt was occupied by a Ford Granada and there was no room elsewhere. So he parked at the kerb in the High Street at the first empty space which was opposite the antique shop with the 'For Sale' board on it.

Inside the saloon he had to push his way to the bar. Saturday night was always crowded, but this one seemed more so than usual. He ordered his regulation pint of bitter. It came to him in a glass tankard, served by a youth he hadn't met before.

'Hold it,' said Peeb. 'Will you pour this into my personal tankard, there's a good chap?'

'Do what. . . .?'

'Look,' said Peeb pointing to the hook on the bar ceiling. Speaking very slowly after the manner of the English when abroad, 'that pewter tankard. . . .'

The young man followed Peeb's gaze.

'What?'

'Pewter . . . p . . . e . . . w . . .?'

'Oh . . . that metal one?'

'Exactly,' sighed Peeb.

The lad took the tankard down and transferred the beer. 'Don't like these. Makes the beer taste funny,' he said.

Peeb put the correct coins on the counter.

Muriel, the landlord's wife came up to Peeb's end of the bar with an order of 'shorts'.

'Two G and T's, two Scotch and ginger ale, and a lager.'

'Evening, Muriel,' Peeb greeted her. 'Where's Bill?'

'Had to go up north, dear,' she said. 'His brother died. At least I think it was his brother.' She put the money in the till and banged the drawer back into place. 'I really don't know his family that well,' she laughed.

'I'm sorry to hear that,' said Peeb.

'It's all right, Bill'll be back tomorrow.' She smiled at an elderly customer. 'Yes, sir?'

Peeb drank some beer and then moved away from the bar to make room for the demanding gestures behind him. He stood near the empty fireplace and lit a cigarette. Three young people next to him were discussing the air display. In due course the planes of the last war were mentioned, and Peeb picked up the cue with unfailing compulsion. Very soon he had bought a round of drinks and the group about him enlarged as he went into his well-worn battle story.

'. . . I turned north-west, and I was nearly home when I spied the BF 109 in the mirror. . . . What? . . . that's the same thing – a Messerschmitt . . . I heard the canon-shells whip over my head. I side-slipped, put on full throttle and shot upwards. Something thumped into the rear of the fuselage, but all the controls seemed to work. I made a tight turn and came back on the reciprocal . . . Yes . . . that's the general direction. In response the Hun made off to the south. We were over the estuary but I was above him by then. I put the Spit into a dive and came up under him. At a hundred and fifty yards I aimed and pressed the button. The last burst was barely a second, but it was enough to set things alight. The plane whipped over on its back and went streaking away down in flames towards the water. It must have happened practically over this very pub. I just made it to the satellite field at Eastchurch.' Peeb made his usual dramatic pause and put out his cigarette. . 'And that was the last plane I shot down.'

It was those following seconds of appreciative silence which he enjoyed most of all, but that evening they were cut short, as it seemed to him later, ruthlessly, mercilessly.

'When you fired at the Messerschmitt, sir, you would have tracer bullets, yes?' asked a precise voice.

Peeb turned round. A man wearing a beret, a bush-shirt and knee-boots was smiling at him under dark glasses.

'That's right. . . .'

'Then you would observe exactly where the bullets hit the enemy plane?'

'Yes. . . .'

'And where was that?'

'I can't remember exactly,' said Peeb irritably. 'What's it matter?'

The other man shrugged. 'It's a good rule to get things absolutely straight.'

'They are,' said Peeb angrily. 'It's all down in the official records.'

'Records can contain errors.'

'Well I suggest you run along my dear chap and look them up more carefully.'

'I have. They record the Messerschmitt went down in flames. So the bullets must have hit the fuel tank under the floor of the cockpit. It could have been good shooting.'

Peeb froze as if a knife had pierced him between the shoulder-blades. His eyes narrowed and his colour mounted.

'What the ruddy hell do you mean – it could have been?' Peeb bellowed.

'If there'd been any fuel in the tank.'

Peeb banged his tankard down on the table and some beer slopped out of it.

'Are you suggesting I did *not* shoot down that Messerschmitt?'

'Well . . .', the man shrugged again.

Peeb looked as if he might explode.

'But I saw the ruddy plane turn on its back and go down in flames. . . .'

'Oh yes, it went down. But not in flames.'

'I saw it go, dammit! Into the drink.'

'Yes. And it sank too.'

'So . . .?' barked Peeb.

'The point I'm making is that it was not shot down.' The man looked round at the listeners to the conversation. 'Running out of petrol can happen to the best of us at times.'

There was an answering murmur of agreement. He turned his smile back to Peeb. 'But it's not the same as being shot down, now is it, my friend?'

Peeb blinked back, sweat glistening on his forehead. The saloon started to sway a little and the voices grew loud and died away like the sound of breakers on a shingle beach. He pulled himself up and jutted his chin out at his questioner.

'Now just listen to me. . . .' Peeb threatened quietly. The man looked at his wristwatch.

'Another time, perhaps,' he smiled and put down his empty glass.

'Hold on,' said Peeb. 'You can't go around saying things like that without an explanation, and without an apology. You're getting into dangerous country, old boy . . .'

'We are all living in dangerous countries, but I must be going now.'

As if paralysed Peeb watched the man adjust his leather gloves. 'Goodnight. Goodnight', he said.

Before Peeb could get round the table, the man had zigzagged his way to the exit. Peeb thrust roughly after him and caught up just as he opened the door. He grabbed the man's arm and swung him round.

'You're not getting away like that,' said Peeb. 'Who the bloody hell do you think you are?'

The man slowly prised away Peeb's fingers from his arm. Then he whispered into his ear.

'I was the Messerschmitt pilot,' he said.

Peeb's jaw sagged open and his hand dropped to his side.

The man saluted and went out. Peeb remained inside for a couple of seconds. Then he flung open the saloon door and ran outside. Some people were just coming in. Trying to sidestep them Peeb tripped and fell onto the tarmac of the parking lot. He struck his forehead. He must have gone out for a second because he next recalled two young men were helping him to his feet.

'Are you all right, guv?'

'OK, now?'

'Yes,' said Peeb. 'Yes, thanks. Thank you.'

He brushed himself down. He thought he saw a vehicle backing out of the park.

'Hey,' he called, 'just a minute.'

A horn hooted as another car came in from the road, narrowly missing him. Peeb dived round the car accompanied by shouts of abuse. He reached the road. But there was no traffic. No tell-tale rear lights. No one walking in the street. He'd disappeared into thin air – like a ghost.

Oh God, thought Peeb. It was one thing being haunted by a plane in the sky, but when a dead pilot came right up and spoke to you while you were having a quiet pint, that was . . . that was . . . that was madness! He didn't believe it. The man in the bar was real enough. There were plenty of witnesses. He'd soon find out who had played such a trick on him, making him look not only a fool, but a liar. He strode back to the door.

But inside the crowded bar he couldn't recognise any of the people who had been listening to his story. They had probably gone. Desperately, he asked one or two customers if they had seen a man in a beret, a bush-shirt, gloves and dark glasses, wearing knee-boots. Peeb asked Muriel but she was far too busy to be of any help. Except that she produced a dressing for his forehead. The old boy looked a bit of a mess, she thought. Especially with the burn scars on the other side of his face.

Peeb felt defeated, confused. He ordered a large Scotch in place of another pint. After a second one his sense of defeat diminished, but his confusion increased. Then he began to feel afraid. It was all pretty unsettling. He was shaking a bit too.

CHAPTER SEVEN

Brian let Susan refill his glass with Amontillado.

'It's a pleasant feeling not to be "on call",' he said.

'How do you manage about that?'

'I have a chum at Minister, the other side of Eastchurch,' he explained. 'Peter Wilcox. No partnership. Just a loose mutual arrangement. I think I come off best,' Brian smiled. 'Peter's married with two small kids. So he's bogged down anyway.'

'And you don't intend to get bogged down?'

'There are bogs and bogs. What about you?' he countered.

'I want to set up on my own. Solo Solicitor.'

'Where?'

'Bishop's Felix.'

'Would you get enough work?'

'If Bishop's Felix can support a doctor, it can support a lawyer. I could defend you, for instance, when a patient sues you for negligence,' she laughed.

'Thanks very much,' Brian laughed.

'A "For Sale" board went up on the antique shop in the High Street this morning. I went in and had a look round. It would make ideal offices for me. The owner's asking a hundred and thirty thousand. I think I might raise almost a hundred per cent mortgage.'

Brian twirled the stem of his glass.

'Anna Household is a patient of mine,' he said.

'I'm not surprised. She has a terrible cough.'

'Chronic bronchitis and emphysema. Smokes like a chimney. Knocks the bottle a bit too.'

'I noticed.'

'I don't want to dampen your enthusiasm, Susan, but every couple of years or so Anna puts up that "For Sale" board, having decided to go and live with her brother in California. Then at the last minute she changes her mind, and the board comes down again.'

'Can't tear herself away from her roots?'

'I have a feeling her husband doesn't want to leave,' said Brian. 'They have a farm and garage about six miles away.'

'Is that for sale too?'

'Susan,' said Brian, 'I'm not an estate agent. But if you like, I can impress upon Anna that her health is such that she really should not delay any longer going to live in a better climate than the Thames Estuary.'

'That could be very useful,' said Susan.

Brian looked at her admiringly. 'You'd definitely be an added attraction in the High Street,' he said.

'You make me sound like an amusement arcade.'

They laughed, sharing their mutual attraction, developing their verbal intimacy. The clock in the hall dispensed eight silver drops of sound. Susan glanced at her wristwatch.

'I can't think what's happened to Daddy. He's usually pathologically punctual. Anyway I'm going to put the grouse on the spit now, or we'll be eating at midnight.'

'Grouse? Marvellous!' exclaimed Brian. 'I love grouse. Even at midnight.'

Susan went out of the room. He looked around the room, the condensation of her background. The books told the story: the fully bound calf of the classics. Brian might have been looking at the bookcase he remembered in his own parents' home.

The pictures bespoke a formed taste of a sort. There was a good oil of boats on a lake, and some watercolours: a Cotswold landscape, a competent flower-painting.

On a fall-front bureau he espied a wartime wedding photograph of Peeb and Susan's mother. Peeb, was in RAF uniform and sported a large moustache. Her mother looked very attractive. The adjacent frame jumped to a picture of Susan at Cambridge wearing academic dress. But otherwise in the room there was nothing to mark the progress of the sixties, seventies, or eighties, his and her generation, save the TV set in the corner. It had all happened inside that box – Rock, the men on the moon, computers, satellites everywhere, transplants, test-tube babies. They had been dispossessed by technology.

The phone rang in the hall and he heard Susan answer it.

'Hello? . . . Yes, speaking . . . what! . . . I see . . .' There was a long pause while he could hear a female voice yacketting at the other end of the line . . . 'Well, is he able to . . . ? Yes, of course . . . You must be, naturally . . . I'll come straight away. Goodbye.'

Susan put down the phone. Brian went out into the hall. She turned round, her face tight and anxious, her slender hand still on the receiver.

'Your father?' he asked. She nodded. 'Road accident?'

'No . . . ', she sounded bewildered. 'He's had some sort of . . . collapse. . . .I don't *know*, Brian,' she ended emphatically.

Instinctively he put his arm round her shoulders. 'Where is he?'

'The Three Crowns . . . but he's not drunk if that's what you're thinking.' She was on the verge of defensive tears.

'I wasn't,' said Brian. 'I'll go and see what's wrong. You stay here.'

'No,' she said. 'But I *would* be grateful if you'd come with me.'

In the car she gave him all the information she had gleaned from the phone call. Peeb had gone outside and come back with a lump on his forehead.

'Had he had a fight?'

'I don't know.'

'When did it all happen?'

'About an hour ago.'

'And since then?'

'A customer has complained about . . . about Daddy's behaviour . . . the landlord's wife wasn't explicit.'

Peeb was sitting at a table on his own with his hands and arms shaking visibly and continuously. It was clear that some of the other customers regarded him as highly infectious.

Susan ran over to her father and put her arm round his shoulder.

'Daddy, what's the matter?' Peeb seemed not to hear her. 'Are you all right?' she asked anxiously, fatuously.

Brian took Peeb's pulse. Fast but regular. Brian was aware of Susan's eyes looking up at him impatient for an answer, a pronouncement. Brian lifted the dressing on Peeb's forehead. There was a one-inch abrasion and the bluish swelling of a small haematoma around it. He turned to the gawping spectators. 'Any of you know what happened?'

'Yes,' said a man of about thirty. 'He came rushing out of the bar as I was coming in. Nearly knocked me over. Then he slipped and fell. We helped him up.' Other heads nodded confirmation.

'Do you think he was unconscious? After he fell?'

'Shouldn't be surprised,' said the informant. 'But it couldn't have been for long because he was back inside here a minute later asking everyone if they'd seen a man.'

'What man?'

'Dunno. Someone with dark glasses and wearing boots.' He made a gesture at his own legs and his friend's. 'I mean it could be anyone, couldn't it?'

'Yes,' said Brian. 'Thank you.' He turned to Muriel but he didn't have to question her.

'He had a pint and two scotches. He's been sitting there ever since – like that – as if he'd seen a ghost.'

'Ghost? . . . Ghost!' The word seemed to bring Peeb out of his trembling stupor. He grabbed Susan's arm. 'He wasn't a ghost, I tell you. He was real all right!'

'Daddy . . .' said Susan.

Peeb looked round at her. Slowly the light of recognition crossed his face.

'Hello Susan . . . what are you doing here?' He glanced at Brian.

'Good evening, Group Captain,' smiled Brian.

'Good evening, Doc. . . .' The trembling died down.

'We wondered what had happened to you? You're very late for dinner,' said Susan.

Peeb shook his head. His manner became more natural.

'My God, I'm awfully sorry . . . ' He looked at his watch and stood up, a little unsteadily. He passed his hand up to the dressing on his forehead.

'Had a little fall in the yard,' said Brian.

Peeb frowned. He didn't remember falling.

'You mean I've had a stroke or something. . . .?'

'Nothing like that at all,' Brian reassured him. 'You ran into someone. Probably had a slight concussion though.'

Brian looked at Susan and gave his professional reassuring smile.

'Don't remember it,' said Peeb.

'You wouldn't. Nothing serious.'

'Come on, we're going home, Daddy,' said Susan.

She steered her father towards the door. Brian picked up his case and followed. He noted Peeb's speech was not in any way slurred. His gait was steady. At the door his patient turned round and in a normally pitched voice, he said, 'Goodnight everyone. God bless.'

Brian came down the stairs at Bluff Cottage and put his medical bag in the hall. Susan was in the kitchen.

'How is he, Brian?' she asked anxiously.

'A lot calmer now. He was very agitated. I've given him a sedative shot. It won't knock him out, but he should drop off into a normal sleep.'

'Thank goodness you were here when they rang.'

'I've been over his CNS with every test I know. I can't find a thing organically wrong.'

'What is it then?'

'If I wanted to show off I'd say he's had "a panic episode in an anxiety-hysterical illness, with phobic delusional and depressive features".'

'And if you didn't want to show off?'

'He's having an old-fashioned nervous breakdown. There's still no better description.'

'But why?'

'I don't know. Age, retirement, resentment at retirement, some guilt somewhere – perhaps part of his bereavement . . .'

'How long will it all go on?'

'Six months, a year. . . .'

'A year. . . .?' She sounded distraught, disappointed. He didn't want to tell her he was letting her off gently.

'What ought to be done?'

'Well . . .' he smiled, 'first we must create an atmosphere of low-key normality. Then we try and get his thoughts and emotions back on an even keel. It's like rolling up a ball of string from a mass of knots and tangles in an old drawer.'

Susan put the coffee and cream on the tray and he carried it into the living-room. She looked up at him, straight, her jaw tense. He held her eyes a second, touched her hand and then went back to stirring his coffee.

'You're keeping something back, Brian, aren't you?'

'No . . . no . . .', he said.

'But. . . .?'

'All right,' he looked at her. He could see a glistening liquid edge to her lower lids. He forced his voice into a flat professional tone. 'While not changing my diagnosis in any single detail, like all responsible physicians, I should like to have it confirmed before committing the patient to treatment.'

'Committing . . .? You make it sound like a sentence!'

He saw her shrink in alarm at the word, because in the circumstances it was loaded with emotional half-informed terrors.

'Susan, I think first your father ought to go up to Queen Square for tests . . .'

'But you said organically there was nothing wrong?'

'Precisely, to confirm there *is* nothing wrong. For my sake if you like. What can he lose?'

'More confidence,' she said intuitively.

'Hardly, if the tests are all normal.'

'Then. . . .?'

'Then I would like him to see Fergusson after all, the psychiatrist I mentioned . . . He could take him into a nursing home for a week or so. . . .'

'Where he has a drug or so, an electric shock or so . . .'

'I promise you, Susan, I should be in constant touch. He wouldn't have anything done that we didn't want . . .'

'No, Brian,' she shook her head violently. 'I can't have Daddy put in that position. I know him. He'd feel degraded. Destroyed. He'd never be the same person again.'

She cried then, put the empty coffee-cups on the tray and went out into the kitchen. He hadn't handled that very well. Not very well at all. He turned as he heard a movement behind him. Peeb was standing in the doorwy in pyjamas and dressing gown. He looked wide awake.

'Hello, Doc,' he said. 'Run out of cigarettes.' He opened the top drawer of the bureau and took out a packet of Stuyvesant. 'I'm afraid your shot hasn't sent me off into a deep snooze, but I certainly feel fairly clear and calm.'

'Good,' said Brian.

'I suppose I couldn't have a brandy though?'

'Not a good idea, sir.'

'Call me Peeb, old boy.'

'Peeb,' said Brian.

'That's better.'

Peeb lit his cigarette and walked towards the window. He slid the glazed panel further open, inhaled and blew the smoke outside. The moonlight on the far Thames estuary was like a silver knife-blade beyond the black clump of the beech trees and the outbuildings.

'The Romans sailed up that bit of water you know. The Vikings came later. The Spanish *Armada* was blown off course and they didn't make it. The Dutch Navy managed to take the wrong turning and forked off down the Medway, lobbing a few shots into Chatham. Napoleon never got anywhere near it. The Huns sent up a sub in the First War and dropped mines all over the place in the Second. But it's still there and it's still ours. In spite of the Common Market; and the Russians, and the Warsaw Pact.' He half turned towards Brian. 'Your generation mustn't ever lose England you know.'

'Daddy,' exclaimed Susan as she came through the door. 'You're supposed to be in bed.'

'I know,' he smiled. 'But I couldn't sleep in spite of the doc's knock-out shot. Besides I don't recall your kissing me goodnight.'

She ran over and kissed him, clearly pleased and relieved to hear him talking rationally, even light-heartedly.

'Well, now you can return upstairs and this time go to sleep properly. You've had quite a knock on the head you know.'

'Yes, I know,' said Peeb. 'And *a propos* of what this young quack here was saying to you about me. . . .'

'How do you know . . .?' began Brian.

'Sorry. Dirty trick. Listening on the stairs. Irrestible when it's about yourself.'

'Come on now. Back to bed,' she tried to guide him to the door, but he firmly resisted her attempt. Looking from one to the other he groped for his words.

'I know that I can't repeat scenes like the one down at the Three Crowns tonight, and . . . and . . .' his voice trailed off.

'Why don't you sit down, Peeb?' said Brian.

Peeb waved the suggestion aside.

'Contrary to what my daughter has said. I'll submit to any tests you like, go into any hospital, if it'll help, if you think it'll help to sort everything out.' He flipped his cigarette stub out of the window. 'What I feel when these things happen . . . is a bloody awful feeling, and . . .' His hands started to tremble. He put one hand up on the aluminium window frame to steady it. The shape was there. Small, black, venomous. It had appeared on the silver blade of the river as he was speaking, growing larger coming straight towards him. '. . . And, and I simply can't . . .' he turned away from the window as the faint sound of the plane reached him. 'Can't go on seeing . . . people . . . and things that aren't there. . . .' He crossed the room, shaking visibly now, and rested his arms on the mantelpiece. He looked up into the mirror which reflected the window and the garden and the courtyard and landscape beyond. The image of the approaching Messerschmitt in the mirror seemed less than a mile away and diving towards the cottage. 'It's too bloody frightening!' shouted Peeb and rammed his face into his arms.

The sound of Peeb's wail of anguish was drowned by the noise of an aero-engine, a piston engine with a finely tuned prop. Brian caught hold of Susan's hand and pointed through the window.

'Look . . .! Look . . .!' he shouted.

Brian ran out into the courtyard pulling Susan after him.

The plane came on relentlessly until it skimmed the top of the beech tree, and adroitly banked to the right with a roar. Something smashed onto the ground ten yards away and Brian heard it bang across the courtyard to the garage. The plane turned and zoomed towards the west, the moonlight suddenly illuminating its previous black silhouette. They saw for a fleeting moment the outline of the pilot's head through the canopy, the white bordered black cross on the side of the fuselage and a number fore and aft and the sinister swastika on the front part of the tail.

Susan clutched Brian watching the plane grow smaller again as it climbed steeply. Then the engine cut out, opened up again, spluttered and finally roared confidently. Soon the sound died away and the plane disappeared from sight.

'Some ghost', said Brian quietly.

'A Messerschmitt. Just like Daddy said,' whispered Susan.

'My God,' said Brian. 'What a terrible mistake I very nearly made.'

They went quickly back into the living room. Peeb was still standing by the mantelpiece but now his hands were over his ears. He was shaking rhythmically, as if plugged into some vibrating machine.

Gently, they eased him away from the empty fireplace and tried to sit him down in his usual chair, but he struggled violently, and eventually they realised he wanted it turned round, so that he couldn't look out of the window. Under Brian's instructions Susan filled a tumbler with a weakish brandy and soda. Brian handed it to him.

'Here, Peeb,' he said, 'drink this. It'll be all right even with the drugs I've given you.'

Peeb stared at him, then took the glass. He drank it avidly in great gulps, as if it were the first draught from an oasis after a long journey across the desert. The shaking began to diminish and by the time he had inhaled a couple of times from the cigarette Susan had handed him, he was fairly steady.

'Better?' she asked.

He nodded weakly.

'Sorry about all that,' he said. He looked at Brian questioningly, seeking if not sympathy, his professional understanding. 'I thought I saw that ruddy plane again. Heard it go over – can't mistake the sound – Daimler Benz engine.' He tapped his forehead with his forefinger and then rotated the tip a couple of times. 'What the hell has gone wrong inside here, Brian?'

'Nothing, Peeb. Nothing at all,' said Brian.

'Come off it – I've told you – I'm not a child . . . It's no joke when your eyes and ears play diabolical tricks . . .'

'They haven't, Daddy,' said Susan. 'That's just it.'

'What are you two trying now?' said Peeb suspiciously. 'Have you both been cooking up some fanciful psychotherapy. . . .'

'No, Daddy . . .'

'That plane you saw and heard just now was a real live Messerschmitt. . . .'

'We saw it . . . both of us. . . .'

'Black cross on it's fuselage . . . swastika on the tail. There isn't any doubt about it,' said Brian. 'I'm afraid I owe you a very sincere apology. You're not suffering from any delusions or anything else of the sort.'

Peeb looked at Brian's apologetic face and Susan's happy grinning one.

'You're OK, Daddy. There's nothing the matter with you at all.'

She put her arm round him and kissed him and he felt the warm wetness of her tears on his cheek. He gave her a handkerchief he found in his dressing-gown pocket.

Eventually he sat up in the chair, brushed back his moustache with his forefinger. His voice was suddenly firm and authoritative.

'That's all very well,' said Peeb. 'But how do you know *you're* not having delusions as well?'

'We saw it. . . .'

'We heard it . . .'

'That's what I said. You saw a plane but was it a Messerschmitt? Apart from the cross what was on the fuselage. Tell me some more about it.'

'Two letters.'

'Letters. . . .?'

'No, Brian, numbers.'

'What numbers?'

'I . . . I don't . . . can't remember.'

'Well, what colour were they?'

'Couldn't tell in this light.'

Peeb sniffed, but he was obviously impressed.

'I don't know,' he said, 'it's all a bit circumstantial, isn't it? I mean we could all be under a collective delusion. . . .' He seemed to relish their discomfiture. 'You know – mass hysteria and all that . . . isn't that possible, Doc?'

Brian pondered the possibility. Then he asked, 'Have you a fair-sized torch?'

'There's one in the kitchen,' Susan replied.

'Would you get it for me?'

Brian went to the windows. Peeb swivelled his chair round and faced the outer world again with interest. Susan came back with the torch. Brian went out into the courtyard and walked over to the garage. He flashed the light on the ground from side to side and then, lodging the torch in his pocket, picked something up with both hands. It looked like a round flat stone. He came back across the courtyard. Halfway, he noticed something else. He bent down and awkwardly picked that up too.

Brian came back into the room and dropped something into Peeb's lap.

'What would you say that was?'

Peeb examined the thin branch and spray of leaves.

'Beech,' he said. 'Copper beech leaves. Broken off here.'

'From the top of your tree,' said Brian, 'and this is what did it.'

With both hands he lowered a somewhat dented and scratched black rubber-tyred circular object less than a foot in diameter onto Peeb's thighs. Peeb rotated it and turned it over almost reverently. Then he smiled up at them.

'What is it?' asked Susan.

'Tail-wheel,' said Peeb. 'BF 109E.'

PART TWO

COMPONENTS OF THE SCENE

'We in our haste can only see the small components of the scene We cannot tell what incidents will focus on the final screen.'

War Poet
Donald Bain

CHAPTER EIGHT

The next day, the Sunday after the Messerschmitt lost its tail-wheel Susan said, 'I shall be back later this afternoon. Brian's trying to cook me lunch. Don't get up to any mischief while I'm out,' she waved gaily.

'Same to you,' Peeb retorted.

Peeb ate the cold lunch Susan had left for him and drank a can of lager from the fridge. Then he sat in the chair in front of the window in the living room and started to read the Sunday papers. But he couldn't concentrate.

The events and revelations of the previous evening certified that the plane was real. Therefore it was being flown by a real pilot. Why had no one else in the village seen it? Probably had. There were a lot of planes about. They wouldn't know it. Anyway, at night they'd all be looking at TV.

This Messerschmitt could not be the Messerschmitt Peeb had shot down in 1940, nor could the man who had spoken to him in the pub be the pilot he had killed. Peeb got up and verified it all, unnecessarily since he knew it by heart, in his well-thumbed copy of Francis Mason's 'Battle of Britain'. The table for Luftwaffe losses on September 15th 1940 under a serial number had a single line entry.

Jagdgeswader 53A Combat Mission. Shot down in flames by Spitfire flown by Peebles-White of 063 Squadron near the Isle of Sheppey at 12.15 hours. Messerschmitt BF 109E-1 (3862) 100% loss. Oblt W. Greifswald killed.

Peeb and Susan and Brian had talked into the small hours wondering how to track down the living pilot, and locate the present plane. And to find a reason for it all.

There seemed no simple answers. It was agreed that anyone could disguise himself, or lose himself in the crowd like the man at the Air Display. Was it the same man? Was there a second, third or fourth man? A whole squadron of Messerschmitts? No. Peeb had a gut feeling it was one man, one plane and Peeb was the target. Could it be one of his old chums in disguise, pulling a practical joke?

At all events it should be possible to find the aircraft. He already had a piece of it. Planes had to take off somewhere. And they had to land somewhere. Peeb picked up the binoculars from the table and scoured the airspace over the estuary. He smiled at the reversal of his feelings. He was no longer fearful lest he should see the thing. He was actively looking for it.

Peeb did not know that all those years ago the 303 de Wilde bullet which had exploded from the outer port-wing Browning gun of his Spitfire had surged upwards through the duralumin skin of the Messerschmitt fuselage, cut through the hundred layers of Willi's silk parachute on which he was sitting, and pierced the back of his left thigh below the fold of his buttock, and out again. The spent bullet was probably still in the cockpit of his ME 109 under ten feet of sea-water.

With fury, Willi had heard his engine splutter and fail for lack of fuel just as the Spitfire gave him a one-second burst. Willi turned the Messerschmitt on its back as an escape ruse and put her into an intentional spin. He never saw the Spitfire again. Eventually Willi corrected the rotary descent and glided silently into that part of the Thames estuary which becomes the river Swale on the south-east shore of the Isle of Sheppey, pan-caking tail-down.

So he had a flesh-wound without bone damage or involvement of major structures. Supplies of the life-saving sulpha-drug prescribed for Anna's father were obtained surreptitiously. Anna's excuse to Doctor Page was that she had accidentally dropped the first lot of tablets he had given her down the lavatory. He accepted the story without question, by the truthful delightful child he had brought into the world over sixteen years ago. Willi's temperature remained normal after several days of treatment and in two weeks the wound in his buttock had healed.

By contrast, Jock Household's infection had not responded. Suddenly, when Anna entered his bedroom one morning to bring him his cup of tea, he half sat up in bed, gave a cry of recognition, and fell back on the pillows.

'Daddy . . . Daddy, don't go,' she said, but he was already dead from his second cerebral thrombosis. She sobbed then, and her sobbing continued through the day and intermittently through the evening.

Anna removed the pistol from the ledge behind the top of the kitchen dresser and emptied out the bullets. With a trowel she made a hole deep in the soil in the water-butt which served as a flower-tub. She dropped the bullets in the cavity and replaced the earth. Still carrying the gun, but by the barrel so there should be no misunderstanding, she went into the front room.

Willi stood up as she came in. He had lost a lot of weight, and his face had a grey, sunken appearance, offset by the sprouting of a beard. But his eyes remained blue and clear. He knew what had happened to her father. She put the Luger on the Davenport table inside the door and sat in the easy chair motioning him to the one opposite.

'Willi . . .', she began.

'*Fraulein* Anna,' he interrupted her solemnly. 'You have my deep and great sadness. . . .'

'Thank you, Willi,' she said.

Willi regarded her long graceful figure and the demure English way she placed her legs parallel to each other, the knees bent and pressed together. He observed the composed positioning of her hands. Her whole demeanour was one of quiet authority. He, Wilhelm von Greifswald, a fighter ace of the all-conquering Luftwaffe, heir to the Greifswald estate and Schloss near Peenemunde bowed and sat in the chair opposite Anna.

'As I told you Willi,' she said 'apart from my younger brother Charles who is in America with my Uncle George, I have no relations. Anna stared straight at Willi. He looked so ill and defenceless. How could the war have anything to do with the two of them sitting there in the sunny front room of an English farmhouse?

'Now father is dead, I am quite alone. Daddy's money will go mostly to Charles but I'll have been left the farm and the petrol station. She looked out of the window towards the river and smiled. 'Every bit of that useless marshland as far as you can see is all mine.' She turned to him again. 'But the other part at the back is not too bad. I shall survive.'

'Of course you will, *Fraulein*. . . .'

'What about you, Willi? What are you going to do?'

'Me? I shall survive too, of course. As soon as the occupation of England is established I shall personally see that you are rewarded as a friend of the Third Reich. . . .'

'Willi! There will be no occupation. It is *you* not *me* who has to worry.' She picked up the Luger and tossed it across to him. 'Here is your gun. I have thrown away the bullets. Now do you want to go?' Her voice was cold and angry.

'Where . . .?' asked Willi.

'Anywhere. Britain is quite a large place.'

Willi put the gun away waiting for her anger to subside.

'Why have you not told the *polizei* about me?'

'I . . . I have been too busy . . . with . . . with father and everything.'

'Thank you, *Fraulein*. I shall always remember how kind you have been to me.' Willi buttoned up his tunic. His boots he had managed to pull on earlier. Using a stick he had taken out of the hall, he limped towards her and held out his hand. '*Auf Weidersehen, Anna*.'

Anna ignored his gesture.

'You can't go like this. You can't escape. England as well as Sheppey is an island, you know. You will be captured almost immediately.'

'Perhaps,' Willi shrugged. 'But I shall soon be released. The war is nearly over.'

'No it isn't!' said Anna vehemently, tearfully. 'We shall never give in. The war will go on for years. And Germany will lose it.' The words were delivered with unassailable conviction. 'It is pointless your leaving now. I am prepared . . . if you decide to stay . . . to help you. And in exchange you can help me with the farm and all the things I have to do.'

After a pause, Willi said, 'I am most grateful, *Fraulein*, but will you not be running a continued risk . . . for yourself. . . .?'

Her expression brightened with a return to childlike enthusiasm.

'I have thought of a way. So that you can go about the farm without anyone suspecting anything.'

'Please explain.'

'You will have to do everything I say.'

'*Ja, Fraulein Kommandant,*' smiled Willi.

Anna went out of the room but was back in less than a minute. Willi had not moved. When he saw what she was carrying, he understood why he had heard distantly the sewing-machine in such use.

'It doesn't matter if they're not a good fit. In winter you will need lots underneath so I have made them on the large side, out of an old pair of curtains.' Willi surveyed the blue sailor-like jacket and trousers dubiously. 'And here is what goes round your neck.' She gave him a piece of bright red cotton which she had hemmed into a neat triangle. 'Put them on,' she instructed.

For a moment he hesitated and then gave her a broad indulgent smile.

'So you think I will make a good lunatic?' he asked.

Returning to Bluff Cottage nearly fifty years later, Susan was not surprised to find her father asleep in his usual chair, the Sunday papers on the carpet around him, a colour supplement open on his lap. Peeb started, and was wide awake immediately.

'Hello, Susan,' he said, 'sit down a minute.'

She did as he asked her.

'You know, Susan,' Peeb began, 'last night I really thought I was going bonkers.'

'I know Daddy . . . We were terribly worried about you.'

Peeb noted the use of the plural. He looked at her calmly. 'You've no need to worry now. I'm quite OK. But I'm going to get the joker who nearly succeeded.'

'You do think it's . . . it's all been intentional then?'

'Of course it's intentional.'

'But why?'

'I haven't a clue,' said Peeb, 'but one can safely assume the intentions of an enemy are basically offensive and potentially destructive.'

'Meaning?'

'He hasn't fired his guns yet.'

Susan felt a cold spot in the centre of her back.

'Isn't that . . . a little far-fetched?'

'More like jokey-crazy. That's what Brian called it. He ought to know. He's a doctor. With special training in nutcases.'

'Yes, that's true but. . . .'

'Well, if I'm the target of a dangerous lunatic, all the more reason not to become the victim too. So I'll have to plan a few counter-measures.' Peeb opened the colour supplement on his lap. 'I know what you're thinking,' he said.

'What. . . .?'

'That I'm getting the whole thing out of proportion again?'

'It's all so fantastic . . .', said Susan.

Peeb opened the supplement. 'If what's happened were a feature in this you'd react quite differently, wouldn't you?'

'How do you mean?'

'Power of the media, old girl.' Peeb paused a moment, narrowing his eyes. He turned over a few pages. 'First of all there'd be a photograph of you in front of the cottage. Then one of me in this room . . . a picture of the boys in the Squadron in 1940; a colour print of a Messerschmitt and a Spitfire in combat over the green and blue patchwork of England way below. . . And then the words. . . .'

Humouring him Susan asked, 'How would the words read, Daddy?'

Peeb looked out of the window and up at the sky. There was some cumulus building up at about fifteen thousand feet over Essex.

'"*Preposterous as it may seem in the age of ICBM's and space shuttles*"', he began. '"*But the preliminaries of an air-battle of World War II are warming up again over the*

Isle of Sheppey on the north coast of Kent. A Messerschmitt BF 109E, a fighter, last seen in the same piece of sky in the Battle of Britain 1940, appears to be pursuing an aggressive programme aimed at a specific target.

'"*The German plane and its unknown pilot materialise at irregular intervals, usually in the evening and keep well under the standard radar scans. On two occasions at least, low-level strafing attacks have been made at roof-top height over Bluff Cottage, the home of retired RAF Group Captain Peebles-White and his daughter Susan, a solicitor in Canterbury. Fortunately so far, no guns have been fired.*"'

'"*The Group Captain has settled into a peaceful retirement – his interests are gardening and a 1937 Lagonda car – in the village of Bishop's Felix where these astonishing events are taking place. It is perhaps significant that this veteran pilot of the Battle of Britain shot down a German fighter. . . .*"'

Peeb paused. The next words he had repeated on countless occasions over the years stuck suddenly in his larynx. Flames. Ruddy flames. Last night in the pub the flames had been contested. Could that be possible? He put his hand up to the scarring on the left side of his scalp. Could his mind that day long ago have confused one lot of flames for another? No. It was in the records. He'd just checked them over.

'"*sh . . . shot down a German fighter in flames over Bishop's Felix, nearly fifty years ago*"', he finished.

'Smashing,' Susan applauded. 'You should go on TV and do it just like that, Daddy.'

'Now listen to me, Susan,' Peeb's voice was abruptly fierce. 'I don't want you or Brian to mention what we saw last night to anyone. You understand?'

'But surely . . . the more people who know about it, the quicker we're likely to find out. . . .'

'Possibly but . . . at the right time . . . when I've got things organised. You understand?' he repeated.

Susan looked into her father's eyes and saw something that frightened her, something akin to . . . she didn't know . . . fanatical dedication?

'Yes, Daddy,' she said softly.

Peeb picked up the binoculars and made a long slow traverse across the whole width of the windows.

'This thing may turn out to be a long job . . . as well as a difficult one. It will need methodical research and patience. But there's no escape.'

'From what?'

Peeb lowered the glasses, turned round and gave her a disarming smile.

'The enemy,' he said.

Throughout October 1940 *Oberleutnant* Wilhelm von Greifswald, late of 3rd *Staffel Jagdgeschwader 26A, 'Schlageter,'* of II Gruppe of the Luftwaffe, based at Marquise in the Pas de Calais area of Northern France, spent his days doing simple tasks about Marsh Farm, near the village of Bishop's Felix on the Isle of Sheppey in Kent, England. The weather varied, some days being thick with mist, others blustery with sizeable waves pushing up the estuary and the Swale in rapid sequence. Dozens of planes still made their trails and sounds above. He watched helplessly the continuing combats of the fighters and bombers. On occasion he saw a German plane dive to earth or a parachute hit the water somewhere in the middle of the estuary.

Willi mixed with the other blue-coated, red-scarfed labourers, digging and dyking in the marshes, learning to match their demented grins with twitches and movements he invented of his own. Arthur prodded him with a stick as unconcernedly as he did the others, and Kim barked no louder, nor licked his hand less affectionately than he did the rest.

At the end of each day, Willi managed to detach himself from the main group, dodging behind a barn door or crawling under a tractor as a temporary hiding place. He watched the figures straggle back along the road to the asylum, where of course he, Willi, was not missed because he didn't start from there in the first place. Whatever stories the poor souls told about an extra in their midst, would be put down to the wanderings of feeble minds. It was a perfect cover.

He tapped on the kitchen window of the farm after darkness had fallen each night and Anna let him in. Rations were no problem because of the farm produce, but Anna had difficulty getting cigarettes in sufficient quantity. Willi had foolishly taught her to smoke and inhale and soon her need was as great as his.

They listened to the BBC and learnt of the nightly tally of mutual bombing, of planes lost or missing and Willi translated for her the claims which streamed out about the destruction of England from Reichsender Hamburg and short-wave transmitter DJA.

'Why is your English so good?' Anna asked.

'I had an English governess. At one time it was very *gemütlich* to have an English governess in the upper classes in Germany.'

'I only learnt French,' confessed Anna. 'I know no German. . . .'

'I know a little French, a little Russian. . . .'

'You know everything don't you?' Anna accused him suddenly. 'Languages, engineering, how to fly a plane . . .'

He put his hand over hers across the kitchen table and gripped it firmly.

'No, I do not know everything. And one of the things I do not know is why sometimes I think you . . . you like me . . . and at other times, you hate me?'

Anna looked at him hesitantly – she must never betray her feelings for this man.

'Perhaps because that's how I feel about you. . . .Sometimes one way. Sometimes another.'

He removed his hand and cleared away the things. He told himself that if the invasion did not come soon, he would have to make a decision about this virgin English girl, who attracted him so intensely.

On October 31st he went with Arthur and four other men from the asylum, all carrying shovels, down to the mudflats. During high tide the last twenty metres of the causeway was under water. There was a low broken wall stretching out on either side from the end of it, built there by Anna's father as the foundation for a jetty he had once planned so that he could add some fishing to the income from the land and the garage repairs and the sale of petrol. But it had never been completed. The barbed wire and the beach-landing defences started half a mile to the east. There was an acre or more of marshland which could be utilised for a root-crop if they unblocked the drains and culverts by the causeway.

That day Anna rode down on her pony to inspect the work. And that day, all the time they were at work there was no plane in sight. Not one. When they finished the stint and started to trudge back along the causeway, Willi stopped behind. It would be November 1st the next day he recalled. For some time the threat of invasion on the German radio had been conspicuous by its absence. He realised suddenly, certainly that it was too late now for an invasion. On the other side of the Channel, so near and yet so far, the idea of a landing this year must have been abandoned. And Willi illogically felt that he had been abandoned too. The next possible time would be May 1941. And next year the operation might be more difficult, its success perhaps uncertain.

The revelation shook Willi, because it was a reversal of all that he had believed up to that moment. Was he really going to have to stay in England, as Anna had prophesied? There seemed quite a chance that she was right.

He watched the receding tidal water lapping the far side of the wall by the causeway. The river was unusually clear and he could make out the sand and mud on the bottom. And then he saw it. The tip of one blade of a propeller projecting above the surface of the water like an old reed. His eye followed it down to the spinner. His eye quickly chased the contours of the mud and sand which marked out with mounds and projections the shape he knew so well. Incredibly it was there. His Messerschmitt. He heard Arthur calling to him. He ran along the causeway to join the blue and red working party, his mind for once as full of crazy ideas as the others.

CHAPTER NINE

That night after they had pushed the dishes to one side, Willi made rough drawings to explain to her how it could be done. She looked at the paper again where he had drawn a tripod of poles with a block and tackle hanging from the apex.

'Why didn't the recovery people see it when they went down the causeway?' she asked.

'They went at high tide. The plane was under water and further out. Now it's moved in against the wall. If we have some rough seas or a storm, it could break up and be gone forever.' Willi set his lips in a firm line. 'That must not happen to my Messerschmitt. You understand Anna?'

Willi screwed up the pieces of paper into a ball and tossed it into the coke-burner.

'OK' he said. 'I have explained the plan. Now you repeat to me what I have told you.'

'Well . . .' she began. 'First we wait for low-tide. The "loonies" dig away the sand and mud from the wings and fuselage. Then you and Arthur set up the block and tackle on the tripod over the engine, because that is the heaviest part, and secure the slings round it. Then we raise the whole plane.'

'No,' said Willi. 'Then we pray and raise the whole plane.'

'Right,' laughed Anna. 'The prayer is answered.'

'Good. Then?'

'Then with the tractor, Arthur pushes the big wagon to the end of the causeway so that the back part of the wagon comes under the plane. Then the "inmates" sit on the front of the wagon to counter-balance the weight as the plane is lowered. We unhook, move the tripod back, lift the plane again and swing it further along the wagon. And so on until it is fair and square in the middle.'

'Correct.'

'The rest is easy. We cover the plane with the tarpaulin. Arthur drives the tractor back up the causeway, across the road and the home field to the bigger Dutch barn. Inside we erect the tripod again, raise the plane and lower it onto the trestles. No one knows it's there. Except the "loonies". And who'll take any notice of them?' she finished with a flourish.

'Arthur knows it's there.'

'Arthur will do as I say,' said Anna. 'I'll tell him we're going to keep the plane and sell it later, when the metal is more valuable. So his share will be bigger.'

'Arthur still worries me,' said Willi. 'The whole thing has to be done absolutely correct if we are not to damage the plane. Everyone has to be coordinated. I don't think Arthur can do that. And he'll suspect me if I suddenly stop being a "loony" and take charge.' Willi frowned. 'No, it's not safe. We'll have to do it without Arthur. Send him off somewhere for the day.'

'We can't do it without Arthur,' said Anna. 'I'm not nearly as strong for one thing. And I can't make the "loonies" do what I tell them. Arthur can. They're afraid of him.'

Whatever would her father have said, if he had known? She felt pangs of sadness at his death, and guilt at what she was doing. If only she didn't feel such strong feelings for this man; her compulsion to help him was overpowing and she knew their was no deluding her heart as to the reasons why. She thought about Willi's plan for the Messerschmitt and the problem of Arthur. The solution suddenly popped up like the sign on a cash register.

'We can't change Arthur. . . .' she said.

'No.'

'But we can change you.'

'What do you mean?'

'So that he doesn't recognise you.'

'Explain. Please explain,' said Willi.

'You shave off your beard and moustache. I cut your hair and dye it brown. I can also dye a suit of father's. And then I introduce you to Arthur as my cousin from Scotland.'

'Have you got a cousin in Scotland?'

'Not till now. He's come down here to help me on the farm.'

'What's his name?'

'William Household. He was named after father and he has an identity card to prove it.'

'It is difficult to get a false identity card. . . .'

'I've got father's. I only had to hand over his ration book. All we need to do is change one or two numbers. It's only for you to use in an emergency . . . if ever a policeman stops you or something like that.'

Willi thought over what she had proposed.

'It might work . . .' he said doubtfully.

'It'll work enough for local gossip, and it'll certainly fool Constable Johnson. You see?' she said like a mischievous child. 'You'd get nowhere without me.'

Willi's face became serious.

'Do you understand where you are getting yourself, Anna? Helping an enemy pilot who is wounded is one thing . . . but disguising him and providing an identity card. . . .' he shrugged. 'If it were the other way round and we were in Germany, you would be shot.'

'But I am not in Germany,' she said. 'And nor are you.'

The point was unassailable. It was all a wild, ridiculous plan which could not possibly work.

'Willi. . . .?'

'Yes. . . .?'

'Supposing somehow you can lift the plane out of the water and on to the wagon and the tractor pulls it back to the farm, and we hide it away, what then?' she asked.

'What then? What then?' he retorted sharply. 'Then I shall repair it of course, and after that I shall get in the cockpit and fly it back to Germany – or that part of France which is now part of Germany.'

'Willi. . . .' Anna's eyes opened wide. 'You'll never do that!'

'Why not? It is the duty of every German officer to escape from captivity. . . .'

'I mean how can you repair something like a plane on your own? For one thing the engine must be full of water and sand and mud. . . .'

'Yes, it will have to be taken completely to pieces and reassembled. You have a garage. You have tools,' Willi's eyes lit up with enthusiasm. 'But most important you have something which is essential for the whole plan.'

'What's that?'

'Benzene. Petrol. You have petrol in the garage tank, yes?'

'Yes, but it's only "Pool" petrol. Doesn't a plane have to have special fuel. . . .?'

'For combat and full performance, of course. But I'm only going to fly it – just across the Channel. To escape. How many litres have you got, Anna? I need at least a hundred . . . to include engine tests.'

'There must be a hundred and fifty gallons left in the store-tank.'

'You must not sell any. Put a notice to say the petrol pump is closed.'

'You can't have all of it,' she objected.

'Why not? The tractor uses Diesel.'

'Because I'm going to start driving-lessons. In Daddy's car as soon as I'm seventeen,' said Anna simply.

Willi stared at her in disbelief at the inconsequence of such a trivial matter.

'And when are you seventeen?' he laughed.

'April the twenty-second, 1941.'

Willi patted her cheek affectionately.

'If you help me, I may even teach you to drive myself. Perhaps I will even teach you to fly, *liebchen*.'

'What does *liebchen* mean?' she asked but suspected she already knew. And she wanted desperately to be right. Willi took her hand, and kissed the back of it.

'It means "darling",' he said.

After a beat she withdrew her hand. Of course it meant darling. She felt the colour rising in her cheeks. She got up and started to put the plates they had used onto the tray. He was smiling at her indulgently.

'Darling, Anna,' he said. 'My little English sister.'

'Why do you make fun of me, like that?' she said fiercely.

Willi pushed his chair back and walked round the table. He put his hands on her shoulders.

'I do not make fun of you, Anna,' he said. 'I call you *liebchen* because that is how I feel for you.'

Willi slowly but gently pulled her to him. She seemed not to resist at all. And then he placed his lips on hers. For a second perhaps he felt her hesitate and then she shut her eyes and responded to his kiss.

The whole embrace lasted less than ten seconds. He did not press her more. When he took away his hands, she opened her eyes again and looked into his with the realisation, the shock of the magic which had happened. Her joy was so intense, so total, that Anna remained for a few moments paralysed by her excitement. Once again the powerful feelings she had for this man threatened to overwhelm her. Then she turned and ran out of the kitchen, up the stairs and into her bedroom.

The matron of Saint Beckett's Asylum for the Insane stood on the steps of the grey-bricked building in which she wielded almost unlimited power over the hundred and fifty inmates. If it weren't for the war they would have closed the place down.

'Goodbye, Matron,' said Tom Page. He got in the old Bentley and drove down the drive slowly in the chilling November mist, and turned right along the road to Marsh Farm. He needed some petrol, for which as a doctor his coupon supply was liberal. But also matron had sent out a patient on the farm working-party in spite of some swelling of his face. 'It's just toothache, Doctor Page,' she had said. 'It won't do Bellamy any harm to be out. Besides, he's not the wit to complain.'

'People with dementia seldom have,' Doctor Page had replied.

He stopped the Bentley by the petrol-pump. The notice on it said unequivocally 'Sorry. Sold out.' Tom Page smiled.

Anna always kept some for him. He gave two long blasts on the horn.

At the end of the causeway Willi and Anna heard the sound.

'What's that?' Willi asked.

'Car horn,' Anna replied.

As she spoke the protective fog surrounding them dissipated with incredible speed. The causeway stretched back, glistening with moisture under the weak sun which broke through. The horn sounded a third time and the farm buildings and garage became clear and distinct.

'That's Doctor Page. 'E'll be wanting some petrol,' said Arthur with the infallible knowledge of local inhabitants. The rotund, trilby-hatted figure of the doctor crossed the road and came towards them.

Willi took a decision and gave a sharp order.

'Lower her down again, Arthur!'

'Why?'

'Don't argue. The wing will catch the wall. I have to adjust the sling.'

'OK, mister.' Arthur turned to his blue-coated squad. 'Let go loonies . . . let go . . . steady, now.'

The chain-tackle made jabs of distinctive sound. Anna jumped off the wagon.

'I'll go,' she said and walked briskly after Kim who tail-wagged his greeting to the doctor all along the causeway. They met about two-thirds of the way back to the road. By which time the damaged Messerschmitt was half-awash on the mud again.

'Stop lowering,' snapped Willi.

Arthur passed on the order.

Willi climbed over the wall onto the far side and busied himself with the unnecessary inspection of the sling he had so carefully placed round the fuselage fore and aft of the cockpit. He was still trying not to worry about future problems. When the Messerschmitt had been lifted from the mud and sand, he saw that the tail-plane and rudder unit had been damaged by something after he had pancaked the plane on the water that hot afternoon in September.

Fortunately the tail-wheel, its castoring, the leg-cuff and the shock-strut were still intact. The rear of the fuselage had a gaping hole from which dangled the torn-off ends of the elevator and rudder cables. Through the hinged canopy he could see brown slime, half-filling the cockpit.

Damn the man, he cursed. Unless they were very lucky, this bumbling doctor was going to blow the whole operation. Willi hoped fervently that Anna could head him off. He put his hand into the water and scooped up some mud and sand, and tried to obscure the white crest on the plane enclosing the black 'S' of his *Staffel* insignia with mud. Water ran over the tops of his boots and his feet squelched in his socks.

He could see Anna talking to the doctor. She was making animated gestures with her conversation, movements he had grown to know and love. Go on, he urged her silently. Take him back to the petrol-pump and send him on his way. For a few seconds he thought he saw them turn to do just that, but then the doctor, laughing, pointed down the causeway and soon Kim was running towards them followed by Anna and her customer. Willi pondered a moment whether he should remain out of sight behind the wall. He decided it was safer to climb back and face the enemy.

'Willi', said Anna. 'This is Doctor Page. He wants to make an examination.' The words made Willi's brain freeze. He searched her face, her expression. Could it be that she was not what he had thought? That she no longer was on his side, that now she was going to betray him, tell all his plans? The continuation of her message swiftly melted his lightning apprehension.

'He wants to look at Bellamy, one of the inmates.' She turned back to the doctor. 'This is Will, my cousin from Scotland, who's come to help me with the farm.'

'How do you do, Mr Household,' said Dr Page. 'Very sad about your uncle.'

'Poor Daddy,' said Anna.

'Oh yes . . . it was very sad, but I did not know him well.'

'Jock was a lovely man,' said the doctor. 'But not as lovely as his daughter. She'll be glad of your help.'

He smiled at Anna and reached forward to shake Willi's hand, but Willi withdrew it in time.

'I'm afraid I'm wet with mud and sand,' he apologised and then made a real mistake. He bowed slightly and said 'How do you do, Mister Doctor?'

As he spoke he cursed himself for forgetting that in English the German *Herr Doktor* is never used. To his relief his ignorance of another English custom saved him.

'*Doctor*, Doctor Page. Not Mister. Never been a surgeon, though my father was.'

'Willi's trying to unblock the drains and culverts,' said Anna. 'Then this bit of marshland will be usable. Daddy was always putting off doing it.'

'Looks a tough job,' the doctor glanced past the wagon to the wall. 'What are you trying to raise from down there? A crashed plane or something?'

'Hope so,' laughed Anna, 'I can probably get some money for salvaging the aluminium from the Aircraft Recovery people.'

Willi was stunned with admiration at Anna's performance, but his heart jumped as Arthur said,

'It's a plane all right, Doctor. One of them Jerry Mizzy-shits.'

The doctor laughed and Anna joined in. She raised her eyebrows fractionally at Willi and he responded speedily.

'Missyshits,' said Tom Page. 'That's a good name for them, Arthur.' Dr Page turned to the four men in blue and red. 'Now which is Bellamy?'

Bellamy's cheeks were blue with the cold and obviously swollen. The doctor put his fingers in front of each of the man's ears. 'Open your mouth,' he said. 'Mouth!' Dr Page opened his own mouth by way of demonstration. The man copied him. 'Tongue,' said the doctor and put his own out at him. From Bellamy a dry coated organ protruded from between some decayed teeth.

'All right, put it away before it frightens someone,' ordered the doctor. 'Mumps,' he announced. 'Nothing to do but wait for them to go. Matron shouldn't have let him come out but he might as well stay now till they return home.

On his own he'd only get lost.' Tom Page looked round the assembled personnel. 'Hope you've all had mumps. Anyway it's the least infectious of the infections,' the doctor observed. 'Well, I mustn't keep you.'

Willi began to feel they were through the danger, but he wasn't prepared for the next question.

'Were you working on the land in Scotland?' the doctor asked.

'Er . . . no. . . .'

'Willy was in the RAF,' said Anna. 'Invalided out.'

'Oh, what with?' asked Dr Page.

'Duodenal ulcer . . . but it's not too bad now, is it Willi?' she prompted him.

'Much better,' he agreed.

'Annoying things. But they're quite right. The RAF I mean. You can't fight with an ulcer.'

'No, sir,' agreed Willi.

'Were you born in Scotland?' Suddenly, surprisingly the question came out like a shot.

'Yes,' said Willi and gave the only place-name he knew. Edinburgh.'

'Like matron. I must introduce you. But *your* accent isn't Scottish.'

This time Willi acted quickly and surely.

'My education was English,' he said.

'Very pleased to hear it,' said Dr Page. 'And now, Anna, if you will kindly dispense me that petrol.'

Anna bestowed a sideways glance of triumph at Willi, and letting Dr Page take her arm they began to walk away along the causeway. Before they had covered many yards the mist started to come in again in swirls and eddies and the two figures were soon lost from sight. Willi climbed back over the wall.

'Right, Arthur,' he called. 'Bring her up again.'

'OK you nits! Pull, pull, pull!' ordered the old man.

Like some strange water-phoenix Willi's Messerschmitt rose again from the mud of the Thames estuary.

* * *

The hacksaw handled snapped at the precise moment the blade cut through the aluminium rivet holding the dented section of the rear fuselage. The serrated edge of the saw came down with force across the back of Willi's left hand and thumb which were holding the tail-wheel shock-strut. The blade tore through the skin. Willi dropped the handle. Cursing with pain, he compressed the main artery at the wrist with his right hand. He walked steadily from the barn across the home field. Inside the farmhouse kitchen he held his hand under the tap and called to Anna.

She came running down the stairs. She saw the stream of blood and water swilling down the sink-drain. She forced herself to look at the back of Willi's hand. The sight of the exposed raw tissues made her stomach contract.

'Tourniquet,' she said. 'You need a tourniquet.'

'Yes,' said Willi.

Anna snatched the oddments of washing off the clothes-line. With the carving-knife she cut a two-foot length of cord.

'Let your wrist go a moment and take off your sweater', she said.

He did as he was told, spotting blood on the floor and the draining-board. She undid his shirt cuff and folded the sleeve back. Then she put a loop of line round his forearm over the two thicknesses of shirt and pulled it tight and secured it. The arterial spurting stopped, a darker venous ooze taking its place. Willi put his hand under the tap again and inspected the wound. He noticed he could not straighten his first and second fingers, nor his thumb. The digits hung down limply and they felt numb and senseless.

'Dr Page?' he queried.

'No. It's got to be the hospital.'

'But that will mean records . . . notes . . . this is just the way I'll be captured . . .'

'Willi . . . Willi darling . . .' the tears came into Anna's eyes. 'You can't lose your hand. We have to take the risk.' She kissed him on the cheek. 'I'll be with you. We'll make it. Don't worry.'

She covered his hand in a towel and they went out to the garage. It was freezing cold and the car did not start without trouble. Willi drove with his right hand on the steering-wheel. Anna knew enough about the gear-lever movements to follow his instructions. They crossed the bridge over the River Swale to the mainland of Kent and after one stop to loosen the tourniquet for a minute and re-tighten it, they reached the hospital in Canterbury without any serious mishap.

They kept Willi in for ten days. He had to have a transfusion and the repair of the tendons and nerves was a long job, requiring the skill of the senior surgeon. Anna visited him daily and no awkward questions were asked. His identity card passed muster and he was issued with an emergency ration-book. Willi marvelled at the totally unsuspicious nature of the nursing-staff and the other patients. Anna told them he had been in the RAF and was invalided out. From then on Willi was embarrassingly treated to the adulation accorded a Spitfire pilot. He refrained from declaring that he flew a plane of another colour.

It was while he was in hospital, which period straddled the Christmas festivities, that he heard the news on the radio of the continuing blitz on London. He also heard the reports of the RAF's attention to Hamburg and Cologne and Essen. At night he listened to the planes go over both ways in the darkness above the building. He looked down the ward at the green-shaded light on the nurse's table and sensed the imperturbable spirits in the sleeping or half-sleeping forms in the beds around him. He thought of the kindnesses he had been shown and the unassuming courage which pervaded the atmosphere. But above all his earlier contempt for an unprepared, inefficient enemy changed to irritation at their refusal even to consider defeat. To this was added a grudging admiration. Finally the first lightning shafts of doubt began to assail him; doubt that the war would be over quickly, but not yet the doubt that Germany might not win it.

When he returned to the farm his hand was still stiff and numb and he knew there were long months ahead of healing and exercise for the repaired tendons and nerves.

He recognised the injury might prevent his resuming work on the Messerschmitt for a year. The prognosis proved somewhat optimistic. When the news came through in June 1941 that Germany had invaded Russia, he suspected that the invasion of England had been called off. When, in the next December, Pearl Harbour was attacked and the Americans started appearing in Britain in 1942 he accepted that any invasion was now likely to go the opposite way across the Channel. All of which made the Messerschmitt project more hazardous, and more urgent. When eventually he resumed work on the repairs it was early in 1943. The task took on the quality of a total obsession.

In the first winter before the accident Willi had methodically assessed the problems, his resources and the chances of success. He remembered looking round the garage at his assets. He found the usual tools. A breast-drill, a set of bits, rat-tail files, ball-hammers for panel beating and the unusual 'find' of some aluminium rivets. There were ring-spanners, box-spanners, tin-snips. There was an oxyacetylene torch without which he could not have proceeded far. The engine had to be stripped down and cleaned thoroughly with tractor vaporising oil. Fortunately, there was paste available for grinding in the valves. He had to fashion new gaskets and these took weeks of painstaking work. He would be on low-grade petrol with retarded ignition. He stripped out the two 20mm MG 17 machine-gruns from the wings and the 20mm cannon from the propeller hub. He was not seeking combat this time.

The flight would be done on direct visual without instruments. There were problems with the undercarriage hydraulics. He had decided to dispense with retraction and fix the oleo-legs in the wheels-down landing position. A supply of glycol engine-coolant had to be built up laboriously from small quantities of glycerine obtained ostensibly for other purposes. He repaired the tail-unit with wood and dope-covered fabric. The knowledge and memory of his days in the Messerschmitt factory at Regensburg before he left for the glamour of the Luftwaffe, was needed and utilised to the full. But of all the factors which encouraged him against these formidable odds, none was more important than the intact variable-pitch propeller blades inserted in their tri-radial disposition into the spinner. To Willi the prop became his symbol of ultimate success. Because of his tail-down ditching it was quite undamaged. He kept it suspended under sheets in the barn and whenever he was feeling depressed or even in despair, he would uncover the shining blades and regard them as a beautiful sculpture in their own right.

The recovery of his hand was laboriously slow. Full skilled coordination took over two years to return. The amount he could do on the plane was severely limited until 1944. By then D-Day, the plot against Hitler and Arnhem had all passed. He now had to fly to the east of the Rhine to find a safe landing-place. Willi's spirit was at its lowest ebb in December 1944 but the sudden counter-attack by von Runstedt in the Battle of the Bulge stiffened his resolve. At last, on Christmas Eve – their fifth together – he was ready to make his first test of the powerful inverted V 1200 h.p. Daimler-Benz engine. In the middle of the afternoon Anna was decorating the small Christmas tree, when he told her.

'I want to be there,' she said.

'I need you there,' replied Willi. 'But please do as I say. It could be very dangerous. Anything could happen. . . .'

'Such as. . . .?'

'Such as the engine exploding, the propeller coming off and killing both of us. . . .'

Willi had made an elevated test-bed from an old steel saw-bench, powered in the past by a traction-engine. At the end of the garage he had constructed extra doors which when open would allow the slip-stream to escape harmlessly into the field. The propeller and spinner were attached to the engine which would later be fitted back into the plane. The whole set-up looked like some fantastic toy, a seasonal present of incredible magnitude.

Willi kept the ignition off and checked the compression of the cylinders by rotating slowly the propeller-blades. Satisfied, he inserted the starting-handle into the starboard side of the engine and switched on the ignition. Sweating with anxiety in spite of the cold December air, he showed Anna how to operate the throttle control.

'When she fires, only increase the speed as I signal. I want to check the revs and the oil pressure and only take her up slowly to flying speed. And keep your head down,' he warned.

He wound the geared handle round briskly, repeatedly altering the ignition timing again and again but the first cough did not come for ten minutes and did not repeat itself. Anna looked sadly on as Willi's rage mounted. Finally they gave up, shut the doors and went into the farm out of the cold and drank large mugs of hot tea.

At length Anna said, 'Well, you did your best, darling. You knew there was a chance that all your efforts might fail.'

Willi banged his cup down.

'I have not failed yet! This engine does not fail. It is one of the finest aero-engines in the world . . .'

'Of course, Willi, of course,' Anna said softly.

'Come,' he snapped. 'We shall try again.'

They went back into the darkened garage. Willi used a torch for inspection of the engine because of the blackout. After a time she heard him curse.

'What is it?' asked Anna.

'It's the damned fuel injection pump. I shall have to take it down and clean it out.'

'How long will that take?'

'I don't know. But I'm going to do it.'

'OK. I'll get some food.'

Anna went back into the house and about ten o'clock returned with some hot soup and mince-pies. Willi scoffed them down greedily. About half-past eleven Anna said she was going to hang up her stocking. 'For Santa Claus,' she added appropriately.

'Don't go now,' said Willi. 'Get on the throttle. I'm ready to try again.'

She did as she was told and Willi started to crank the engine. At about the sixth turn the engine coughed. coughed again, fired and then the blades of the prop started rotating.

Slowly he turned to Anna and signalled. She depressed the lever gently. The blades picked up speed until the revolutions became invisible except as a circle of grey where the torch light was reflected. The roar of the engine built up to a deafening pitch and the slip-stream tore at their faces and hair. Willi said something but she couldn't make out the words in the din. He switched off the ignition. The engine sound died away and the air settled quietly round them.

'What did you say, Willi?' she asked.

'We have an engine. We have a plane. Now we have to marry them.' He kissed her, and holding her away looked into her eyes. '*Heilige na*cht, *liebchen,*' he said.

'Merry Christmas,' said Anna and then burst into tears.

CHAPTER TEN

On Monday morning, Peeb had outlined his mock article for the media. Susan made two impulsive decisions. She told the senior partner of her firm that she wished to leave in six months' time. Then, dispensing with a surveyor's report, she made a verbal offer over the phone for the shop in the High Street. It was five thousand less than the asking price. She gave the figure to Anna's husband, who said his wife was not available. When Brian came round for dinner he said,

'Anna just managed to crawl into my surgery this morning with an acute flare-up of her bronchitis. I sent her straight home to bed – antibiotics, a Ventolin inhaler and ordered the District Nurse round with an oxygen cylinder and mask.'

'Will she be all right?' asked Susan.

'Oh, she'll get over this attack. I'll get her x-rayed again when it's over. But there's no cure. And she won't stop smoking. I shall press her hard about the trip to California as soon as she's reasonably able to fly.'

'More coffee?' Susan handed him a cup before he had responded. She had got to know this man so well – a man so serious and dedicated to his patients and yet a man capable of tremendous passion as she had recently discovered. She knew she was in love with him – a fact she had been aware of some time now.

'Thank you,' he said, catching her eyes for a moment.

'Is your chum in Eastchurch on call for you tonight?'

'No, unfortunately. He's gone to a BMA dinner. I've had all calls transferred to this number temporarily.'

'Oh,' said Susan simply.

'Until nine o'clock surgery tomorrow morning,' Brian added and looked at her steadily.

'Oh. . . .' repeated Susan. She returned his look for a beat and then they smiled at each other. 'I should tell you; even when Daddy's here breakfast in this establishment is at seven-thirty sharp. I have to be in Canterbury by nine.'

'Yes, darling,' said Brian. He removed her hand gently from the coffee-jug handle, and pulled her to him without awkwardness. He kissed her in several ways over a considerable length of time. Why did this woman arouse him so? He had had a number of relationships in the past but never before had he experienced this sense of belonging, this great physical attraction and most importantly a deep need of this woman. As they broke their kiss, they eyes met. Tenderly Brian removed a strand of hair that had fallen across Susan's face. Gently, breaking their embrace Susan asked,

'How did you know Daddy wouldn't be coming home tonight?'

'You told me over the phone that he'd called from the RAC Club in London that he wouldn't be back to dinner.' Brian gave her a broad grin. 'So I took a gamble on the rest.'

'In fact he said he wouldn't be back for a couple of nights.'

Brian's grin became broader.

'I'm getting very fond of your father,' he said, and put his lips once more over hers.

Later, when they were lying side by side in the dark listening to the downpour pounding the roof, Susan said,

'I'm still worried about Daddy. . . .'

'There's nothing wrong with him, I assure you. Do you know what I think, Susan?'

'What. . . .?'

'That you should start letting your father fight his own battles, past or present.' Brian turned towards her, over her. 'And concentrate on your own.'

He kissed her breasts and her neck and she responded vigorously and put her legs around him. Then she drew him into her and it was much later when she noticed that the rain had stopped.

* * *

Normally, if he had any business in London in the daytime, Peeb would avoid the appalling traffic problem when he got there by taking the train from Sittingbourne. But because part of the purpose of his visit involved carting the tail-wheel of the Messerschmitt with him, he went in the Lagonda.

Before he had left on the Monday afternoon, he had telephoned Mart Beddows – now Sir Martin Beddows – an old schoolfriend. Mart was one of the permanent mandarins in the Ministry of the Environment, kept on in spite of his age and Margaret Thatcher. Peeb just wanted, if not actual information, which he knew he would not get, but an impression, a lead if there was one, on his present quest from Mart's lighning-conductor of a double-first brain. If there was any aspect of the affair which was official, Mart would know about it.

As if they had last spoken ten minutes instead of ten years ago his old friend's voice, following a gauntlet run through several secretaries, PA's and assistants, came through the phone.

'Hello, Peeb. You must stop ringing me all the time like this,' he said.

Peeb took up the joke and played it back.

'Mart. Are we scrambled?'

'You sound positively *poché*. How are you? Where are you? And for how long?'

'Cracking form. In Kent, but I'll be in town tonight. Two days. Might be three. Can you make dinner? RAC?'

'No. With me. Athanaeum. Tomorrow. Tuesday. Seven o'clock.'

'Willco.'

The line snapped off and without more ado the meeting had been arranged.

Peeb left the Lagonda, its locked boot housing the tail-wheel, in the RAC underground park, and walked briskly across Pall Mall and St James's Square, and up into Piccadilly. Hatchards was as reliable a bookshop as ever. He found a volume on the war-planes of World War II, another on German fighters which detailed the development and modifications of the Messerschmitt 109 from the thirties to the end of the War. For good measure he bought an extra copy, since it was now in paperback, of Deighton's classic 'Fighter'. He also purchased the Ordnance Survey Map Sections – the old one-inch-to-the-mile, covering the Estuary, the Essex and Kent coasts and the 1:25,000 sheets of the Isle of Sheppey itself. He asked for everything to be parcelled up and delivered pronto to the RAC. No problem. Hatchards complied without a murmur.

From the bookshop he went up Bond Street to Dixon's Photographic and obtained something he'd always wanted, but never quite afforded: a 125 millimetre telephoto lens for his old Pentax. The current price knocked him back a bit, but he obtained some free advice on the new fast Japanese colour films and he was also sold a couple of rolls of professional very fast black-and-white which would really be more useful if he was going to have to shoot at one five-hundredth at least, in evening light.

Back in the RAC after dinner he took his books to the reading room and browsed through them while he had his coffee and brandy. Half an hour later he was nodding off in the chair and well before ten he was in bed and fast asleep.

He awoke refreshed and managed a fashionable jog round St. James's Park, a swim in the pool, and an English breakfast, before he nosed the Lagonda up the Edgware Road against the incoming commuters.

At that early hour on a weekday the RAF Museum car park was virtually empty. He parked facing the arch-windowed façade which reminded him of a hotel in Tunis without the sunlight. He spoke from the phone at the entrance desk to the Assistant Librarian and asked if he could have a ticket in half an hour's time. Then he walked across the tarmac to the Battle of Britain building.

He went down the aisle where the German planes were displayed at an oblique angle to the roped-off barrier. He spotted the Messerschmitt 109 immediately. It suddenly struck him how small and inoffensive it seemed compared with the large bombers further down. But when he saw the swastika on the tail and the *Schwarz Kreuz* on the fuselage, his belly muscles tightened and he heard in the eerie silence of the Museum the percussive snap of the 20 millimetre cannons. He had taken careful measurements of the tail-wheel and its broken-off piece of castor. Looking furtively round to make sure the uniformed attendant was out of sight, he ducked under the rope and tiptoed across to the plane. Using a steel tape-measure he quickly took the dimensions of the tyre and the piece of castor and counted the number of spokes. He jotted the figures down on the postcard he had brought for the purpose and on which he had put the measurements of the wheel in the Lagonda boot. The two columns tallied exactly. He was back in the aisle before the attendant re-appeared. Peeb gave a token salute to the Spitfire and Hurricane further down the gallery, and then made his way round past the Heinkel III, the Dornier 217, the Wellington and the Stirling.

Well, there seemed no question that the wheel he possessed was to all appearances the tail-wheel of a Messerschmitt. Now he needed professional confirmation.

The Assistant Librarian was not more than thirty-five. He was obviously used to showing appropriate respect to veterans of the War which had begun long before he was born, but he was also used to dealing with many other types of enquiries.

'I merely want an official confirmation,' said Peeb.

'Of an unidentified flying object?'

'No. Of a Messerschmitt BF 109E.'

'Er yes. Have you any photographs, sir?'

'Not yet. But I've got a piece of the plane – a tail-wheel. It's in my car outside.'

'Ah, I see,' smiled the man with dawning revelation. 'You want the aircraft archaeology people. It's something you've dug up?'

'No it's something that came down,' Peeb said. 'As I told you.'

'Hold on a minute, sir.'

The man went over to someone who looked like his twin brother and exchanged a few whispered words. They both returned beaming.

'This is Mr Conway. He is somewhat of an authority on World War II aircraft.'

'Morning,' said Peeb and shook hands. 'Would you like to have a dekko at this bit of Hun I've got downstairs?'

'Hun?'

'Messerschmitt.'

'Ah, yes. Glad to, sir.'

When they got to the Lagonda Peeb unlocked the boot, unwrapped the old blanket he had tied round the tail-wheel with cord, and exposed it to view. Conway heaved the wheel half out of the car and inspected it with care. Then he stood back and shook his head.

'I don't understand it,' he said.

'Look, old boy,' said Peeb. 'Is it a BF 109 tail-wheel or not?'

'Certainly. Certainly, but it's in such excellent condition. It's from a 109 Emil late '39 or early '40. It's been fantastically preserved and looked after. . . .' Conway glanced at the gleam on the Lagonda's bodywork. '. . . like a vintage car. I suppose you've kept the tail-wheel as a souvenir of your war days, sir?'

'This wheel collided with a tree next to my cottage two days ago and landed in my front garden.'

'It couldn't . . . I mean I'm afraid that's impossible.'

'Why?'

'Because there are only two BF 109's of this vintage in existence. One's in the museum over there. And the other's in Luftwaffe Museum near Bonn.'

'Well,' said Peeb 'Now there's a third one. Flying about somewhere with part of its arse missing.'

'But that means it's being kept, serviced and fuelled somewhere. . . .' Conway rubbed his finger around the surface of the tyre, and looked at the deposit left on his finger. 'It would have to be some sort of Flying Club. There's a publication listing all of those.'

'I've thought of that', said Peeb. 'But they'd never keep this secret. Why should they? The publicity would bring funds into the Club like billyo.'

'Then it must belong to a private owner', Conway picked up some small dried lumps of earth and grass and straw strands from inside the blanket. 'And he doesn't take off from a runway. But these planes and the Spitfires and Hurricnes, as you already know sir, could take off from any fairly flat field if it was dry and firm enough.'

'Sure', agreed Peeb. 'But landing wasn't so easy.'

Peeb saw the younger man glancing at the old scarring on his scalp and the recent bruise and abrasion of his forehead.

'No, sir', said. 'I don't expect it was.'

Peeb wrapped up the wheel again and secured it with the piece of rope. Then he locked the boot.

'Thanks for the info,' he said.

'Not at all, sir . . . just a minute, I've remembered something. There were three or even four old Messerschmitts obtained from Spain and used by a film company some years ago. But I think they were earlier 109 B's built under licence by Hispano-Aviacion after the Civil War.'

'What happened to them? After the film?'

'I don't know. Some were written off certainly. Perhaps one could have survived. We've no official information from Spain. I suppose you could try the film companies.'

'Do you know the title of the film?'

'"The Battle of Britain", I think.'

Peeb grinned and shot out his hand. 'Thanks a lot, old boy. Most helpful.' He got into the Lagonda and drove off with an unnecessary flourish.

Peeb had plenty of time to think while crawling back through the traffic of central London to the National Film Theatre on the South Bank.

He found out there was a rumour that at the end of shooting "The Battle of Britain" some stunt pilot had bought back the plane from whoever owned it in Spain, presumably the Spanish Government for probably quite a reasonable sum, and had kept it somewhere, so that when the next demand for a war film with a Messerschmitt came up he'd have the only one on the market all ready to fly. 'And he's recently been getting in a bit of practice round Bishop's Felix,' thought Peeb. It would also explain the pilot in the pub. Stunt flyer/actor, same man or two chums having a spot of fun at the old boy's expense. Yes. That could be it but it was a joke Peeb didn't appreciate. In fact, it made him bloody livid.

The girl in the Film Archives Department was charming and very helpful. She turned up promptly all the information on the Battle of Britain film, which listed the whole production team, including the names of the two fliers used and the members of the air-camera crew. But she couldn't tell him what happened to the planes when it was all over. She happened to know where the same Director of Photography and Lighting Cameraman had an office. She rang through and very persuasively fixed up an appointment for Peeb to see him at three o'clock.

He left the Lagonda in the Festival Hall Park and took a taxi. The office was just behind the Savoy. Peeb was not kept waiting.

'If you had to make another film about World War II where would you get a Messerschmitt 109?' As with the Venus of the archives, Peeb had prepared his question in order to avoid stating the real reason for his enquiries.

Barry Huxtable lit a Rothman's and pushed the packet across the desk at Peeb.

'I shouldn't bother,' Barry said. 'No point.' He shook his head sadly. It was an unencouraging reply.

'You mean with all this peace stuff . . . another film about World War II isn't very interesting any more?'

'Oh no. There's a new surge of interest in the WW II genre. Especially after this year's 50th anniversary of September 3rd 1939. But if we shot a film now we wouldn't bother with the actual planes. We can do virtually anything with models – did you see Star Wars?'

'No, I missed it,' confessed Peeb.

'Models. Static studio mockups of an ME 109. Back projection. All the old tricks and all the new ones. And we've got miles of aerial combat shots from all the other films. The actual real-war footage is no good of course because it's black-and-white.'

'I see,' said Peeb. He thought of the vapour trails in the blue of the sky and the red stabs as the Brownings fired on the wings. 'Do you remember what happened to the Messerschmitts you used in the "Battle of Britain" film?'

'Yes. Two were write-offs. The other two went back to the Spanish Army.'

'But they wouldn't still be using those, would they?'

'Not unless they were crackers. They'd shake to bits at any speed. That is if they could be got off the ground.'

Peeb decided to take the risk.

'So if you saw a BF 109 diving on Tower Bridge and pulling out just in time and then back over St Paul's and head down river again, what would you think?'

'I think I'd go out and take a taxi to Harley Street.'

Peeb grinned. 'I thought you might say something like that. But if I told you it really was so. The plane – real I mean?'

'Then there'd have to be some nut who'd rebuilt a whole new Messerschmitt, for some peculiar personal reason. And he'd also have to be something like a multi-millionaire nut to pay for it.'

Peeb stubbed out his cigarette. He felt deflated. The film idea had turned out to be a dead-end trail.

'Thank you for your help, Mr Huxtable,' he said, getting up.

'A pleasure.'

They shook hands and he followed Peeb to the door. As he opened it he asked,

'Are you in touch, Group Captain . . . with some finance . . . er . . . for a world War II film. . . .?' I mean . . . it might . . . it'd have to be a block-buster to make any money. They all have to be. But I could certainly. . . .?'

Peeb realised the tramlines along which the other man's mind must always be running.

'Thanks . . .' he repeated. 'Not at the moment I'm afraid.' Peeb felt suddenly sorry for the grey hopelessness in the hopeful question. He produced his best Squadron-reunion smile. 'But if I do . . . get involved, I'll be on to you like a flash, old boy,' he said, and beat a retreat down the flight of stone stairs to street level.

There were no messages for him back at the club. He took an *Evening Standard* from the porter and went up to his room. There was a time for an hour's kip before he needed to get ready for Mart at the Athanaeum. He lay on the bed and listened to the distant sounds of the Pall Mall traffic below. Without any effort at all he dropped off to sleep. He couldn't remember exactly what he had dreamt about, but he awoke with a start and found he was repeating a phrase to someone. 'Landing wasn't so easy . . . landing wasn't so easy'. Then he recalled the conversation with Conway up at the RAF Museum and he knew he had taken no action about the most important aspect of it.

Peeb got off the bed, put on his shoes and jacket and retied his tie. From the drawer of the writing-desk in the room he found a couple of envelopes. As soon as he reached the Lagonda in the RAC garage, he opened the boot, unlashed the cord round the blanket which enclosed the tail-wheel. Carefully he scooped up some of the dried soil with his hand and put a sizeable sample into each envelope. He sealed them, re-wrapped the wheel and went back to his room to change.

He had only to walk along Pall Mall to the little square which led to the Duke of York's column and the steps down to the Mall. In the towering hall of the Athanaeum with its overpowering stairway and the famous oil painting of Charles Darwin, he found Mart waiting for him. Mart had gone bald. The sight shocked Peeb a little and he wondered how he had altered.

'Mart . . . Haven't changed a bit.' They shook hands warmly.

'You're as good a liar as ever, Peeb,' Mart chuckled.

They were served prettily by the waitresses in the dining room; a simple English meal but of best quality – sherry, soup, lamb cutlets, house claret, no sweet, Stilton cheese. They climbed the staircase to the long reading room. Mart sat opposite him in another leather chair and beamed benevolently.

'Well, Peeb. Out with it. What's bothering ye, laddie?'

Peeb took out one of the envelopes he had prepared in the garage and handed it to Sir Martin Beddows. His old friend took the envelope, but didn't open it. Slowly he held it to his ear and shook it gently.

'Ah. Letter-bomb,' he smiled.

'Wrong,' said Peeb, 'but don't open it now.' Mart shook the envelope a little more vigorously listening to the sound of the moving contents.

'Hemp seeds?'

'What a suspicious mind you've got.'

'I'm paid to have one. Jumping beans?'

'Much simpler. You might say quite basic.'

A look of faint distaste came over Mart's face.

'Oh no, Peebles-White. Not that. You'll have to be beaten after lock-ups.'

Peeb laughed at the school-time allusion.

'Of course not. It's a sample of earth.'

'Earth?'

'Soil.'

So. . . .?'

'Well, ground is presumably part of the Environment and that's your Ministry, so I wonder if you could find out more or less exactly where it comes from?'

Mart shook the envelope again, then made a note with his biro on the outside, and put the envelope into his breast-pocket.

'Might take a few weeks. Now tell me the rest.'

Peeb summarised as briefly as he could his recent disturbing experiences.

'What's the Messerschmitt flight-range fuel-wise?'

'365 to 460 miles,' said Peeb.

'Unless he has an auxiliary tank?'

'No sign of that. So I estimate, taking Bishop's Felix as the target, he must take off from a place not more than 230 miles radius. But he does a lot of zooming and to-ing and fro-ing and uses more fuel because of the low-level stuff. That reduces it to about 150 to 170 miles to give him any margin of safety.'

'Liverpool, Amsterdam, Paris, St Malo,' said Mart. 'Hell of a lot of soil.'

'You can't do it?'

'Yes we can do it, but we're talking in months now and it would shorten the time if I had more samples.'

Peeb gave him the second envelope. Mart smiled.

'Thanks. You were going to keep that? If you vacuum the blanket you'll get a lot more.'

'Right,' said Peeb and smiled with satisfaction. 'I knew you'd come up with something helpful.'

The evening was dry and balmy after the previous night's rain and storm, and Mart strolled back with Peeb along Pall Mall to the RAC. He refused the offer of a final drink and hailed a taxi. As he said goodbye he added,

'I don't want to depress you, but it's just occurred to me that our calculations of distance could be wildly out.'

'Why. . . .?' asked Peeb.

'Well, theoretically, the plane could land near you and refuel for the return trip. That would mean Edinburgh, Dublin, Dijon, Frankfurt, Bremen.'

'Under all that radar? The whole of Nato would have to be asleep!' protested Peeb.

'Some people think it is. Goodnight. I'll be in touch.'

'Goodnight, Mart,' said Peeb. 'And many thanks.'

He watched the taxi break out into the traffic. Inside, the porter gave him his key and he went up in the lift. Frankfurt, Bremen. The names faintly flicked distant apprehensions.

CHAPTER ELEVEN

Just after his return from meeting Mart Beddows in London, Susan ran the Metro into the garage beside the Lagonda, walked across the forecourt and let herself into the cottage.

'Daddy. . . .' she called.

'Up here,' came a voice from above. 'Unpacking. You're early. Everything OK?'

'Fine. I've taken an afternoon off for a change.'

'A letter came for you. About five minutes ago. Pushed through the box.'

Susan picked up the brief-size envelope marked 'By Hand' from the hall-table, where Peeb had put it. She knew what it was. With a little scud of excitement she opened it. A neat hand-written note was clipped to the main bundle of photostat papers.

Dear Miss Peebles-White. My wife asked me to drop this in to save time. She is feeling a great deal better. Should you care to ring her at home, please do so. Yours sincerely, William Household.

Susan went into the living-room, sat down and began to study the copy of the Deeds to 'The retail premises situate at 31 High Street, Bishop's Felix on the Isle of Sheppey in the County of Kent. . . .'

The shop had been conveyed to Miss Anna Household in 1950 from the previous owner, Michael Swan of Leysdown. In 1960 this was changed to joint ownership, Mr William Household and Mrs Anna Household.

With a professional eye Susan rapidly read through all the clauses in the papers. Peeb came in, pecked at her forehead, sat in the chair by the window and lit a cigarette. Susan put the documents back in the envelope and smiled with satisfaction.

'How did you get on?' she asked her father. 'Anything exciting to report?'

'Going to ask you the same thing, old girl.'

Susan tapped the envelope.

'Deeds to the shop in the High Street. No restrictions. No easements. . . .' She stopped. Something in her father's expression gave her the embarrassing clue to his remark. She felt her face colouring up. 'Oh. . . .' she said. 'You've seen it.'

'Seen what?' asked Peeb with apparent innocence.

'Brian's dressing-gown . . . behind the bathroom door.'

Peeb pursed his lips and shook his head slowly.

'Not a very pleasant . . . combination of colours.' He broke into an indulgent smile.

'I'm sorry Daddy. . . .' apologised Susan.

'You can't be responsible for someone else's taste.'

'I meant I'm sorry I didn't put it away.'

'Needn't be, darling,' said Peeb. 'But it . . . gave me a bit of a shock. Then I said to myself 'Well . . . she's a grown woman . . . got her own career . . . self-sufficient . . . it's her home . . . She can do what she likes.' He gave her an affectionate glance. 'And if it's of any importance . . . or significance . . . I think Brian's a splendid chap.'

'I definitely want the shop.' Susan changed the subject. 'It's ideal for my office.'

'What's happened to your offer?'

'Anna Household has been quite ill. Over the worst now, thanks to Brian.'

She passed the note from Mr Household to Peeb, which he read quickly and handed it back.

'Sounds as if they're in a bit of a hurry. Good time to haggle.'

'I'm going to ring her,' said Susan and went out into the hall to use the telephone.

'Household . . . Household? The name rang a bell somewhere in Peeb's head, but he couldn't pin it down. When she came back into the room, she said,

'I'm going to see her now.'

'I'll take you,' said Peeb.

'Turn left here, then fork right,' said Susan when they were on the way. He turned the first corner as instructed. Shortly they approached a gaunt nineteenth century building of some size, three storeys high with an encircling drive.

'What's that?' Peeb enquired.

'It's half-empty. The other half is an Old People's Home. Way back it used to be a "loony-bin".'

'All in Brian's territory?'

'Yes. He goes there twice a week.'

Peeb looked at the staring curtainless windows and sensed the desolation and depression which must lie behind them. As they passed the entrance he prayed he would never end up in an institution of the welfare state.

'Look out!' shouted Susan.

They were about twenty yards from the fork when a dilapidated saloon shot out from a concealed drive. Peeb slammed on the brakes and threw the wheel over and then held the Lagonda as it bounced along with one wheel on the verge. The saloon tore past as if it owned the road. There was a glancing impact at the rear of the Lagonda. Peeb stopped dead and leapt out. The other car was fast disappearing into the distance.

'Bloody hell!' he swore, as he found a long scrape in the carefully polished door and bodywork. Susan got out and came round the car.

'Oh dear,'she said unhelpfully, 'Will it need panel-beating?'

'Certainly. Couple of hundred quid at least. And bang goes my no-claim bonus,' said Peeb. 'I suppose you didn't get the number?'

'Afraid not.'

'Ruddy idiot,' said Peeb. 'Nothing we can do about it. Unless we see the car again.'

They climbed back into the Lagonda and Peeb drove on and as always after any accident, at a somewhat slower pace. He took the right fork and pursued a long straight road between fields of stubble. The smell of the marshland and the Thames mud became stronger and the wind fresher, with a cold bite in it. The road began to descend a gentle gradient as it curved slightly to the east. A group of farm buildings, two Dutch barns, a house and the bright colours of petrol pumps came into view.

'Here we are,' said Susan.

'I know this!' exclaimed Peeb. 'This is where I got the petrol when I came back from the reunion dinner.' He came up to the garage and pumps. 'William V. Household,' he read out from the sign, 'Specialist Repairs.'

'Anna's husband,' said Susan.

'Awfully nice chap,' said Peeb. He drove onto the forecourt, stopping beyond the pumps in front of the open garage doors. It seemed a more extensive place in the daylight. At the side there were a number of farm and earth-moving vehicles neatly lined up in an open lean-to, under a notice "For Hire". Peeb saw a figure in light overalls working on the underside of a car which was jacked up on a hydraulic lift. 'In fact I think he's just the man I need.'

'Good,' said Susan, getting out. 'I'll go along to the house while you play about here.'

Susan found the front door ajar. She rang the bell and pushed the front door open.

'Hello. . . .? Anna?' she called.

Anna called down from the bedroom.

'Is that you Susan?'

'Yes. About the Deeds to the shop. I've got them with me.'

'Go in the living room. I'll be with you in five minutes.'

Her asthma was particularly bad that morning. She lay on the bed using her puffer. Then she took a tablet, gathering her strength for the business deal. Selling the shop was an emotional as well as a financial affair. The attack would soon pass. Her mind went back to the morning in 1945 when, long before her present afflication had developed, she had awoken early in the same bed, in the same room and Willi had lain beside her.

Then the early sun had made an exclamation mark of light between the curtains. First the sparrows, then the wood-pigeons and finally the seagulls greeted the April morning. Anna had slept deeply in the night after Willi had made love to her, until doubts and fears had broken her tranquillity. Anticipation of the day ahead jerked her into consciousness. She stared into the dark of the bedroom, her mind numbed with despair. This was the day that Willi would go; the day that he might die in the attempt; the day that if successful he might never return; the day that whatever happened would be followed by the night, when she would be alone.

'No you will not, *liebchen*.'

The unexpected sound of his voice, made her jump.

'How long have you been awake?' she whispered.

'Enough to know your thoughts.'

'But how could. . . .?'

'You have been telling me not to go for weeks now.'

'I haven't said so. . . .'

'Oh yes, *liebling*. Not in words. You are too brave for that. But your eyes, the break sometimes in your voice, the corners of your mouth have told me to abandon the whole plan and stay here with you in England. After all I have been safe for four and a half years, why should things ever be different? I can continue to lie, dye my hair, trim my beard. . . .'

'Yes, Willi!'

'No Anna, you know that is no life. A life of pretence, and secrecy and fear of discovery.'

'Yes, Willi, it is! It is better than our being apart. . . .'

They lay still and silent for several minutes. He had to speak to her about the future and the unknown, and his total love for her.

'The war will soon be over,' said Willi. 'Germany will be defeated. I know that now. In nineteen-forty we had conquered the whole of Europe. It seems incredible that since then we should have lost everything. I do not understand how it has happened, but it has. I suppose soon I will learn the reasons. . . .'

'You have lost because of the evil of Hitler and the Nazis. . . .' said Anna.

'I do not know . . . I do not know what is the truth any more . . . There is so much propaganda. . . .'

Anna picked up his hand and brushed it with her lips.

'You are not like that Willi. You are not a Nazi. . . .'

There was a long pause before he replied.

'I am a German officer. The Fuhrer is my Commander-in-Chief. I owe allegiance. I obey orders, Anna. I must continue to fight my country's enemies until I am either killed, captured or ordered to surrender. Only in one of those ways, can I, Willi von Greifswald retain my honour, and respect for my family name.'

He spoke softly, the sentences punctuated by small caressing movements of his hands. With infallible feminine insight Anna drove through the words.

'Then I too am your enemy, Willi.'

'No, no, you are my sweet darling mistress. . . .'

'Who has betrayed her country by keeping its enemy. . . .?'

'I am not an enemy of yours, Anna. We have discussed this. We are outside all these things, but that does not mean they do not exist, that they are not important, that they do not have to be considered. I love you, Anna. . . .'

'Do you love your wife too?'

'Wife? . . . Wife? I have said I have a wife? That I am married?' He spoke quickly, indignantly.

'Willi . . .! There is a photograph in your wallet of you in uniform and a beautiful girl in a wedding-dress.'

'You have looked through my wallet. . . .?'

'Of course. Doesn't a mistress always do that?'

'I don't know,' he said sharply. 'Perhaps English mistresses do. I have never had an English mistress before.'

'But you have had a wife?'

'How do you know the girl in the photograph is not my sister?'

'Because that would mean you are a liar. And I don't think you are a liar.'

'Of course not. I am not a liar. All right!' he shouted. After a beat he went on quietly. 'Yes, Anna. It is my wife in the picture. Renate and I were married in Berlin in March

1940. After Poland, and before France. We had a five-day honeymoon in Kitzbuhl. I had another two weeks' leave in July. Renate was a champion skier. You do not ski, do you, Anna?'

'No,' she said sullenly.

'One day I will teach you. After the war I will take you skiing.'

'With Renate? All three of us? Or with some of your other mistresses? That will be lovely.'

'No, *liebchen,* no. Don't be like that.' Willi kissed her on the cheek. 'I never saw Renate again after that July. I had a few letters during the campaign in France, and then nothing more. My *Geschwader* was moving about all over the place. Then I came to England. It was not much of a marriage. It is a long time ago. Too long. Obviously by now Renate believes I am dead. I must be dead officially. She might even have re-married.

'And she might not. And you're going back to find her. . . .'

'If she is alive. . . .'

'She will be alive . . .'

'Then I will tell her, our marriage has finished, that I love you. When I have settled up my family affairs and seen to the estate, I shall come back to fetch you to Germany and marry you.'

There was a long silence between them. Eventually Anna whispered, 'If only that could happen. If only I could believe that. If only I could believe *you.*'

Willi took her face in his hands and kissed her lips slowly and tenderly.

'Anna, I promise you. I will come back for you. Whatever happens I will come back. The only question is will you wait for me?'

She nodded.

'However long it is?'

'I promise you Willi.'

'Good,' he said. 'You understand that somehow I have to go back to Germany first? I want to see my parents and sister again. Maybe they are not alive. But I have to find out. And if I have to surrender, I want to surrender with my comrades in arms, with dignity, with honour. You understand?'

'I understand, Willi.' Anna started to cry quietly. 'But still I cannot bear to think of you going today.'

'I am not going today.'

'What. . . .?'

'How could I go today? I shall leave tomorrow. Just as it gets light. That is the safest time. Today is your birthday. Your are twenty-one, yes?'

'Willi . . . I thought you'd forgotten. . . .!'

'Germans do not forget these sort of things,' he laughed. 'And because it is your birthday, and it is my last day here, we are going to do something special.'

'What do you mean?'

'I am taking you up to London. You know I have never been. You will show me London. We shall have lunch at a restaurant with champagne. Then I shall buy you a ring, and then we shall go to a theatre . . . not the opera of course, but something jolly with music. . . .'

'Isn't it too dangerous?' Anna asked excitedly.

'It is dangerous, of course. Just the smallest bit. But I think I am pretty good as an Englander now. . . .'

'Englishman.'

'Englishman. Thank you,' he said seriously. 'But one thing I command you. If . . . if I should be stopped or questioned, remember I am just a stranger who spoke to you – who "picked you up".'

'But Willi. . . .'

'Oh yes, Anna. Our secret must never be discovered. In no way must you be in danger or trouble on account of me. For you I have never existed.'

'After we have spent four and a half years together? Practically all the war. . . .?'

Willi smiled as a thought occurred to him.

'Do you know something, Anna?'

'What?'

'You and I have probably had the best war of any two people in the whole world,' he said.

* * *

Willi used two keys to open the separate locks he had fitted to the side-door of the larger Dutch barn. Anna followed him inside, and closed the door behind her. Willi touched the switch which started the small generator. To the casual observer the irregular shapes under their tarpaulins gave the overall impression of a group of stored farm machines, the big one being perhaps a traction-engine or a harvester.

Willi removed the covers from the Messerschmitt. As it had done every day for the last few weeks the sight of the plane evoked a feeling of intimate satisfaction. There she was, engine-tested, fuelled, ready to take off, ready to lift him back over the alien sea till the wheels touched down on the soil of Germany. It had all been an incredible test of patience, endurance, and faith. Unarmed she may be but she was a survivor. He had not tested her in flight. There could be no trial shots. But he knew both as an aircraft engineer, and a pilot that she would fly. He had to be especially careful of the take-off. The ME 109's had an unhealthy reputation for lurching, but the surface of the field in front of the barn was at least still hard from recent sharp frosts.

Willi walked round the plane assessing the final camouflage. He had decided that confusing identification was the safest bet for his low-level flight. On this side of the *Kanal* he didn't want to be a sitting duck for a Spitfire, but equally, on the other side he wanted to avoid the irony of hostile Messerschmitts shooting him down for a maurauding Hurricane.

He had sprayed a blue and white pattern on the under surface of the wings, tail and fuselage; green and brown on the upper surfaces. He had left his white and black *Staffel* badge forward of the cockpit. The black and white German *Kreuzer* he had toned down. He planned on banking to expose them to friendly aircraft. He had painted out the crosses on the wings, and the Swastika on the tail-fin. On the rudder he had proudly touched up the seven black rectangular kill-markings with their little red, white, and blue RAF roundels above them. The reconstruction of a new tail unit had been perhaps the most difficult part of the whole job. All the enemy bullet-holes he had painstakingly patched over.

Willi climbed up into the cockpit and unnecessarily checked the wing-flaps, tail and rudder controls. He bounced up and down on the pad he had made on the seat in place of the absent parachute. There would be no bailing out this time any more than last time. Today would be memory tomorrow. He looked down at Anna and smiled.

'Climb onto the wing, *liebchen*,' he said. She did as instructed. He took her hand and directed it to the fuel switch on the control panel. 'Now remember,' he said. 'Put the parcel you will make of my uniform, and all my belongings, wallet, everything, here in the cockpit and then switch on the juice. Understand?'

'Yes, Willi,' she replied miserably.

'I am leaving the canopy open to make it easier for you.'

She nodded.

'Get down,' he ordered.

Anna climbed back to the ground. Willi got out and jumped down beside her. He showed her the two petrol canisters near the side-door.

'You can easily lift these. Try.'

Anna obeyed.

'Unscrew the top.'

She did so. He replaced it.

'You will have to cut open the bails of straw and spread it under the plane and put a trail to the other machines. The petrol over all the straw. The whole barn will have to go up to make it look right. Then come back to the side door – switch off the generator and stand outside – whatever you do don't stand inside. Then light the petrol-lighter I gave you and throw it in; slam the door and run for your life back to the farm. Go to bed and lie still. Let someone else, it doesn't matter who – Arthur, the Home Guard, Dr Page, anyone – give the alarm. You come out in your dressing-gown when the fire-engine arrives. It will be too late for them to save anything. And don't forget to claim the insurance otherwise it will look very suspicious.'

Anna nodded sadly. Willi put back all the tarpaulins neatly in place, bedding the bird down again. He threw his arm round her and switched off the generator. They went out into the sunlight and slammed the little door.

'Willi?' she said. 'I'm not going to have to do all that am I?'

'Of course not,' he laughed. 'I do not intend to be captured on my last day. But one always has to have a plan. An unbrella makes the sun shine. Come on. Let's catch that train.'

CHAPTER TWELVE

As soon as the train reached the outskirts of London, Willi began to notice the gaps in the terraced houses where the loads from the Heinkels and Junkers had landed. The bomb-sites, legacies of the Blitz were not over three years old. Weeds and shrubs had grown on them, and he saw children climbing on the heaps of rubble, enjoying their new-found playgrounds. But what surprised him more were the untouched acres of intact roofs, and regular streets where bright red buses passed each other in unhurried procession. According to the German radio, all of London was devastated. Nearer the centre there were admittedly some truncated church spires, but the absence of any balloon-barrage – the silver blobs he recalled from the summer of the Adlerangriff – showed that no Londoner now in early 1945 expected the attentions of the Luftwaffe. But when the train stopped momentarily by a recent V2 hole stretching across six house-widths, Willi realised that the world had moved on into the rocket age, more horrific than the one he knew – remote, pitiless.

Surveying the scene he considered the possibility that the official British news of German cities laid waste or even annihilated, were likewise so much propaganda. The train jerked forward. In the distance he spied St. Paul's dome, and was reassured. In Germany, Berlin must still be there just like London. Then his eyes caught something which doused his elation like the flame of a match discarded on a wet pavement.

The man sitting beside Anna was reading *The Express*. The banner headlines on the front page hit Willi like a punch in the stomach. 'Belsen. Nazi Atrocities.' Nothing else except a blown-up photograph of hundreds of wasted skeleton-like human bodies, filling a long pit, ten deep. A British Tommy stood on one side surveying the obscene distorted limbs, the incredible positions, the twisted necks, the staring sightless eyes and the toothless open mouths, with a blank expression, his hands on his hips, his tin-hat tilted back at a rakish angle.

Willi stared with incredulity. This could, could not conceivably be true. This was not Germany, not his country. This sickening picture was a diabolical piece of trick-photography, used by the enemy, the enemy sitting all round him, as a propaganda exercise of outrageous proportions. The reader turned a page and the picture was lost to Willi's view. He looked at Anna who smiled at him happily. The other occupants of the compartment, two middle-aged women, a navel petty-officer smoking a pipe, a mother and her small daughter all appeared complacent, seemingly unaware, unconcerned, but essentially harmless and friendly. Clearly their intelligence and common sense did not allow them to believe or subscribe to the coarse inept efforts of the sensational press. As if he needed further reassurance, further safeguard against the shocking protest and anger which had begun to rise up in his throat, the man with the paper, the same paper in which was printed this unjust, unreal, ridiculous accusation, folded it into a more compact shape, took out a pencil and with hardly a pause solved the first 'across' and the second 'down' clues of the crossword puzzle.

By the time they reached Charing Cross Willi had countered his first numbing reaction to the horrors which had been so casually presented to him. They were a lie. They had to be a lie. He accepted them as a lie. He would therefore ignore them. By the same token he would not let a lie colour the day ahead, his last in England for some time. With a rush of sadness he knew that also meant his last day with Anna for some time. He tried to reassure himself about the future. The day would come when he would take her boating on the little lakes near the Baltic coast of Pomerania, ride on the chestnut thoroughbreds through the woods his family owned, ski with her in the Tyrol. It might be a few years, but it would come.

Germany may again have lost a war but Germany was never defeated.

With the wages Anna had sensibly paid him for his work on the farm, he bought her a solitaire diamond ring at a jewellers in the Strand. He had heard of his father staying at the Savoy Hotel when he had visited England before the war. And so at a table in the bar – perhaps the same table – Willi von Greifswald, son of a German Junker, ordered a bottle of French champagne for the daughter of an English farmer, during the second cataclysmic conflict of the three respective countries. He raised his glass to Anna. They drank some of the cold bubbling liquid. Then Willi solemnly placed the ring on her finger and kissed her.

'Thank you, Willi,' she said. 'Thank you, darling,' and kissed him back.

She drank some more champagne. She was a woman in love. She was with Willi the man she loved, the only man who had loved her, and who was more important to her than country, than religion, than life. Defiantly she held out her glass and the waiter materialised and filled the fluted tulip nearly to the top. Then he replenished Willi's glass and the bottle was abruptly empty and upturned in the bucket and they were both half-drunk, and happy and carefree. The mood was perhaps better defined as careless, because Willi was beginning to speak with a slight German accent.

'I will order another bottle,' he said.

'No Willi,' warned Anna. 'I am drunk.'

'Nonsense. You are lovely. And after another bottle, you will be more lovely.'

'No, Willi.'

'Come *liebchen* . . .'

'Willi. . . .!'

'This is your birthday, Anna. There is nothing to fear.'

'Willi, I'm hungry. Let's go.'

She got up, knocking over her glass.

'*Achtung*!' said Willi.

The waiter retrieved the glass as it rolled on the carpet.

A little ostentatiously Willi put some pound notes on the table and followed Anna out of the bar.

'Please, Willi, be careful,' whispered Anna. 'Don't say things like "*Achtung*".'

He put his arm through hers and whispered into her ear '*Ich liebe dich*. Is that better?'

She nodded and they went out of the hotel by the revolving door. They were not saluted nor even noticed by the cockaded porter who was far too busy signalling taxis for uniformed Americans, an activity which attracted the largest tips.

Anna and Willi crossed the busy street. On impulse they went into the Vaudeville Theatre in the faint hope that there were some tickets left for the first house. It was a sell-out, but luckily as they enquired, two returns on the front row of the circle came into the box-office. Willi bought them and gave Anna hers.

'There,' he exclaimed. 'Not only is it your birthday, but they *know* it is your birthday!'

'Why?' she asked.

'Look at the number – A21 "Anna. Twenty-one".'

'What number is yours?'

'Twenty-two.'

'You're not twenty-two.'

'Of course not.'

'You see. . . .'

'But it is not *my* birthday.'

Anna laughed and held out the ticket. 'No. You keep it. As a remembrance. And I'll keep mine.'

Arm in arm they went out of the foyer into the sunlit Strand, and turned up Southampton Street to Maiden Lane. Unaware of its fame the shabby glass-fronted façade of Rule's seemed to Anna to offer an inconspicuous place to eat. She did not trust Willi taking any more risks, and made him promise he would behave.

As soon as they were inside they were engulfed by the jostling crowd in the bar. There seemed no hope of getting a table. Willi told the head-waiter they were prepared to wait, if necessary all day. The passage of a ten-shilling note also helped the process and in something under half an hour, Anna and Willi were sitting side by side on one of the red-plush Victorian banquettes. Again Willi ordered a bottle of champagne.

Gradually however, the mellowing effect of the wine allayed her unformulated apprehensions. The excitement of the occasion made her forget temporarily the fear of the morrow and the loneliness which would follow. Her teenage years, which should have been so full of carefree gaiety, had been usurped by the untimely responsibility of the farm after the loss of her father. The separation from Charles, her brother who had grown to six feet, a process she had watched in photographs from America, had accentuated the essential loneliness of war. This outing to a restaurant in London was a novel experience. It gave her a glimpse of what peace-time could be like, perhaps would be like. She regarded Willi her eyes dancing with affection. His hand made a strangely demure gesture of squeezing hers under the table. With alcoholic solemnity he raised his glass to her for the umpteenth time and toasted her birthday. She felt him rotate the ring on her finger.

'*Das madchen ist schön*,' said Willi, slurring a little.

Two army officers at the next table glanced at them, but whether it was because they overheard Willi's compliment she did not know. In any event, the men both smiled and nodded imperceptibly to her when they rose and left the restaurant, which was beginning to empty. The waiter came and poured some more wine. He also smiled and she and Willi responded politely. Then abruptly, with exquisite clarity Anna perceived the essential precariousness of their situation. Uncertainty and danger swooped from the silk-lined walls and the decorated ceiling like fell birds of prey. She asked fearfully,

'We *will* get married, won't we Willi . . . I mean one day?'

Willi let go of her hand and re-sought it across the table. She drew hers out from underneath and placed it between both of his.

'I have given you my word,' he said seriously. And then more lightly, as if such a mood-change were appropriate he added 'But one day . . . one day may be a long time.'

Anna blinked back the hotness behind her lids.

'However long it is . . . I . . . I don't mind,' she lied.

Willi nodded and let her hand escape his.

'Dear Enemy,' she said, and then becuse he sensed she might burst into tears, he asked briskly, 'Now! How would you like some coffee?' Willi rolled his eyes and waved his finger round and round. 'We need some coffee.'

Anna went upstairs to the Ladies. He sauntered back to the bar near the street entrance having paid the bill. There were three officers in uniform having their last drinks before closing. A discarded newspaper on one of the tables shouted its savage photographic message about the camp at Belsen. '*Ten thousand unburied corpses*', was the caption. Willi picked up the paper and studied it intently, unflinchingly. How had they managed to produce such a picture? Was it an old photograph of a natural starvation disaster taken years ago in some far-flung British colony? It had to be a diabolical exercise in misinformation to label the Germans as the monsters of the human race, never to be forgotten, never to be forgiven. Rage and disgust at the perpetration rose with uncontrollable fury inside him.

'Disgusting, isn't it, sir?'

Willi looked up and saw the white-coated barman polishing a glass on the other side of the counter.

'Yes,' replied Willi. 'It's an abominable disgusting evil thing to do.'

'You know what I think?' said a voice with an Australian accent. 'When we've finally beaten these Jerry bastards. . . .'

'Which won't be long now. . . .' The American of the trio was swaying visibly.

'Only one thing for it,' said the British major in the Gunners. 'And that's to put every German over the age of twenty up against a wall and shoot him.'

There was a general bibulous murmur of approval.

'Well that's what one'd do with any other sort of filthy vermin, what?'

Folding and refolding the paper until it was in a tight strip Willi looked from one bleary-eyed face to another. There they were, the Allies in force, passing moral judgement on Germany, on the Third Reich, on him, a member of a distinguished family, with no record ever of a dishonourable deed, just because of a series of dirty lies, cleverly calculated to engender implacable hatred. It was perhaps in the end a profound feeling of injustice, of innocence possibly, in the face of what he believed to be dishonest, untruthful accusations which tipped Willi over the edge. All the caution, the patience, the dogged perseverance towards survival of the previous four and a half years evaporated.

'*Verflugte Scheisse*!' Willi shouted and brought the folded paper down on the bar top with a sound like a rifle-shot. 'You don't believe this foul filthy propaganda, do you?' Willi barked out the question at his astonished audience. 'This is not true.' He smacked down the paper again. 'This isn't happening in Germany. I can tell you, because I know Germany. I know because I am a German.'

Out of the corner of his eye Willi saw the head waiter lift the phone at the desk and make three stabs with his finger at the dial. Willi guessed he was calling for the police but he couldn't stop the tide of anger which engulfed him. The blank impassive expressions on the faces of the three pie-eyed officers seemed to incense Willi even more.

'It is ridiculous, unsubtle, despicable,' he continued vehemently. 'Germans would never do this sort of thing to anybody . . . do you understand. . . .?' Willi slapped the bar-top again with the paper. And then he made his real mistake. 'Not to anybody,' he repeated, 'Not even Jews. . . .!'

'Oh no?' yelled the American. 'My name's Goldberg, you Kraut!'

He lunged forward and swung a fist at Willi's chin. The punch had been too well signalled and Willi easily warded off the blow with his left arm and drove his scarred right fist under the American's ribs, who staggered backwards knocking over a bar-stool. The Australian followed up with a wild swing at Willi's head. Willi ducked and shoved his shoulder into the other's armpit. The barman tried to grab Willi by his coat-collar, but Willi swept him away with a backhanded sweep. As the barman disappeared behind the counter he tried to save himself by grabbing the display cabinet on the bar-top, and brought it down with a shattering crash of broken glass.

'Willi!' screamed Anna.

She had appeared at the bottom of the stairs.

With split-second recognition Willi knew he must keep Anna out of everything. He had burnt his own boats but he did not intend to involve her in severe or long-lasting penalties. Willi turned and made for the street door. The movement at long last stimulated the gunnery officer into action which he both understood and in which he was well practised. His qualities as an officer had not so far been in evidence, but like the good Rugby full-back he certainly was, he shot after Willi and tackled him with precision, bringing him down on the carpet.

Anna ran forwards just as two uniformed policemen, a sergeant and a constable came in from the street. They picked Willi up. One held him by the arm. As the others recovered their equilibrium, the head waiter now emerged from behind the protection of the desk.

'Is this the gentleman?' asked the sergeant.

'This is the gentleman,' said the head-waiter.

'May I see your Identity Card, sir?' the sergeant asked Willi.

'I haven't got one,' said Willi.

'In that case I shall have to ask you to come along to the police station.'

'But why?' asked Anna. 'What has he done?'

The sergeant glanced round at the broken glass, and the general effects of the fight.

'Disturbed the peace by the look of it, miss. . . .'

'What else have the Germans been doing since 1939?' asked the army officer. 'And this character says he's a German!'

'Does he now?'

'He's wearing civvies . . . but I've an idea he's an officer. . . .'

'He's been wounded,' pleaded Anna. 'Let him go . . . I can tell you all about him. . . .'

'You don't know anything about me,' snapped Willi. 'How could you? I only picked you up a few hours ago.'

'Is that correct, miss. . . .'

Willi opened his eyes wide and looked straight into Anna's. He did not know if she got the message, but he wasn't going to risk her making any further attempts to save him from what was now a hopeless position. He slipped his free hand in his breast pocket and in one swift movement wrenched his other arm out of the constable's grasp. He lurched past Anna back towards the restaurant knocking her handbag out of her hand onto the floor, where half the contents spilled out. The sergeant closed on him and with the help of the now recovered constable secured him by each arm behind his back.

'Obstructing a police officer, assaulting a police officer, resisting arrest. . . .' said the sergeant. 'Come on. Let's go.'

Willi disappeared through the door between the two policemen. Anna bent down to pick up her handbag from the floor. Amongst the fallen objects she saw Willis's Identity Card. He must have purposely dropped it when he pushed past her. Quickly she scooped it up with the rest of her things and put them into her handbag, closed it and stood up. Without acknowledging or meeting any of the surrounding stares, she walked out of the restaurant.

Before she could properly absorb the shock of what had happened, and its devastating implications, instinctively Anna felt she should distance herself quickly from the scene of Willi's arrest. She crossed Maiden Lane and darted down a narrow alley which led to the Strand. When she reached the thoroughfare she stopped after a few yards and gazed into a shoe-shop window so as to keep an eye on the exit to the alley.

After five minutes she was satisfied that none of the people she had seen in Rules had followed her. She turned away and began walking, aimlessly, hopelessly along the crowded pavement towards the Aldwych. Willi had gone. Willi had been snatched from her. And she didn't know where or when or if ever she would see him again. The tears started to come, and she made no effort to stop them. She felt so miserable and forlorn that, like a child, she let her tongue taste the salt in the tears, and sniffed back those that ran down inside her nose, and with sobs she swallowed the fluid from both sources.

By the time she had reached the Royal Courts of Justice the extreme intensity of the emotional storm had abated. If still with a leaden weight in her chest, she told herself that in any event Willi would have been going the next day. Perhaps what had happened might be a blessing. It might have saved him from being shot down or crashing in the Messerschmitt.

Anna started to speak softly to Willi as if he were beside her. 'Darling Willi, what can it have been that caused the trouble just now? That made you break cover? I should never have left you alone. Dear Willi, you were so gallant, so solicitous of my safety, saying that I had only known you for two hours. But it's your safety not mine that matters. That is something you can't understand. I've never worried whether we should or should not have loved. What was patriotic, what was *richtig* didn't bother me. Our love is not concerned with these things. Even you sometimes said that.'

'Dearest Willi, I will respect your wishes . . . if only you will come back in the end. You will come back Willi?. . . . You will come back as you've promised?'

Anna's private soliloquy, sentimental and immature as at another time she might judge it to be, calmed her. She gave a long shuddering sigh which terminated her histrionics. Gradually she became again the practical resourceful person she also was. She walked into a café by Temple Bar and in the Ladies restored her shattered make-up. She had a cup of tea and a plain bun and smoked a cigarette. When she opened her handbag to pay at the till she found a ticket to the Vaudeville. On the instant she decided she would use it. She just had time. The curtain would go up in fifteen minutes. Willi would like her to do that. Willi would approve.

When however, she was sitting in A21 on the front row of the full crowded seats, she wished she hadn't come. The empty seat beside her was too eloquent and sad, and she had

had enough sadness for one day. She gathered her things and was about to get up and retreat, when someone came along the row, apologising for the disturbance and sat down in Willi's seat. Immediately the house lights went out and the music blared out and the chorus was high-kicking across the stage.

Anna sat down again, her mind racing, not taking in any of the performance. She looked at the main in Willi's seat. If he was there and Willi wasn't, the ticket must still have come from Willi. Her heart leapt.

Did it mean that Willi was at large again and was trying to tell her so, but in order not to compromise her had nevertheless conveyed the information to her by giving this anonymous messenger his ticket? It was a heart-warming prospect, but it turned ice-cold at the notion of a more sinister interpretation. The man could be a plain-clothes policeman. Though Willi had successfully got rid of his identity card which would have led them to her because the address of the farm was on it, he had forgotten the theatre ticket. Whatever he had said they'd suspect he was unlikely to go to a theatre alone, and after all she had been with him. They had failed to take her at the restaurant and that was a mistake on their part. She might know quite a lot about Willi. And so this man had been sent along just on the chance that she would show up in the seat next to A22 – either A21 or A23. She glanced across at her neighbour. A23 was fifty-year old obese matron with glasses and a laugh which cackled indiscriminately at everything the comedian said. No. Not A23. She, Anna in A21 would have to be the suspect.

Her heart thumping she began to prepare possible replies to questions which might be put to her. But the more she observed surreptitiously Willi's surrogate, the more she felt her fears were unfounded. He was young and chubby-faced and when the lights went up at the interval and he took off his raincoat in which he had sweltered through the first half, she saw he was wearing an Able Seaman's uniform complete with bell-bottomed trousers. Far from asking her any questions, when he caught her eye on him, the boy blushed and looked away shyly. But whoever or whatever he was, he must have seen Willi, talked to Willi, perhaps had touched Willi. That was excuse enough for instant enquiry.

'Enjoying the show?' asked Anna.

'Yes . . . yes, thanks . . . it's marvellous,' he spoke nervously with a north country accent. 'Are you?'

'Oh yes,' she lied. 'I was very lucky to get a ticket.'

'You couldn't have been luckier than me,' the boy laughed.

'Why is that?'

'Well, I was at Bow Street Police Station . . .' he laughed again. 'No, I haven't done anything. I was enquiring about the address of an auntie of mine who'd been bombed out by one of these doodle-bugs, when they brought in a fellow they'd arrested following a fight in a restaurant. . . .'

'Oh . . . I see . . .' said Anna encouragingly.

'They made him turn out his pockets and there was this theatre ticket. So he picked it up, showed it to the sergeant behind the desk who was booking him in and asked, 'Am I going to get out of here in time to use this?' The sergeant said 'You're not going to get out of here at all.' 'In that case,' said this bloke. 'It's ridiculous to waste a good seat' and turned to me and put the ticket in my hand. 'Here. Like to see a show?' he asked. 'Sorry I haven't got one for your girlfriend.' 'I haven't got a girlfriend', I said. 'Well perhaps you'll find a beautiful girl in the seat next to you', he said. So I took it. The sergeant said 'OK'. And here I am.' The boy smiled shyly and blushed. 'And . . . and you must be the beautiful girl he talked about.'

'Thank you. . . .' Anna smiled, the lump hard in her throat. Thank you for the . . . compliment.'

'I mean it,' he said.

'Yes,' replied Anna. 'Excuse me . . . I must go now. . . .' She stood up. Impulsively she kissed the boy on the cheek. 'Goodbye and good luck,' she said.

'Aren't you going to stay for the second half. . . .?' she heard him say as she stumbled along the row and up the gangway.

Her eyes were filling again but when she got outside the theatre, the cold night air in the darkness of the street, stemmed the tide of emotion. She walked away towards Charing Cross. She found the two return rail tickets and passed through the barrier. The train was packed and she had to stand in the corridor. As the carriage moved forward she threw Willi's ticket out onto the line.

'Oh Willi,' she whispered. 'Willi darling. . . .'

Nearly fifty years later Anna put on her dressing-gown, dabbed her eyes in front of the mirror, blew her nose and went down the stairs into the living-room. Susan got up.

'Sorry I was such a long time,' she said, 'but today's not ideal for the old bronchioles.'

'That's quite all right,' said Susan.

'Do sit down.'

Anna sat on the couch beside her.

'Well, are we going to do a dal?' she asked with a smile.

'I think so,' replied Susan and arranged the papers on her lap.

CHAPTER THIRTEEN

While Susan was in Marsh Farm William Household went back under the car on the lift, gave two final squirts with the grease-gun, stepped clear and then flipped a switch. The car floated down to the ground. Peeb recognised the vehicle immediately as an early Bugatti. Peeb stared at the car in silent admiration and went into the garage.

'What a little beauty,' he said.

'Isn't she? Belongs to a stockbroker at Chilham. Doesn't appreciate it. Bought it as an investment. I love cars . . . and engines.'

Peeb looked round the garage. He was surprised at the unusual tidiness. The tools in racks gleamed brightly and were sized meticulously. The floor was uncluttered with obstruction, and free of oil patches. The place had more the air of an operating theatre than a workshop. At a bench at the end someone finished using a welding torch. As he took off his goggles Peeb saw that he was a young Asian. The old man with the shock of grey-white hair matched the almost unmarked overalls . . .

'Can I help you, sir?'

'I'm sure you can,' said Peeb. He recognised the voice straight away. 'We've met before, Mr Household.'

The man gave him a blank stare which slid into a warm smile.

'Yes, I remember. One damp early morning.' Household nodded at the Lagonda.

'Glad to see you're driving a decent motor-car this time.'

'Come and see what I've collected on the way here,' Peeb led him out to the Lagonda. Household went down on his haunches, rubbed one gloved hand along the scrape and carefully felt under the rear wing with his other. He stood up.

'Bloody bad luck . . .' he said.

'Bloody bad driving,' said Peeb.

'You?'

'Of course not.'

'Of course not.'

'Know anyone with a dilapidated green Ford Cortina?'

Household shook his head. 'Not my kind of client. 'Fraid you'll need a panel beat. You've dented the inner skin of the rear wing.'

'I thought so,' said Peeb.

'The maroon colour . . . I'd have to send for that. There's a place in Whitechapel which keeps all these old shades. . . .'

'Moorecambe's. Cable Street.'

'That's right.'

'How much would you need?'

'A litre.'

'I've got two pints,' said Peeb. 'Always keep a supply. Just for touching up, you know.'

'Good. Then if you'd like to leave the car, I can have it done in less than a week. How's that?'

'Unbelievable,' said Peeb.

'Want me to give her a tune up as well?'

Peeb nodded.

'You're . . . you're not English, are you?'

'Why do you say that?'

'Well, you're too obliging . . . too efficient . . . and there's just the trace of an accent. It isn't German, is it?'

'Might be. I was a POW in Germany in the war. Perhaps I picked it up from the Goons.'

'Goons?'

'German guards,' lied Willi.

'I see,' said Peeb sympathetically. 'Anyway,' he laughed awkwardly, 'you couldn't get a more English name than Household.'

'That's right. Any other questions you'd like to ask?' The voice had developed a hard edge.

'No, no . . . of course not. I'm sorry . . .' said Peeb. He felt embarrassed by his own curiosity.

'I'll start tomorrow then,' said Household. 'Will you get

the paint to me not later than the day after?'

'You can have it now,' said Peeb. 'I keep it in the boot.'

He took his bunch of keys out of the ignition lock on the dash, and selected the one he needed. Household stood at his side as Peeb unlocked the boot. He reached down to find the two cans of paint, but he couldn't get to them properly without lifting out the bundle tied in the blanket. This he did with some difficulty. The rope slipped off and exposed the tail-wheel of the Messerschmitt. He placed it on the ground, found the tins and handed them to Household. He saw that the man was looking at the wheel with a puzzled expression. On an impulse Peeb asked:

'Do you know what that is?'

Household put down the tins and examined the wheel and its stubby inflatable tyre.

'Where on earth did you get this?'

'It dropped from the sky into my garden.'

'A stacker-truck wheel?'

'That is not a stacker-truck wheel.' Peeb squatted down and began wrapping up the wheel again in its blanket and tying the rope round it. Somehow he felt he should not tell the fellow what it was. But then what harm could it do? Perhaps it was because he was afraid not just of disbelief, but of being laughed at. He put the wheel, now blanketed firmly again, back in the boot and locked it. 'That wheel Mr Household', said Peeb, 'is the tail-wheel of a Messerschmitt BF 109E.'

Household's eyebrows lifted slightly. His stare was level, steady and icy blue. The bluff was irresistible and he played for its full value.

'So you're the madman who flies over here at roof-top level and terrifies my wife . . .?' he asked.

'Don't be ridiculous', laughed Peeb.

'It's no laughing matter. . . .'

'Listen. . . .'

'It's also illegal. And damned dangerous. I don't think you know what havoc you cause. . . .'

'I'm doing nothing of the. . . .'

'The last time that damned Messerschmitt came over the

marshes it was so close to the ground its slip-stream flattened out the reeds behind it, it put up flights of geese into the sky, not to mention seagulls, rooks, crows and every other kind of bird. It came towards this place like a guided missile. Parakhat Singh back there dived under a tractor and cut his head. Then whoosh, it went over the house rattling the slates, leaving the dogs barking, the chickens going mad and the cats having proverbial kittens . . .' Household slapped his hand on the back of the Lagonda. 'Where's the joke? What's it for? Why do you do it?'

Peeb pushed Household's hand off the surface of the bootlid.

'It's not *my* Messerschmitt. I am *not* the pilot.' He enunciated each word sharply and clearly.

'Why should I believe that? I hear you're always boasting about your flying exploits in the RAF.'

'I haven't flown for years. . . .'

'That's no answer. Once you can swim you can always swim. Once a flyer, always a flyer.'

'Listen, Household,' said Peeb, 'I've been plagued by this ruddy thing too. In fact I'm about to start a systematic search for its base.'

'And how are you going to do that?'

'Among other things I propose to ask selected local people if they've seen the plane. I thought I'd form them into a kind of . . . of Observer Corps, plot the sightings. . . .'

Peeb stopped speaking as a Cessna executive jet temporarily drowned out his voice. It passed above them at about two thousand feet on its way north to Southend Airport.

'See that?' observed Household. 'There are too many planes – RAF, commercial, private – going over here one way or another all the time. I've already asked people about this Messerschmitt. Even the police. A complete blank, of course. The English wouldn't even recognise a Messerschmitt if it landed in the High Street. Not any longer.' He looked at Peeb with a more friendly expression. 'Of course, you and I are different, Group Captain.'

'You . . . and I?' asked Peeb.

'Well, you shot down a Messerschmitt in the air. So did I.'

Household took off his gloves. He saw Peeb notice the raised irregular scar across the back of his left hand. 'Not without certain mishaps,' he added and directed his gaze unmistakably at Peeb's cheek.

'Pilot?' asked Peeb.

'Tail Gunner. Lancasters,' said Household. He tilted his head and regarded Peeb questioningly. The game was on now and there was no holding back. 'Perhaps we can join forces. Tracking down this Jerry?'

'Why not?' Peeb gave a smile. 'Glad of the help.'

'The plane's not kept at any of the flying clubs around here. I have made enquiries.'

So his guess about that had proved right, thought Peeb. Household pointed across the marshes to the water.

'Our land goes down to the Swale, over the marshes and mudflats.' He swung his arm through a hundred and eighty degrees. 'The little beauty comes first from the north and then turns east before doubling back from the opposite direction.'

'Does it return the same way?'

'I don't know.'

'It could come from further north still. Suffolk or even Norfolk. . . .' commented Peeb.

'It could be a long search,' said Household.

'Looks like it,' agreed Peeb.

'Unless we shoot it down.'

Peeb glanced at the other's straight face.

'You're not joking.'

Household produced a sly grin.

'If it were a Spitfire and we were Jerries in Germany I bet we'd take a pot at it.'

'Not nowadays,' said Peeb. 'The Jerries are good boys now.'

'Don't you believe it. In East Germany, they'll shoot down anything. Believe me.'

Peeb pondered Household's observations and then shook his head.

'The pilot of that Messerschmitt is someone who knows me and who's having a joke at my expense.'

'Why do you think that?'

'Just a hunch. Probably some crazy Yank. Their sort of Joke. There were nine of them in the Battle of Britain you know.'

Peeb suddenly felt he did not wish to discuss the matter any further. He handed his car keys to Household, who got into the Lagonda and drove it to the far end of the garage. A familiar minicar came into the petrol pumps. Brian got out.

'Hello, Peeb,' he said. 'What are you doing here?'

'I brought Susan. She's with your patient.'

'Right. I'll go and see them both. Fill me up, Parakhat, would you?' Brian shouted to the Asian.

While the little car was being attended to, Peeb wandered across the road. It looked as though when the tide came in it flooded the stretch of marshland right up to a raised causeway leading down to the river bank. The early evening breeze wafted the pungent smell of the mud towards him. Two labourers came round from the field at the back and picked up their mopeds from inside the garage. Peeb heard them wish their employer goodnight and then they steamed off. Peeb was beginning to feel chilly when a beaming Susan came out of the house with Brian.

'One hundred and twenty-seven five,' she whispered in his ear. 'It's a bargain.'

CHAPTER FOURTEEN

Willi's conversation with Peeb flicked up the past like a photograph found at the bottom of a drawer.

Camp 13, used mainly for aircrew shot down over Britain was the official commandeered Shapwells Hotel, in Cumbria. No Colditz, the three storey edifice with its courtyard just below the summit of Shap where the railway line climbs over to Scotland, was formidable in its isolation. It was set in the midst of deserted grouse-moors, and beset by cold and rain. There was also the interminable sound of rushing water over rocks as the Berk Beck tumbled southwards. A foot-bridge crossed the torrent to the huts occupied by the British soldiers and guards.

Willi arrived from London at the same time as a crew of a recently captured U Boat on May 7th 1945, the day Germany unconditionally surrendered. On May 8th the British Commandant of the Camp made the announcement to the assembled prisoners.

Willi took some time to settle into the routine of the camp, he took more time to settle with the idea of being a prisoner; the longest was the time he took to accept what had happened to Germany, to reverse so many of his beliefs, eliminate so many illusions. It was a painful process. But like nearly all the others who shared his captivity had noticed, there was an atmosphere in the Shap camp, which gradually weaved its spell about him. Slowly the dye grew out of his hair and beard and none of his fellow prisoners saw fit to question him about it. They were quite well fed. They were certainly well-housed. There were abundant facilities for reading, learning, attending lectures by visiting academics and personalities, pursuing hobbies, games or other interests. Gradually the values of the Third

Reich began to disintegrate. The compulsory film of Belsen was shown and Willi came to believe it.

Willi also found an exhilaration at being again, after so long, amongst Germans in a German atmosphere. But he was careful not to give his own experience away. He remained suspicious and wary of anything which might in the most devious manner trace him back to Anna. Ever mindful of censors, British, German, Russian or any others, Willi wrote long but careful letters to his parents in Greifswald, his wife in Berlin and his sister in Dresden. They brought no reply. It was painful and depressing that he dare not write to Anna. And of course there was no way, no hope that he would hear from her.

Time lost its meaning of measured moments. There was no beginning and no end to its punishing continuum. How long would they be incarcerated? 1945 became 1946 and then 1947. Even a criminal knew the length of his sentence. But all the time he thought of the marshes and the mud-flats. He smelt the muddy river smell of the Swale and the Thames with a nostalgia as if indeed the Isle of Sheppey were his home. If Anna was still there, then perhaps it was his home. Second home he corrected himself. *Heimat* was Germany. That would always be so.

In late 1947 the barbed wire came down and the prisoners were allowed to wander where they liked. The dispiriting attacks of *Lagerkoller* subsided. Willi volunteered for work on a nearby farm. Farming seemed a tangible activity which would keep him near in spirit to Anna.

With a squad of others he picked up potatoes where they had been turned out onto the surface, watched by the tall lean farmer. To his surprise the man approached him, and in perfect German asked if he would like to stay on the farm and continue to work there on a permanent basis with full pay, as estate manager.

Willi vaguely sensed a trap, puzzled at the suggestion. He looked round at the others still bending to their task, putting potatoes into their baskets.

'Why me?' Willi asked in English.

'I can arrange it. You will be more comfortable on the farm.'

'What makes you select me? There are others.'

'All the others from time to time tread in a potato. You never do.'

'Of course not.'

'Exactly. It is not *korreckt*. It is not *gemûtlich*, *Oberleutnant von Greifswald*.'

The man held out his hand to Willi. 'Colonel Sir Walter Hildersley. Ex-Intelligence.' Willi stiffened. 'Retired,' smiled the older man.

There was a pause and then Willi wiped his hand free of soil and shook the one offered him.

And so by 1948 the German fighter-pilot was established at Welbeck Farm in the North-West of England with an English Colonel's family in an English home. He found a light-hearted but strangely deep warmth there. He also found respect and eventually self-respect. It had nothing to do with politics or ideologies or even patriotism. It sprang from his genes. It went back to his childhood to his upbringing, and his family motto. *Honeste Audax*.

Willi threw all his effort and ingenuity into work about the farm. His engineering skills soon found an outlet in the repair of farm machinery, tractors, cattle-cake crushers, milking machines and separators. But though Willi felt trusted, and in return he spoke freely about many things, his trust did not extend to the revelation of Anna. To expose her to any danger was unthinkable. He dare not write, he dare not telephone; he dare not confide in a third party to take a message. He wanted desperately to signal to her that he constantly thought of her, that he was keeping his side of the promise.

His position on the farm suddenly offered the opportunity for some form of communication. Fanciful it might be, but Anna was intelligent and sensitive enough to get the message. Some illustrated flower and shrub catalogues arrived. He discussed possible orders with Mrs Hildersley. The English name of one flower intrigued him. 'Sweet William'. She made a joke about it. Later, amongst many orders on the telephone for other things, Willi directed the farm's seedsmen to send to the Householder, Marsh Farm, Isle of Sheppey, Kent, a single packet of the seeds of *Dianthus barbatus*. He stressed the fact that no other gratuitous literature or information should accompany it. It was a month later that the uncertainty about repatriation was at long last resolved.

Willi said goodbye to the farm on the fells and the Hildersleys with promises, faintly believed, that one day he would re-visit the family of which he had been temporarily a part. Hildersley suggested that after he had been back to Germany, he should return and settle in England.

'Thank you, Herr Colonel. It might be nice,' said Willi. 'But I have my own estate in Greifswald to look after.'

'Of course,' said Hildersley. 'Good luck.'

Willi felt the genuine warmth of the handshake but noted the tinge of pity in the eyes, as it was given.

Willi forgot the handshake but remembered the look when, having shipped from Harwich to the Hook, he arrived next dawn at the frontier of Germany. There they had to change trains, into standing wagons over a hundred men to a wagon. For something like ten hours, they could not get out. Willi felt a rage of personal distress and disgust.

'This is what we used to do to the Jews,' someone muttered.

'But we are Germans!' shouted a young voice.

And the other ninety or so sweating stinking men reserved their thoughts and said nothing.

Through the open parts of the truck Willi saw the devastated countryside, the broken houses and factories. Sometimes when they stopped, thin coughing women came up to the trucks asking for cigarettes and even thinner boys begged for food.

At *Munsterlager* POW's from all countries were processed. Willi came across his first Russians. They looked at each other with dead eyes and made no expressions. He was given a medical, a combined identity card and certificate of release, and a ration-card for food and clothing, and some Deutschmarks. Willi also had two bars of soap, three bars of chocolate and three hundred cigarettes. All his other belongings had been compressed into a small suitcase given him by the Hildersleys.

At last he was on his own in his own country. At the station he managed to get a seat in a dilapidated carriage. With a jerk the train moved forward. The line ran north to Osnabruck before east towards Berlin. At Helmstedt the unforgiving realities of the war returned. Passing through the frontier into East Germany was a shock. Willi watched his uniformed countrymen of the new *Deutsche Demokratische Republik*, serving their Russian conquerors with all the purblind *Ordnung* he knew of old. He was bundled out of his carriage, searched, and bundled back again minus one bar of soap, one bar of chocolate and one packet of Players.

It was dark by the time he got out at Charlottenburg in West Berlin. The streets were dimly lit. Few people were about and those that were moved quickly and furtively. His footsteps echoed, for there was little traffic. It seemed like a worked-out mining area with pyramids of rubble instead of slag. Willi walked east where the lights were brighter. He reached the Kurfurstendamm at the corner of Leichnitzstrasse.

Here, there were some cafes and restaurants open. Wearily he sat down at a pavement cafe table and ordered a coffee and cognac. A raincoated tart in high heels, one of the perennial survivors of all wars and disasters sat down in the chair on the other side of the table. She raised her pencilled eyebrows, crossed her legs provocatively, the hem of her tight skirt slipping up above her knees.

'Got a cigarette chum for a lady?' she asked in heavily accented English.

'*Bitte schôn*,' said Willi and offered her one from a packet.

She lit up eagerly, running an eye over his clothes and suitcase.

'*Kriegsgefangenen*?'

'Yes.'

'America?'

'England.'

'Looking for old friends?'

'Relatives.'

'Wife?'

'Wife, sister, parents.'

'All in Berlin?'

'No. Only my wife. We had a flat. . . .'

She laughed. Willi noticed her teeth were not too good.

'That's where you're going to stay?'

'If it's still there.'

'You'll be lucky. Where was it?'

'By the Oranienberger Tor.'

'That's in the Russian zone. Have you got a pass?'

Willi showed her the papers he'd been given at Munsterlager.

'The Russians will make you wait days, weeks with just those. You need a city pass.'

'Where can I get one?'

'I can give you one.'

'How much?'

'Fifty.'

'Marks?'

'Cigarettes.'

'OK,' said Willi.

He handed them over.

'I said a hundred cigarettes,' she said glimpsing his supply.

'You said fifty,' said Willi.

She shrugged and got up.

'If you don't want the pass. . . .'

'All right. All right. Give it me.' Willi felt too defeated to argue. She held out her hand took the cigarettes and dropped them into a worn capacious plastic handbag. He gripped her arm and held it firmly, till she handed over the card.

'*Danke schôn, Herr General*', she said sarcastically.

As she teetered away she spat on the pavement. Willi paid for his coffee and cognac and the café owner showed him the way to the YMCA.

Surprisingly he slept well, and next morning he was almost first in the queue at Checkpoint Charlie. When he reached the Russian zone he was searched, and had his documents stamped. The East German Polizei sent him to the Missing

Persons Record Office just off the re-named Marx-Engels Platz.

'. . . von Greifswald. . . .?'

The man was in his fifties, grey, haggard, but precise, official, full of "*Ordnung*". Once a Civil Servant, always a Civil Servant. At least always a German Civil Servant. He took down the appropriate volume and went through it methodically.

'Renate Gerda von Greifswald?'

Willi could feel his hands sweating.

'That's right.'

'Reported missing, 17th June 1943. Air Raid. No subsequent records.'

'Does that mean. . . .?'

'Killed? Of course. If she had not been killed she would not be in this file. She would have to re-register for food and other things. . . .'

'She could have . . . have remarried . . . have a different name?' Willi's voice was thick.

'Impossible. There would be a cross reference here. There is nothing. Your wife is dead Herr Greifswald.'

'Thank you,' said Willi.

'Now, your parents?' The man looked at the file again. 'No record. They lived in. . . .'

'Griefswald. It's an estate outside the village of Greifswald.'

'The address you're going to? The address I have?'

'My home,' said Willi.

'How old are they?'

'Now. . . .?' Willi made a rapid calculation. 'My mother sixty-two. My father seventy.'

The man shrugged, a quick Teutonic jerk of the shoulders lacking the sinuous French expressiveness.

'You could be lucky.'

Willi swallowed. Lucky? Lucky . . . How do you assess lucky anymore?

'And now your sister, you said.'

'Yes . . . yes. Giselle. She was not married. . . .'

'Where did she live?'

'Dresden.'

'*Ach*, Dresden. There are no records for Dresden.'

'Why not?'

'Dresden does not exist any more my friend. Don't you know that?'

'No,' said Willi.

'Give me her full name. Did she have children?'

'No. She was unmarried.' Poor Giselle. She was so good with children.

The man sat and produced a line sheet from the desk drawer and began writing.

'It will probably be useless but I'll put out a tracer sheet.'

Willi told him everything he could remember.

'Right. Enquire again in six months.'

'Thank you,' said Willi.

'Anyone else?'

Willi looked round as if he might see an uncle, an old schoolfriend, a comrade from his squadron. But the room was mostly full of middle aged and elderly women. The man looked into his eyes. He wore suddenly a human expression. A man, old and sad and alone.

'They come every day, some of them. It's a waste of time. But time's about the only thing which isn't rationed.'

Outside it was sunny. Willi made his way to Albrecht Strasse near the University where for those few weeks in the spring of 1940 he had lived in a flat with Renate. The building had disappeared. What did he expect?

The train journey north for no obvious reason took two days. The more eastern route via Prenzlau and Arklam which would have taken him directly to Greifswald was not in use at all. The more western route through Neu Strelitz was slow and unreliable. In the end he got out at Grimmen which was twenty kilometres from his home. He rode on a cart hitched to a tractor for five of these, but the rest he had to walk. In town, there were some trams running. He had just sat down when he saw the notice "*Nur fur Arbeitender*". The conductor was onto him like a flash.

'Are you a worker?'

'*Nein*.'

'*Raus*!'

The conductor punched the bell. The tram stopped and Willi jumped down. Along the last two kilometres on the road to Greifswald Willi began to notice houses here and there which he remembered as a boy. Some were almost untouched but others were pitifully half-repaired. There were other landmarks he remembered. Eventually he saw the silver streak of the Baltic ahead and smelt the wind fresh off the water. The familiarity of it all lifted his heart and he made the effort to disguise his limp.

As soon as he turned the corner by the gatekeeper's lodge where the drive curved away up to the house, he stopped dead. A blackened shell confronted him. The whole building had been gutted by fire. So this was what he had dreamed of bringing Anna to? A voice behind him said,

'Willi. . . .? Is it you Willi?'

Willi swung round. His sister was standing on the step of the lodge, the door open behind her.

'Giselle . . . Giselle!' Willi cried out and ran to her and they put their arms round each other. Willi kissed her again and again. 'They said you were in Dresden. . . .'

'I'd got back here. They said you were killed. . . .'

For a second or so they looked at each other, observing the familiarities of their faces, and trying to ignore the changes.

'Mama and Papa . . .?' asked Willi. Giselle shook her head.

'So it's just us?'

'No,' his sister smiled. 'It's not as bad as that.' She called into the hall behind her. 'Klaus. . . .? *Komm hier, Klaus*.' A blond haired boy, about seven years old appeared at her side and looked up at Willi with grey uncurious eyes.

'Say hello to your Papa,' she ordered him. The boy hesitated. Willi held out his hand.

'How do you do Klaus?' said Willi.

The boy gave Willi's hand a brief shake and then withdrew his own quickly.

'Are you going to stay?' he asked.

'I have your file in front of me,' said the *Grenzpolizei Kommissar*. 'I am aware of your war record as a Luftwaffe pilot, and your spell as a prisoner of war in England. I know of the personal losses you have suffered – your wife and parents. . . .'

'And the loss of my property and land which have been in my family for generations,' said Willi.

'And now rightfully belong to the State.'

'Stolen by the State,' muttered Willi.

'Handed over lawfully to the State,' Kommissar Schildt corrected him icily. 'You are a German patriot, a hero even, but all that is history. It is the future that counts. Now you are something much more important. You are a citizen of the German Democratic Republic, Herr Greifswald. . . .'

'von Greifswald,' said Willi.

'Comrade Greifswald,' emphasised Schildt.

Willi shrugged. 'OK, Comrade von Greifswald.'

'Are you trying to be funny?'

The fat bald man behind the desk eyed him balefully. By his cavalier attitude, Willi knew he was reducing his chances of getting what he had come back to Berlin for, but he couldn't help it. The man had all the hallmarks of the unscrupulous opportunist. Willi imagined him in the twenties as a minor Civil Servant; in the thirties as a Nazi informer. In the war, his obesity making him conveniently unsuitable for service at the front, a willing administrator in a KZ camp. Now he was a communist lackey wielding the frightening power of the petty official.

'I asked if you are trying to be funny?'

'That would be a waste of time, Comrade Kommissar,' said Willi.

'I'm afraid your application is also a waste of time.'

'I am only asking for a Day-pass to West Berlin. It is a small simple thing.'

'It is a simple thing, not a small thing.'

'But the ridiculous blockade is over now . . . the airlift has finished.'

'Protection of the Peoples Democratic Republic is not ridiculous. . . .'

'Protection from what?'

'Our enemies, *naturlich*.'

'Comrade Kommissar Schildt,' said Willi quietly holding down his temper. 'As one German to another, I ask you to reconsider my application.'

The man's pudgy hands fingered the documents in front of him.

'Why do you want to go to West Berlin?'

'To try and find some old friends.'

It was vital to arrange a contact on the other side.

'You applied for passes at two *Grenzposten* in the North. Why?'

'For the same reason,' Willi replied in exasperation. 'To find old friends of my parents . . . if they are still there . . . who now happen to live in West Germany.'

'As a one-time engineer you are *unabkommlich* – indispensable to the DDR.'

'Comrade Kommissar,' said Willi. 'I was once an aircraft engineer. I was once a figher-pilot. The job I've been offered is that of a mechanic in a tractor-factory!'

'We need tractors.'

'We need freedom,' said Willi.

Schildt looked across the table sourly.

'Unauthorised attempts at crossing the border always fail. We capture a hundred a day.'

'Capture? Germans trying to get to Germany? Is this what I fought for? Is this what you fought for?' rasped Willi. 'Or did you fight? What exactly were you doing in the war, Comrade Kommissar?'

The Kommissr banged his fist on the desk and shouted.

'You are not here to interrogate me!'

Willi shrugged, his anger dissipating hopelessly. 'I am not really interested in your war record.'

There was a long pause while Schildt stabbed with his biro at a form and then attacked it with two different rubber stamps.

'Comrade Greifswald', he said. 'Application for a pass refused. You can re-apply in five years' time.'

'Five years . . .?' Willi asked incredulously.

'Please hand me your Passport.'

It was all the same, Willi thought. Different uniforms. Same oppressive, aggressive *Ordnung*. He handed over his Passport, which Schildt stamped and handed back. Willi was then given a thick plain envelope with a number on it. He opened it. All his letters to Anna which he had sent from East Germany were inside. He looked up to see the man watching him.

'You . . .' Willi began. His stomach tightened. Anna would have heard nothing apart from the Sweet William seeds.

'Don't write any more, Comrade', said Schildt. 'They will not get past the Censor. We have copies of course.'

'But it's diabolical. . . .' said Willi.

Schildt must have pressed a hidden button because a uniformed constable of the *Schutzpolizei* appeared. The Kommissar stood up. Willi rose to his feet.

'She will have to wait a little longer, your *Englische Madchen*.' Schildt paused sneeringly.

Willi tried not to clench his teeth. The constable touched his arm. They went out of the elegant room formerly used by one of Himmler's subordinates.

Willi forced himself to let his rage ebb away. He walked out of the building along the drab streets where there were hardly any motor vehicles. When he reached the Unter den linden, he stopped and glanced towards the Brandenburger Tor, through which Hitler's motorcades had once passed. Now, blackened and scarred the neo-classical columns merely demarcated the limit of one occupied zone of the capital from another. Willi remembered the '*Sieg Heils*' of the spell-bound crowds over a decade ago. But now he picked up faintly a deep undifferentiated sound coming from beyond the gate. It was the composite noise of cars, and trams, and buses and people, the bustle and activity of a crowded city going about its peaceful business. It was also the sound of freedom. Willi thrust his hands into his overcoat pockets, and one of them closed fiercely on the bundle of letters to Anna. Any faint doubts which remained as to what he intended to do now were emphatically dispelled. He had tried to comply with the regulations. He had 'played the game' as the English would say. And his reward was virtually a prison sentence for five years in his own country.

Willi turned off the main thoroughfare and walked northwards towards the Oranienburg Station. He began to review the various means of escape through the iron curtain, as Churchill had already dubbed it. It struck Willi as ironical that he had spent the war preparing a German plane to fly home from England; now he needed it in Germany to travel the other way. But he saw little chance of 'borrowing' a plane in Eastern Germany. He had heard of a freight-pilot and a crop-duster managing to hop over the border, but such defections were made by people who were already trusted to fly aircraft. Besides he had to find a safe way to include Giselle and Klaus, above all Klaus. He could steal a vehicle and try a bust through a border road; he believed an ambulance had managed it, but the hazards were very great. What one really needed was a tank. He dismissed wryly the fanciful idea of spending twenty years reconditioning a burnt-out Panzer. There had to be simpler ways, diplomatic ways. Other people had to be involved, other people who could be trusted. Disguise and false papers? A train? A tunnel? Willi felt a deepening depression the more he thought of the difficulties and dangers. But his resolve was unshaken. He pulled his shoulders back and his walk became a marching step.

He noticed a queue beginning to form outside a shop. He couldn't see what kind of a shop it was, but his sister had taught him in the months since he had returned to East Germany, that if ever a queue formed, then join it. A queue meant a shortage, and everyone was in the market for a shortage. After standing and shuffling for twenty minutes, he reached his goal. It seemed at one time to have been a toy-shop. On the walls above the empty shelves were pictures of dolls and teddy bears, trains and engines, but today his ration of joy was one toilet-roll. Just as he was leaving the shop he spied a box of assorted objects, tennis rackets, a pair of roller-skates, a sailing boat, a bow without an arrow and several different sized coloured balls. He picked out the largest, the size of a football and bounced it on the floor. 'How much?' he asked.

The shopkeeper shrugged.

'Whatever you like, Comrade', he said. 'Balls are not rationed yet.'

A few people behind Willi sniggered. He put a note down on the counter, and left the shop carrying the toilet-roll for Giselle in one hand and the ball for Klaus tucked under his arm.

The gate to the little lodge creaked as he opened it, and before he reached the door Klaus ran out.

'Papa!', he shouted and leapt onto his father, flinging his arms round his neck and his legs round his buttocks. The sheer exuberance and force of the physical greeting nearly brought Willi down. He dropped the ball and the toilet-roll and catching hold of the boy's wrists, swung him off his feet round and round faster and faster until he was flying horizontally through the air. Klaus shrieked with delight and when he was lowered to the ground staggered away with the effect of the rotation.

'Don't you attack me like that again or I'll throw you over the roof,' said Willi.

'Is this what it feels like in a plane?' asked Klaus rolling his eyes histrionically.

'Possibly,' admitted Willi. 'Here, I've brought something for you.'

He picked up the ball which Klaus had not noticed, and kicked it high in the air out of the garden into the paddock which stretched away to the burnt-out ruin of the once solid but elegant house Willi had known throughout his own childhood.

Klaus rushed across the grass after the ball. He picked it up and kicked it into the air. Willi watched him with affection and saw the facility with which the boy played, reminding him briefly of Renate and her graceful slaloms at Kitzbuhl. Immediately he thought of Anna, and whether she would take to Klaus and he to her. But Giselle's greeting behind him pointed to the complexities of his relationships and the difficulties ahead. As he kissed her and gave her the toilet-roll, he wondered if all of them, Anna, Giselle, Klaus and himself – would ever come together in one place.

'Did you get the pass?' asked Giselle.

'No,' said Willi. 'No chance.'

'I thought not.'

Willi noticed the look of indifferent resignation on her face. She was so unlike the sister he used to know.

'We've got to have a long talk tonight,' he said.

'What about?'

'Everything. What we're all going to do.'

'Yes Willi,' said Giselle. 'When Klaus is in bed.'

'OK.'

Klaus shouted from the field.

'Are you coming to play, Papa?'

'Of course,' Willi called, and climbed over the fence. The action produced pain in his right buttock, a reminder of old battles lost and won. He joined combat with his son, dribbling the ball round the boy, keeping it just out of the child's reach.

The next morning the men came and roped off a large area. It included the paddock, the drive up to the house, the burnt-out building itself, and the ornamental garden behind it. All his childhood in fact, thought Willi. He watched with a surly eye from the lodge window. They erected a wooden hut in which to keep their tools and eat their rations. Willi envisaged with distaste the new prospect which would appear when the planning vandal's work was complete – a grey concrete block of featureless workers' flats rising to ten storeys. At midday two bulldozers arrived. The monster machines were parked on each side of the house like sinister sentinels.

'Like the tanks,' said Giselle.

'What tanks?'

'The Russian tanks. In 1945.'

'I didn't know there was a battle!'

'There wasn't. None of our soldiers had been seen for more than a day. The gunfire faded out too as the retreat went on.

We were just thinking we'd been lucky. . . .'

'We?'

'Mama and Papa. . . .'

'And Klaus. . . .?'

'And Klaus, of course. We were all here in the lodge.'

'Why weren't you in the house?'

'It was too cold in the house. We had no fuel all the winter. And not much food either. But we were together. And we had survived. And we were just thinking we'd somehow missed the fighting when suddenly two tanks with about twenty troops riding on them came round the end of the wood, and stopped on each side of the house. The officers got out and stretched their legs and looked at their maps and smoked cigarettes. The soldiers wandered about and some of them broke into the house. It was all very casual.'

'A sitting target for our Stukas,' said Willi.

'We hadn't any Stukas, Willi . . . not even one Messerschmitt!'

We had one,' said Willi sadly. 'But it was a long way away.'

'After about half an hour the soldiers came out of the house again, and climbed back on the tanks. We prayed that if we kept down and hidden, they wouldn't bother even to look at the Lodge. Smoke and flames started to come from the house and it was obvious they were burning it down as a matter of routine before they continued their advance. I don't know why they didn't fire a few shells into it. It would have been much quicker.'

'Waste of ammo,' said Willi. 'Burning was cheaper. Typical of the Russians.'

'Well, it was too much for Papa. When he saw the flames, he became completely agitated. We tried to stop him, but he snatched up his walking-stick and ran out of the door shouting "Wait! Wait! There is something I have to get. . . ." Mama ran after him "Come back Johann", she called. "It doesn't matter. Come back. What do those things matter now?" But Papa didn't come back.' Giselle started to sob. 'And Mama ran after him across the paddock. . . .'

Willi could picture the scene. The two elderly people, breathlessly stumbling over the frozen rough grass, their grass, their land, his land . . . Willi's parents running to the house built by his great great grandfather after Waterloo.

'Did Papa . . . did Papa go inside, into the flames?'

'No . . . no,' said Giselle. 'He got to the steps by the front door and then one of the Russians fired a burst at him.'

'And Mama?' asked Willi thickly.

'She reached Papa's body . . . I could see her lifting his head. I think she . . . she was comforting him, though he must have been dead. Then they shot her too. Almost immediately part of the blazing front wall of the house collapsed on top of them.

'God. . . .!' said Willi. '*Die blutige Bars*!' the words choked in his throat. 'Did Klaus. . . .?'

'No,' replied Giselle. 'Klaus slept through everything.'

'And what about you?'

'The Russian officer came in here. He saw where Mama and Papa had come from. He assumed I was Klaus's mother . . .', Giselle broke off and looked at Willi as if asking permission. 'Well, I am in effect aren't I, Willi?' He recognised the question for what it was – a desperate appeal.

'Yes, Giselle. You certainly are. How old was Klaus when Renate was killed?'

'Eighteen months. It was 1942 when I left Dresden.'

'Poor Renate,' he said.

But poor Giselle too. She had always wanted children but she was 'unblessed' as Mama used to say. And she hadn't ever found a husband. Perhaps one of the Russians . . . he had heard stories of rape . . .

'Did any of them. . . .?'

'No,' said Giselle. It was a defiant voice. 'No one tried. No one dared to touch me. I held Klaus's tiny hand and said 'We are both von Greifswalds'. They didn't understand but that wasn't important. I made the point, didn't I, Willi?'

'Yes,' he said. 'Quite right. Quite right, Giselle.'

'So they took what food there was and . . . left us to starve.' Giselle smiled suddenly and said, 'But as you see, we didn't.'

Willi kissed her gently on the forehead. In spite of her remark Giselle looked thin and undernourished. But Klaus, though thin, was growing into a wiry boy. Willi could see how she doted on him. And the boy on her. He noticed he called her '*Mutte*' at times. The bond between them had been forged good and strong; maybe indissolubly. He, Willi, Klaus's real '*Vater*' felt the odd one out. He understood the strength of her feelings when the previous night they had talked seriously about defecting to the West. They had reached no conclusion. And they had to decide on a plan.

'Have you thought about what you are going to do?' he asked.

'Willi, I told you. They have agreed to let me keep the lodge. That is marvellous nowadays. To have even one room to oneself is marvellous. You don't understand, Willi. We are all right here . . .'

'But Klaus. . . .'

'Klaus is all right here,' she raised her voice. 'You go Willi if you want to, but you can't take Klaus. He is all I've got. Things will get better . . . perhaps you will come back later . . . in a few years . . . Klaus will be fine . . . things are bound to get better. . . .'

'Things will not get better,' Willi cut her short brutally. 'They will get worse. The Russians will never give up their half of Germany.' He made a contemptuous sound. 'In spite of everything, they are still afraid of us, you know.' Willi gave her a brief smile of pride. It was an expression of an old emotion; one he hadn't felt for a long time.

'Oh Willi . . .,' sighed Giselle. 'Not another war!'

'I don't know,' he replied thoughtfully. 'Maybe. But Germany will not start the next one.' Willi turned to her pleadingly. 'Giselle. Don't stay here. It is going to be terrible here. And now is the time. It is going to get more and more difficult, don't you understand?'

'Why don't *you* understand? I feel tired and exhausted. I don't want to run. This is my home. I accept that life will be different now, but it is still my life. In my home. And this is Klaus's home. He is happy. He is getting on so well at school. All the teachers say he is learning to be a good citizen. . . .'

'You mean he is learning to be a good Communist!' shouted Willi. 'That is precisely why I don't want him to stay here. I do not want my son to be a good Communist. I don't want him to be any sort of a Communist.'

Giselle was silent for a few seconds.

'Willi . . . how would you feel if we were caught, and all sent to prison . . . or if Klaus were killed when we tried to get away? It is all so dangerous.'

'It need not be dangerous,' said Willi. 'There need not be any crawling under barbed wire, or climbing electrical fences, or dodging searchlights and bullets. An escape can be bought you know.'

'With what?'

'Money. How much have you saved?'

'Two thousand. I got them in dollars. Never mind how. You can have them. And a diamond ring that Mama and Papa gave me. Please. . . .' Willi looked at his sister and nodded slowly. He knew he was going to accept her offer. There was nothing else to do. Poor Giselle.

CHAPTER FIFTEEN

After she had finalised the deal on the shop with Susan, and waatched her and the young doctor go back to the garage, Anna felt a lump of sadness in her chest. So the shop had gone. Well, she had had a lot of fun out of it for many years. She recalled the day when she had first had the idea of buying it; the day her brother Charles came back from the States just after the war had ended.

'Are you going to stay?' Charles had asked.

'Stay. . . .?'

'Over here, in England?'

'Of course,' replied Anna.

'Jeez. . . .', said Charles.

Anna regarded the 1946 edition of her remembered 1939 brother with a kind of disbelief. The stripling boy of eleven had become the hulk of nineteen. The metamorphosis to an American was complete; accent, gestures, outlook.

'I thought when you finally came home, Charles, you'd want to stay.'

'I came to take *you* back with *me*,' he laughed. 'Uncle George said 'Go get Anna. She's a good-looking kid. She can stay with us until we've rustled up someone to marry her!'

'Like one of the cattle on his ranch.'

'It's a great place, Anna,' said Charles missing the innuendo. 'There are thousands of acres. Not like this little old farm. Takes a whole day to ride right round Uncle George's place. You'd love it. It's great, really great.'

'Don't you feel at all that you belong here?' she persisted.

'It's over seven years for God's sake. . . .'

'Eight since Daddy died.'

'I know,' said Charles. 'It must have been tough for you when Daddy died, but . . . well I don't remember too much about him. . . . I missed *you* most . . . I've always missed you, Anna, but I didn't miss this place,' went on Charles. 'It doesn't mean anything special. . . .'

He looked out across the marshes to the estuary. In a flash Anna saw her brother astride a horse, gazing from under the shade of his wide-brimmed hat at the golden distances of California. 'I guess I just don't feel British any more.'

And that just about sums it up, she thought. For you Charles anyway. And for you Willi? *Heimat*, Homeland you said was the place where you feel deep in your guts you belong. But I don't believe that, Willi. It's people not places that count. *Heimat* is people. Anna turned to Charles trying to keep the emptiness out of her voice.

'You've only been here a week and you just can't wait to get back, can you?' It sounded like an indictment.

'Anna, I didn't mean that . . . it's great being with you.'

'Got a girlfriend over there?'

'I have lots of girlfriends.'

It wasn't a boast, just a casual observation. They continued to saunter down the causeway.

'Not one special girlfriend?' Anna was relentless.

'I guess so,' Charles said.

'What's her name?'

'Miriam.'

'Miriam who?'

'Miriam Rubinstein.'

'That's Jewish isn't it? Is she Jewish?'

'I don't know. I haven't asked her. All I know is she's absolutely fantastic to look at,' he grinned, and took out his wallet and showed her a picture.

A very glamorous girl. There it was. The freedom from prejudice, the freedom from all that had just happened here in Europe. She returned him the photo.

'Congratulations, Charles. Hungry?'

'Sure am.'

'Shall I see if I can make a Hamburger?'

'Jeez. . . .' said Charles. 'That'll be great.'

They walked back to the farm, a very old Kim leading them along the causeway. When they had eaten and were smoking their cigarettes over the coffee he had brought her, Charles said,

'Well, if you won't sell up, why can't you come over for a short trip? Get the feel of the place. Where's the harm in that?'

Where was the harm? Only the harm that Willi might come and not find her, and go away and never come back.

'Who'd look after the farm?' she asked.

'How about the guy that lives in the cottage?'

'Rodney? Arthur's son. You remember Arthur?'

'No, but Rodney looks OK. Doesn't he practically manage the farm, anyway?'

'Yes, but. . . .'

'Well, what's stopping you?'

Faith, loyalty. The Sweet William seeds. A sign Willi that you are keeping faith. At least until then. Why haven't you written since? Have you found your wife, Willi, and gone back to your old life, in your own country? I'm so terribly afraid.

'Perhaps I'm afraid,' said Anna.

'Of what?'

'Of liking it too much in America,' she said truthfully.

After the drab war years, half of her yearned intensely for a taste of the ease and comfort, the sunlight and affluence of Los Angeles and San Francisco, magic names in a magic landscape.

With sudden insight, Charles said, 'I guess you've got a boyfriend hidden away here somewhere, Sis and that's why you won't come.'

A boyfriend, a love, a life, a totality. How could she tell him? How could he understand?

'No such luck,' she said.

In the afternoon they went into Bishop's Felix. Anna bought the week's groceries and then crossed the road to where Charles was looking at the antique and junk shop. Anna knew the window by heart: three Japanese netsukes, a copper and brass Tibetan horn leaning on a Victorian rocking-horse; a wheel barometer. On a tray were some silver vinaigrettes, wine-labels and spoons. There was a stuffed cock pheasant in a glazed case. Charles was attracted by a sword described as 'Mid 17th century English pillow-sword with 31 inch blade'.

'Guess that'd come in handy on the ranch for prowlers,' he chuckled. 'Change from a six-shooter.'

'I'd love to have a shop like this,' said Anna. 'Come on. I'll buy you something to take back for Uncle George.'

They went in and she quickly struck a bargain with the proprietor. The object was wrapped up and Anna handed it to Charles.

'Gee thanks,' he said. When they were outside again he asked, 'What the hell is it?'

'Don't you know, Charles?' Anna replied as if such a thing were in everyday use. 'It's a silver George II marrow-scoop. Uncle George'll love it.'

'You don't say?' observed Charles.

They walked down the street together, as they had often done as children. Daffodils were out in the vicarage garden and the rooks were making a din in the elms against the windy April sky. The *Evening Standard* purchased at the newsagents told them the Russians had opened the routes again to Berlin and the airlift was over. That was it, she told herself. That was the good news she had sensed in the spring air. Anna felt uplifted. She would hear from Willi soon, one way or another. The phone would ring and he would say in his precise accent. 'Hello, Anna. It is I, Willi. I am here, in London'.

She and Charles got in the car where she had parked it by the War Memorial. The only stonemason in the district was chipping out fresh letters, almost white in their newness against the general grey of the granite. He was going to be several days on the job. He had nearly completed the heading, 'World War II 193 . . .

Anna watched the man as he worked away. Willi's war she thought. Her war. Their war. Our war. Part of history. Her mood of optimism plummetted. Was Willi the past? Had she not better cut her losses, put the past away in the old world and go with Charles to the new? Charles was looking at the War Memorial.

'Thank God you missed that,' she said to her brother. She pressed the starter, let in the clutch and drove up the High Street.

Anna walked down the platform at Charing Cross Station. The previous day – her twenty-ninth birthday – she had said goodbye to Charles and his wife Miriam who had been staying with her at Marsh Farm at the end of their six-week trip to Europe. They had left her a house full of flowers and other ephemeral gifts.

'Now listen honey,' the younger Miriam had said to her confidentially. 'You don't mind if I speak to you girl to girl, do you?' Before Anna could assent or object, she went on. 'What you're doing is just plain crazy. You may think you're young – you *are* young – but you're wasting your life all on your own with this little farm and its one-pump filling-station. Oh, I know it's cute and rural and genuine old England, and it's where you and Charles were born, but it's time to pull out, before you just vegetate. As far as I can see you don't have much fun at all. You don't meet anyone, there's no neighbourhood activity. You're simply not going any place at all. Now, am I right, Anna?'

'I don't know', she had said. 'Perhaps. . . .'

'It isn't as if you have any family here. Charles is your only close relative. He *is* your family.' Miriam had put a hand on her arm. 'He and me too, honey. And I know one thing for sure, you'd just love our new place at Palm Springs. Why don't you sell up and come over and live with us in California?'

'That's sweet and kind of you Miriam. . . .'

'You've never even visited with us. It's crazy honey! And you're so easy on the eye. I guess you'd be hitched to someone in less than a twelve month. . . .'

'I'm not sure I want to be hitched. . . .'

'You have to be kidding. . . .'

'To just someone. . . .'

Miriam's mouth had opened and for a second no words emerged. Then the flow had continued.

'Well, I don't know of course, but the situation is a bad situation for you to be in. It can go on for years and years and in the end you can wonder what happened to your life. Still,' Miriam had shrugged expressively, 'it's your life. . . .'

Brashly as it was expressed, Anna was quick to recognise her sister-in-law's perceptive insight. If she had dared to confide the truth of the situation about Willi, Anna was certain Miriam would not have held back from giving even stronger advice. She could imagine the precise words. 'You haven't seen the guy for years? He's a Kraut – excuse me – a German? He must have been repatriated to Germany now but you don't know exactly where . . .? Honey, you need your head examined!'

And ever since Miriam and Charles had gone, Anna had examined her own head, and her heart too. After all, in a lifetime, was eight years so long? And Miriam's voice spoke loud and clear 'At twenty-nine honey, it's hellish long!' But though their visit had not diminished Anna's deep longing for Willi nor her faithfulness, she felt she had reached a crisis point. She had to find out where Willi was and talk to him and see him. If that involved risks for her, now she would accept them.

She took a taxi outside Charing Cross to the new German embassy in Belgrave Square. She was impressed by the courtesy and concern of the junior official who dealt with her simple request.

'Some relatives of mine in California are related by marriage to *Oberleutnant von Greifswald, Wilhelm von Greifswald*, and are anxious to trace his whereabouts.'

'You say he was a Luftwaffe pilot and was a prisoner of war here in England?'

'He must have been repatriated to Germany.'

'Did the letter say where the *Oberleutnant* was making for?'

There was no letter. Just some seeds.

'Greifswald. He had an estate there.'

The man pulled down a large roller-map of his country. An aggressive black line pursued a sinuous course southwards from just east of Hamburg to the Czech border north-west of Pilsen. The official pointed out Greifswald. It was beyond the line near the Baltic coast not far from Peenemunde.

'Your relative is no doubt in East Germany. I am afraid I am unable to help you.'

'But. . . .?'

'It is sad, but Germany is divided into two.' The man smiled at her wanly. 'But we mustn't grumble. After all, Caesar divided Gaul into three parts did he not?'

The Consulate for the DDR was a short taxi-ride away in Rutland Gate. There the official was also polite, but his suit appeared to have been made for someone else. A second stone-faced man was present during the interview. He sat in a chair near the wall with folded arms.

Anna was asked interminable questions, most of which she couldn't answer and to some of which she chose to profess ignorance. There seemed to be great irritation that she would not supply details of Willi's appearance – though she reiterated that she herself had never met him. Under pressure she said her relatives had given her a photograph. She showed her questioner the picture of Willi and Renate on their wedding day. In spite of her protests the man took the photograph out of the room and she was left alone with the silent 'gorilla' under whom the Louis Quinze reproduction chair seemed just about to collapse.

After half an hour the official returned and gave her back the photograph. He checked once more all Anna's details including those on her old Identity Card. Then the man gave her a stiff little bow and wished her goodday.

'But you haven't given me any information at all?'

'If Herr Greifswald is in East Germany we shall find him. There is no doubt about that.'

'But how long will it. . . .?'

'That is impossible to say. We shall inform you Miss Household.'

The interview was over.

By the time she reached home a profound despair had settled on her. She sat down in the living-room and faced the probability squarely that she might never see Willi again. Sadly and bitterly she also accepted the possibility that if they did meet, they would discover they were both different people; people who had once had an affair; and that the affair was over.

She went to the bureau and started a long letter to Charles and Miriam, but it was really to Miriam. Across the marshes the water of the estuary was steel-grey.

CHAPTER SIXTEEN

Peeb settled into his usual place at the end of the bar.

'I hear you had a spot of bother while I was up north?' Bill Mitchell put the brimful tankard in front of Peeb without spilling a drop.

'I wish you'd been here actually.'

'Yes . . . well we always get a few strangers in on a Saturday night. Not to worry.'

The landlord glanced at the fading mark on Peeb's forehead.

'How are you then, all right?'

'Not even a headache.'

'That's all right, then.'

With the repetitive formula phrases the incident was officially closed. Not that it sounded very much. Experience had taught Bill that a cool attitude to such events was best for business. Peeb wanted to ask Bill if he knew anyone like his questioner of Saturday night. But he shied off it. Truth was he was a shade embarrassed now by the whole affair. It had even taken a little courage to come back to the Three Crowns again. So he said nothing.

As the pub began to fill up and Peeb approached the end of his second pint, the familiar performance took place. The last one-second burst was sending the Messerschmitt down in flames, when Brian and Susan arrived. He bought them a drink. Susan had been showing Brian over the shop premises. She had come to rely on his help and support quite considerably as their relationship had developed. They both seemed very excited. But there was more to their excitement than merely Susan's celebration having acquired the shop. They had both been aware of their growing love for one another, and over the past weeks they both knew they would have to tell Peeb of their intention to marry. Brian had insisted they should tell him in a conventional fashion, for he would appreciate the formality, despite Susan's insistence that it was not necessary. But she knew Brian well enough to know that if he felt it was the right thing to do, then it would be done his way. Smilingly, she had agreed, and tonight would be a good occasion to break the happy news. Brian drove them all back to Bluff Cottage. Peeb tried to look surprised when Brian requested to see him alone.

'May I have your consent to marry your daughter?', he asked formally.

'Certainly,' said Peeb. 'Congratulations. Must say you haven't let the grass grow.'

'I've always excelled at spot diagnoses,' grinned Brian.

'Good for you,' laughed Peeb. 'Glad to have you aboard.'

Susan came in then and all the appropriate gestures were exchanged. Peeb fetched up from the cellar the last Bollinger, kept for such an occasion. The wedding date was fixed for the following June 1990, when Susan also hoped to open her new offices in the High Street.

After Brian had gone and Susan was upstairs, Peeb went out into the forecourt and looked up at the sky. He felt peaceful and happy and just a little pissed. He raised the binoculars to his eyes and scanned the night reflections on the distant estuary. There was nothing there except two cargo vessels coming downstream from Tilbury, no shapes, no shadows, no disturbing sounds. For a second the alcoholic haze which perfused his contentment almost persuaded him that perhaps after all he had imagined everything. But when he went back into the living room he saw the broken-off piece of the beech-tree, the leaves now withering, which Susan had quixotically put into the empty vase on the bookcase over a week ago.

Within a week, as promised, Household delivered the repaired and tuned Lagonda to Bluff Cottage. Peeb was down at the Three Crowns. Susan was preparing dinner when the bell rang. She took off her apron and opened the door.

'Good evening Miss Peebles-White. . . .'

'Susan is much shorter, Mr Household,' she smiled.

She noticed for the first time the discerning gaze of the older man's expression. His hair though white was startlingly thick and springy. She had no difficulty in imagining how handsome he must have been as a young man. He held up the Lagonda keys and dropped them into her hand.

'She's in the garage. There was half a can of paint left over. I've put it on the floor behind the driver's seat. Tell your father it's a beautiful engine but he'll need the brakes re-lining after another two, three thousand miles. Dooley's in Ashford are safe for that, as I shan't be here.'

'Of course, you're going to California next week. How is Anna?'

'Fine. Well . . . much better. Her solicitors will formalise everything on the shop direct with you. So I'll say . . .' he seemed to hesitate and then chose his words, '*Au revoir*.'

'*Au revoir*,' said Susan and shook his proffered hand. 'Give Anna my love and I do hope she'll respond to the climate.'

'Yes,' said Household. 'I'm going to stay with her for a few months. We have a good headman who'll run the farm. If the climate does the trick we'll come back, dispose of the farm and garage and then go out there for good.'

Household strode briskly to the gate. Susan noticed he limped slightly. He climbed into the Land Rover, where the Asian mechanic sat at the wheel. The vehicle backed into the drive and disappeared down the lane.

Half an hour later, when he came back from the Three Crowns driving Susan's new Fiat, Peeb inspected the Lagonda. It was a perfect restoration job and re-spray. The envelope containing the bill was taped to the outside of the windscreen. The account was quite substantial, but then, it was a specialist repair. There was also a short note from Household, giving his California address. '. . . in *case you track down the BF109. Meantime, good hunting*' it said.

When he got back to the farm Willi found Anna in the midst of the chaos which always precedes packing for a long journey. She stood in the bedroom darting from case to wardrobe, clothes on the bed, back to the cases.

'Not so fast, *liebchen*,' he said. 'Take it easy. We're not leaving till tomorrow.'

'I know,' she said. 'But I can't help it. I'm excited and sad. . . . I'm afraid too.'

He put his arms around her and they stood together like that for some moments.

'Can you imagine,' he asked, 'how afraid I was when I finally left East Germany to come back to you? Knowing I'd never see my son or sister again. Would I get here? Where would you be? Were you alive? Would you have gone?'

'But you did come back, Willi. And I was here, wasn't I?'

'Yes, *liebling*, you were,' he said softly. 'But it was a hair-raising journey. And I was so afraid.'

The two Swedish businessmen wore steel-grey suits, steel-grey Trilby hats set on the head without a millimetre's deviation from the horizontal, thick-soled brown Scandinavian shoes, fawn raincoats folded over their arms and brown leather gloves. They carried bulky black brief-cases and walked in step to the centre-point guarding the docks at Rostock, the main Baltic port of the Deutsche Demokratische Republik. One of the men, the taller, appeared to have a slight limp, but this may have been due to the cobbled surface of the quayside which was also criss-crossed by railway lines.

To the Customs officials they opened their cases exposing swatches of cloth and fabric which declared their commercial interests; to the Polizei they submitted to a personal search for weapons; to Passport Control they showed their papers and current Swedish passports. All documents were duly stamped. They repacked their things, closed their briefcases, and made their way to a five-thousand ton Danish ship, the motor vessel Ebjerg, which was one of the passenger ferries to Copenhagen. The voyage took just over five hours. They spent most of the time in the refreshment saloon exchanging views on non-controversial topics. The language they used was German. The shorter of the two had a Swedish accent and was not very fluent. They talked some business which involved the transfer of files. Inside one of them were concealed ten one hundred laundered dollar bills.

When the boat docked at Copenhagen, the men shook hands and separated. The shorter went out of the docks into the city; the taller wandered about and eventually located a grimy twelve-thousand ton British cargo vessel, the ancient S.S. *Rangoon*, built in Glasgow in 1918. The salt-caked funnel emitted some black smoke. The boilers were getting up steam. She was bound for Newcastle-on-Tyne. The grey-suited taller traveller walked up the gangway, and in perfect English asked a deck-hand to take him to the Master of the vessel, giving the name on his passport, Olaf Svensen. The captain was a bearded Scotsman called Joachim McTaggart, but inevitably known as 'Auld Jock'. In the privacy of his cabin he invited his only passenger to identify himself. This being done, the next procedure was predictable. A thousand dollars were carefully counted and tucked away in a deep Scottish pocket. Then a bottle of Glen Farclas malt whisky appeared, several drams were downed and the visitor was shown to a cramped makeshift cabin for'ard, in fact a converted paint-store, with that very legend inscribed on the outside of the door, which was locked behind him until three hours later, when the ship was rolling tipsily in the Kattegat.

So that he would not be accused of entering Britain illegally and also to protect McTaggart from suspicion, the day before they were due to reach Newcastle, Willi formally asked the captain of the *Rangoon* for political asylum from the East German Communist State. With not inconsiderable histrionic flair McTaggart handed Willi over to the authorities on arrival and Willi was escorted to a cell in a Police Station in Newcastle. The next day he was taken to a similar accommodation in Durham where he awaited the Special Branch officers who came and questioned him. For a referee of *bona fides* he gave the name of Colonel Hildersley, who came across from Westmorland on the other side of the country. After that the Home Secretary allowed the formalities to be completed.

Willi, once more Wilhelm von Greifswald was issued with documents registering him as an alien immigrant. He was given a work permit and set free, at large in the country of his wartime enemy. Hildersley took him to lunch at an old coaching inn in the town.

Willi looked round the comfortable shabby restaurant, with its casual service and wholesome unsophisticated food and experienced a familiar sensation, which was that odd mixture of isolation and security which made England feel different from all other European countries.

'What are your plans, *Oberleutnant*?' asked Hildersley.

'Willi, please. . . .'

'What do you intend to do, Willi?'

'Thank you first for . . . well, for backing me up.'

'I was sure you'd return here. I mean to England. The job at Welbeck Farm is still open if you want it.'

'I am very grateful for that, Colonel Hildersley, but. . . .'

'But you have another farm you'd rather go to?'

'Another farm? No, I. . . .'

'I'm sure Miss Household needs your help more than I do.'

Willi stared at Hildersley. Was it some trap? Were the British the perfidious Albions of French myth after all?

'Don't look so suspicious, Willi,' laughed Hildersley. 'The war's over. We've closed the file.'

'You knew about her?'

'Oh yes.'

'When?'

'After you left. Your signal might have slipped through, but my wife has never been fond of Sweet Williams and she's pretty hot on accounts. The item stuck out like a sore thumb. When questioned, the seedsmen told us where the order had been sent. Local enquiries on the Isle of Sheppey confirmed the presence of a wounded "cousin" from Scotland throughout the war, and then his sudden disappearance after the day you were picked up.'

'Did you question Anna? Did she. . . .?'

'Not necessary. After all you'd helped our war effort on the land, her land. It would probably not have been so productive without you. There was no espionage, no breach of security. So we wiped the slates clean. Yours and hers.'

Willi absorbed the information with surprise. He thought Hildersley had retired. Never underestimate your enemy, he reminded himself.

'Have you been in touch with Anna?' Hildersley asked matter-of-factly.

Willi thought bitterly of the bundle of letters returned to him so triumphantly by Schildt.

'All my letters were stopped.'

'And so she cannot possibly know, or guess, that you've come back?'

'No. Except that I told her I would. However long it took.'

Hildersley asked for the bill and paid it.

'There's a telephone-box in the hall,' he said. 'You'll be quite private. Here are some coins.'

Willi picked up the shillings and sixpenny pieces Hildersley pushed across the table.

'Thank you,' he said. 'You're very kind.'

Willi went to the kiosk and asked for the number. He stacked the coins in a neat pile on top of the black metal pay-box. He could hear a continuous sound. It broke off and started again. After about a minute the operator spoke in a north country accent.

'There's no reply, sir.'

'Are you sure? Are you certain?'

'Yes, sir.'

'Are you ringing the right number?'

Willi enunciated again the exchange and number precisely.

'Bishop's Felix one one six.'

'Hold on. I'll check it again for yer.'

After what seemed an interminable delay, the girl came back to him.

'Are you there, caller?'

'Yes.'

'Bishop's Felix one one six is reported disconnected, love.'

'Disconnected. . . .? What does that mean?'

But he knew what it meant. And it was as though he'd been shot through the chest. The phone clicked off and a sad continuous note sounded in his ear.

Willi got out of the train at Swale Station where he caught the last bus going over Kingsferry bridge to the Isle of Sheppey. He alighted at the bus-stop where the road branched south to Bishop's Felix halfway between Eastchurch and Leysdown. The habit of lifts and hitch-hiking he remembered during the war had dropped out of fashion with the ending of petrol-rationing; not that more than two or three vehicles passed him. He walked the three and a half miles to Marsh Farm. The familiar smell of the estuary mud and the sea pricked his nostrils. He realised he was hurrying. He slowed to an easier pace. It was absurd that a final five minutes saved out of all the years could make any difference. And yet he could not control his fears that he was right nor repress his hopes that he was wrong.

It was nearly dark when he reached the cluster of buildings he knew so well. As he had done ten years ago, he darted across the road and rang the bell by the front door of the house. But this time there was no dog bark, no chink of light at the side of blacked-out windows. The curtains were not drawn. He rang the bell again. The sound had an echoing quality confirming his worst apprehensions. He tried the locked door, then cupped his hand against the glass and peered through the tightly-shut windows. Dust sheets covered the furniture.

Willi went round to the back of the house and looked across the home field. The distant silhouette of the two Dutch barns was unchanged. So she had not burnt one down. Or was it that new barns had been erected on the old site; new barns by a new owner? The field was no longer simple pasture. Its barley crop had been harvested. Mechanised box-like stooks were scattered across the expanse of stubble. A crack of sound like a rifle shot reached him from the direction of the barns. Willi ran across the field zig-zagging between the string-tied bales of grain. On the far side of the larger barn the side door to which he had once fitted two locks was ajar. He could hear the hum of the generator.

He went inside. Immediately he smelt the petrol and saw the straw had been spread about over the floor and bunched round the tarpaulined shapes of the farm machinery just as he had instructed. He looked at the Messerschmitt which was uncovered. Anna was sitting in the cockpit gazing upwards through the open canopy. Her right arm hung down over the side of the fuselage. In her hand was the Luger pistol.

'Anna. . . .! he cried out.

To his astonishment she raised her head and turned her face towards him. She smiled drunkenly.

'Willi,' exclaimed Anna. 'Willi, you've come back at last! I knew you would'.

When they got back to the farm Willi saw that the bottle of Scotch on the kitchen table was half-empty. There was a glass beside it. Anna found another one, poured a drink for Willi spilling a little whisky as she did so. She was half giggling, half sobbing and swayed unmistakably.

'You'd better not have any more,' he said.

'No, darling. Darling, Willi. I don't need any now . . . now you've come back. And now you've come back, I don't need anything at all,' she said repetitively. 'You're thinner,' she added.

'Sit down, *liebchen*,' he smiled at her indulgently.

'No, I'm going to make some tea.'

She went over to the sink and filled the electric kettle. Willi drank some Scotch.

'I tried to ring you yesterday,' he said.

'I'm sorry, darling. I told them to disconnect the phone.'

The door-bell rang.

'Hire car,' said Anna. 'His name's Leonard. He was going to drive me all the way to Heathrow.' She opened her handbag and gave Willi some notes. 'Tell him I'm not going now, but I'll pay him just the same. I'll have to send Charles a telegram tomorrow. Miriam *will* be surprised.'

Willi went down the hall past Anna's piled suitcases and paid off the driver. When he returned she was putting the milk and sugar in the cups. The scene was very prosaic, very commonplace, but their expressions gave the lie to such epithets. They regarded each other solemnly, unflinchingly, and knew their hearts had survived their separation. But they could not refrain from seeking reassurance.

'You thought I wouldn't come back?' he asked.

'No Willi I never thought that . . .'

'You're all packed up. . . .?'

'A visit to my brother. *Only* a visit,' she said plaintively.

'I might just have missed you,' he accused her.

'You would have found out where I had gone. Why didn't you write Willi? Why did you leave it so long?'

He put his hand into his breast-pocket and handed her the bundle of letters in their thin air-mail envelopes addressed to her.

'Returned. Re-sealed. Read by the Censor.'

'But why? What did you write? Secret information? What is in them?'

'Love,' smiled Willi.

Anna counted the letters.

'When I do read them I shall read them very slowly, one after the other. In the right order. Again and again.'

He put his hand over hers. She ran her finger along the scar.

'Does it hurt any more?'

'No.'

She took her hand away.

'You haven't told me about Renate.'

'She was killed.'

'I'm very sorry.'

He took her hand again.

'It's made it easier for us.'

'Easier . . .?'

'To get married.'

'You still want to, Willi?'

'*Naturlich*.'

'Oh so *naturlich*,' she laughed and kissed him. 'Did you find your other relatives?'

'Only my sister, and . . .' he stopped because he had not yet decided how he would tell her about Klaus or when he would tell her; or if he would tell her.

'Your sister and . . .?'

'What . . .?' he stalled.

'You said you only found your sister and . . . someone else?' she persisted.

There was no escape.

'My son,' he said.

'Oh,' she said. 'You didn't tell me.'

'I didn't know. How could I? He was born after I came to England. He's nearly ten.'

'Of course,' she said. 'He would be. I don't mind, Willi. I don't mind at all. What's his name?'

'Klaus.'

'Klaus,' she repeated, watching Willi's face. 'You must be very fond of him.'

'I hardly know him. . . .'

'Then proud of him.'

'I don't know, Anna. It depends what he will become.'

'He must visit us,' she said.

'No! No!' Willi's expression of pleasure clouded over. 'It would be very difficult to arrange. Even impossible. It was very difficult for me to get here. I have decided that my son, and sister and that part of my life are over. It will be better for all of us.'

Anna looked at him along the pain of his decision on his face. Eventually Anna got up. 'Come on, Willi, you'll have to help me make the bed.'

He rose to his feet and put his glass and cup on the draining-board. Carelessly Anna had left the Luger there when they had come in.

'Why hadn't you burnt everything as I told you? Someone might have found the Messerschmitt and then. . . .'

'I couldn't do it, Willi. The plane was you. When I felt lonely and sad and . . . and bitter sometimes . . . I used to go in the barn and lock the door, take off the tarpaulin and look at her. And it used to make things seem better. Even if you wouldn't come back for me, I was sure you'd come back for the 109.'

'And nobody ever found out?'

'Nobody.'

'But you were going to burn her tonight?'

'I was going away. But I don't think I could have set her alight. I felt so miserable. So I had a few drinks and felt more miserable.'

'Did you often get into the cockpit?'

'Tonight was the first time.'

Willi opened the magazine of the pistol and ejected the remaining shells. He could smell the cordite.

'Where did you get the bullets?'

'I hid them – years ago.'

'Why did you take the pistol to the barn?'

Anna shrugged.

'It was all part of you, darling.'

'But you fired it? What were you aiming at?'

'Nothing. Nothing at all,' she laughed. 'It was just a gesture . . . a signal . . . to you perhaps . . . wherever you were.'

'If a bullet had gone into a petrol can you might have set the whole place ablaze, and never got out!'

She put her arms round his neck and kissed him.

'Oh, Willi. . . . I've been so lonely.'

Willi whispered in her ear. 'Well you won't have to be again,' he said.

'I think we should always keep her.'

'Who?'

'The Messerschmitt. She's lucky for us. I have a feeling when she goes, our life will be over.'

'You are a superstitious little thing, aren't you?'

'Yes,' she said.

Willi continued to embrace her. He noticed he was still holding the empty Luger.

CHAPTER SEVENTEEN

During the rest of 1989 and the early part of 1990, Peeb spent a great deal of time searching for his Messerschmitt. In the Three Crowns he kept a wary eye on the door whenever it opened. He experienced a flip in the chest on a few occasions, whenever large dark glasses, a black beret or knee boots were a feature of the incoming customer's gear. When one night a pronounced German accent ordered '*Zwei biers und a sossage sandvitch*' it belonged to a genuine tourist, just over five feet tall and weighing at least fifteen stone.

Peeb purchased more maps and motored hundreds of miles in Kent and on the north side of the Thames in Essex and Suffolk. He took dozens of photographs of distant planes.

Several exposures with the telephoto lens at 1000th of a second near Burnham-on-Crouch looked very suspiciously like a 'rotte' or pair of Messerschmitts in attacking formation. But when he had the pictures blown up, they resolved into two Jet Provost Trainers, a long way from their base at RAF Cranwell.

So for month after month Peeb failed to discover either of his quarries. As time passed he entertained the idea that perhaps the attack had been called off or the plane that had earlier made his life so unsettling had crashed into the Thames or the North Sea and sunk without trace. Or perhaps it had taken itself off to another part of the world and become caught up in sporadic battles of barely reported wars, and been destroyed by some guided missile.

By January 1990, Susan and Brian were making day trips to London, looking at carpets and kitchen equipment for their joint home. They were married on June 1st in the church at Bishop's Felix, had three weeks' honeymoon in

Crete, and returned for Susan to open her office in the High Street. Peeb found Bluff Cottage a little lonely without his daughter. And less comfortable. A daily was not the same thing at all.

One evening in July when Peeb arrived back at the cottage as usual from the Three Crowns, he found a letter had arrived from Sir Martin Beddows. Jocular and cryptic, it contained disappointing information.

'*Dear Peeb*', it read, '*Your phantom would appear to emulate the yum-yum bird of ano-rectal fame. After exhaustive sampling encompassing most of Western Europe, the rear claw was contaminated with only very local excrescence. The report confirms that the contents of your envelopes contained soil from clay farmland with alluvial river deposits, the percentages indicating North Kent or South Essex. I suggest you send me further washings from the wheel and also a sample of earth from a local field or two and we may by comparison get a precise match. Keep your ear to the ground and your feet on it. As ever, Mart.*'

Peeb put the letter away and went back to the Lagonda and unlocked the boot. He lifted out the blanketed bundle tied round with cord which he had left there all these months, and placed it on the ground. As he did so he had the impression there was something different about the cord. It was tied securely enough, but the knot was not the simple reef-knot he invariably used. It was a much more complicated affair. A short sheep-shank he believed it was called. He had some difficulty unfastening it, but two thoughts began bleeping in his head like an anxious transmitter. If the knot was different then the cord had been unfastened and re-tied. He was sure he had not looked in the boot since the car was returned by Household as long ago as the previous September. Peeb at last got the thing undone, and pulled open the blanket. The wheel was there but it too looked different. He stood it on its tyre. It was just too small to be right and the spokes were the wrong shape. It was also faintly smeared with oil. It was a stacker-truck wheel. Household was in the know. Household was the bastard's accomplice. Household the motor engineer serviced the airplane!

Peeb slapped the boot lid to, got in the Lagonda, savagely reversed out and shot off down the lane into the village. He ripped along the High Street, his exhaust making an unholy disturbance, which matched the turmoil in his brain, the conflicting implications of his discovery. He turned off into the road towards the marshes. He was just passing the old loony-bin building when he saw the Messerschmitt. It was coming straight at him, diving from about a thousand feet. Peeb held his breath and his course, snapped on his headlights and accelerated. They must have been approaching at a combined speed of some four hundred and fifty miles an hour. The shock wave hit him like an explosion, rocking the car as the plane cleared him by ten feet. Peeb's offside front wheel banged into a pothole and he heard the report as the tyre burst. He went into a long sliding skid and came to rest with the Lagonda's nose in the ditch and its arse in the air, the rear wheels spinning. Swearing, Peeb switched off and clambered out. He seemed all right except for some sharp tenderness of his ribs where they had struck the steering wheel, and a pain in both thumbs which had gripped it forcefully. The 109 had made its turn and was coming at him again along the reciprocal. This time he could feel his hair prickling with sweat inside the back of his collar. He expected any moment to see the small orange flashes from the MG 17 machine-guns in the engine mounting and the 20mm cannon on the leading edge of the wings. There was no firing, but instinct was too strong. Peeb shot across the road and flung himself onto the opposite verge and rolled into the ditch, where his chest struck a stone. The impact winded him. The Messerschmitt screamed over and in the now darkening sky he saw it perform a perfect Victory Roll.

Breathing heavily and painfully Peeb got up, spitting mud and grass out of his mouth.

'You bastard,' he said, 'you ruddy bastard!'

He heard the engine throttle down and watched the plane begin a landing approach behind the distant line of trees. He knew where that was. A number of possible actions confused his brain and tore at his emotions. Peeb crossed the road, switched off the car lights and locked the door. Then he headed for Marsh Farm. He estimated it was one mile away. When he approached the building he slowed up, sucking in the air in gulps, paying off the oxygen debt. The movement of his ribs gave him a vice-like sickening pain in his chest.

There was a 'Closed' notice on the garage and the house looked deserted.

He went along the path and rang the house bell just the same. There was no answer.

Still with pain, he went round to the back. A long field stretched away without obstruction for well over a furlong, perhaps a quarter of a mile. At the end in the gathering dusk he could see the distant shapes of the Dutch barns. For a second he thought he saw a glimmer of light. After he had covered fifty yards or so he stumbled on the uneven turf. He picked himself up painfully. In spite of the dark he determined the cause of his fall. Recently-made wheel-tracks went off into the blackness. He followed them to one of the barns, which as he drew near, he observed had been closed off at both ends and along the sides. When he reached the building he could just see a fine pencil-slim streak of light at the top of what were now clearly twelve-foot high doors.

Cautiously Peeb eased round one corner of the barn. In a brickwork frame was an ordinary-sized door, which looked as if it was made of steel, which indeed it was. He began to breathe heavily again each breath a stab in the chest. He thought he was going to vomit. Peeb slowly turned the recessed handle. To his surprise the door gave inwards.

Peeb was aware of a high floodlight which shone down into his eyes. Slowly he opened the door and went inside. Against the flood Peeb could make out the shape of the Messerschmitt. He felt the heat from the recently-used Daimler-Benz engine, and smelt the aviation fuel and the glycol coolant. Half in the shadow in front of the port wing, sitting in a canvas chair facing Peeb, was a figure wearing a leather flying-jacket, breeches and knee-boots. On his head was a flying helmet. The man still wore his flying goggles. He motioned casually to Peeb with a Luger pistol held in his right hand. Peeb felt dizzy and swayed a little when he heard the voice.

'Ah, it is you, Group Captain. I was beginning to think you would never find me.' He got up and pushed another canvas chair towards Peeb. 'Sit down. We must drink to a certain occasion.'

'What. . . what occasion?' asked Peeb. The pain in his ribs was building fearfully.

'September the 15th 1940. The day you officially killed me.'

Peeb's brain whirled with fury. That bloody joker again. Alive? Twin brother? Actor? Well, he wasn't going to stand any more of it this time.

Peeb stood still, assessing the distance between the end of the revolver and the fraction of time it would take him to jump the gun.

The man in front of him stood up, clicked his heels and gave an outmoded formal bow.

'*Oberleutnant Wilhelm von Greifswald. Drei Jazdgeswader zwei und funfzig – A*.'

Peeb lunged forward at the gun. There was a star-burst in his chest and then a cold extinguishing blackness.

PART THREE

THE BATTLE OF BISHOP'S FELIX

'*Just then I saw the bloody Hun*
You saw the Hun? You, light and easy,
Carving the soundless daylight. . .'

Combat Report
John Pudney

CHAPTER EIGHTEEN

Still holding the unloaded Luger, Willi caught Peeb as he lurched forwards. Dropping the gun he lowered the dead weight into the chair. The floodlight accentuated the pallor of the face, and reflected the sheen of sweat on the sagging features. There was no doubt Peeb was unconscious, and it occurred to Willi he might also be dead; as effectively dead as if he had shot him with the Luger, or loosed a few cannon-shells at him through the spinner of the Messerschmitt. Lightning spurts of imagination sent ripples of guilt through Willi's mind. The death of his one-time adversary was not what he desired. He slipped down the knot of Peeb's tie and put a finger inside his collar and ripped it open, sending the button flying. Willi had half-informed ideas about the kiss of life and older methods of resuscitation but when the circumstances presented themselves, like most people he found himself floundering, inept and indecisive. He temporised by undoing Peeb's shirt, having some vague idea about massaging the chest, the heart, anything. His dilemma was abruptly resolved. Peeb's eyelids flickered, and his chest began to move. He gasped noisily for air and coughed up some blood. His eyes opened and Peeb brought Willi into focus.

'*Wie geht's*? *Wie geht's*?' asked Willi. 'Feeling better now?'

Peeb nodded assent.

'My God! . . . It's you, Household.'

Peeb put his hand on his bare chest.

'I thought . . . I thought you . . . sh . . . shot me,' whispered Peeb.

The effort of speaking increased the pain and he winced.

'*Nein, nein*,' Willi shook his head. 'There was no intention of that.' Willi picked up the Luger and demonstrated the emptiness of the magazine. 'See? There are no bullets. It is harmless. Like the Messerschmitt here. No ammo. Though I have put the guns back. It is perfect but it's shooting days are over.'

Peeb glanced up at the wing of the plane above him and saw the white-bordered black German Cross painted as fresh as new.

'But not its f . . . f . . . flying days,' he said.

'Maybe not quite,' smiled Willi.

'But what . . . but why? . . .' The effort of trying to find an explanation, an answer to all the questions that jostled in his mind, defeated Peeb. He shut his eyes again and slumped in the chair. 'Pain, chest . . .' he muttered . . . 'I think I'm having . . . a heart attack,' he managed weakly.

'I think you are, my friend,' said Willi. 'Do not speak any more. I will explain another time. Leave everything to me.'

Willi bent down and lifted Peeb forwards. With great care, almost gentleness he eased Peeb's body upwards until it was over his shoulder, thighs firmly held and arms hanging loosely down Willi's back.

'OK?' asked Willi.

'Roger', said Peeb feebly.

Willi straightened up and carried his burden past the gleaming airscrew blades to the side door of the barn, stepped out into the night air and at a brisk pace made his way across the long home field towards the farmhouse.

Anna came back from her trip to her Canterbury solicitors, parked the car by Willi's Land Rover and went into the house. She switched on the lights in the hall and called out for him. There was no reply, but she heard a banging on the back door. She ran into the kitchen.

'Who is it?'

'Me. Willi. Open the door quick!'

She turned the key in the lock. Willi stumbled in carrying Peeb.

'The Group Captain. . . !' exclaimed Anna.

Willi pushed past her and took Peeb into the front room and placed him on the couch. Anna switched on the light.

'My God, he looks awful. I saw his car in the ditch down the road. Is he dead?'

'No. He swerved madly. I saw him get out.'

'Then what's he doing here?'

'He followed me to the barn.'

'The barn? . . . So you've been flying again. . . ?'

'Anna, for God's sake. . . The man's collapsed. I've just carried him all the way across the field. . . .'

Willi felt Peeb's pulse. It was still there.

'Willi! You promised me!'

'It was my very last flight, Anna.'

'You dived at his car as he came along the road. . . !'

'He didn't have to go into the ditch. I wasn't firing at him. . . .'

'He didn't know you couldn't.'

'I didn't know his heart wasn't OK.'

'It must have been terrifying for him.'

'Nonsense. He's a fighter-pilot.'

'You said you were going to let the whole thing drop. My God, Willi, I hope you're satisfied now you've settled your petty personal score at last.'

'There's nothing petty about it.'

Peeb made a low groaning sound and moved restlessly on the couch.

'He needs a doctor,' said Anna.

'He needs morphine,' said Willi. 'The Armageddon pack. Get it. *Schnell*!'

While Anna ran out of the room, Willi fetched a rug from an old chest by the window and put it over Peeb. He seemed to be coming round again. Willi poured a glass of brandy from the decanter in the drinks cabinet and tried to get some fluid between Peeb's lips. Anna came back with the neatly labelled kit. Willi ripped it open with the attached tape and took out one of the sterile disposable syringes. Each contained three times the lethal dose of morphine. He had to guess but he assumed it would be safe if he injected just under a quarter. He pulled up Peeb's sleeve and stuck the needle in the outer side of his arm. He pressed the plunger a little way and then pulled the needle out. He handed the syringe to Anna.

'How do you know that's the right amount to give him?' she asked.

'I don't. Look at him. What is there to lose?' Willi went out into the hall and dialled for an ambulance. When he came back into the room, Peeb had opened his eyes again.

'Breathing . . . I . . . I can't breathe,' he announced.

'Don't talk,' ordered Willi.

'Will . . . will you send for my. . . ?'

'Daughter?'

'My son-in-law, Dr Bayliss.'

'Of course,' said Anna. 'I know the number.'

She went out to use the phone.

Willi said, 'Take it easy my friend. An ambulance is also coming.'

'The Lagonda . . .' said Peeb.

'I'll deal with it tomorrow.'

Peeb nodded and shut his eyes. It was exquisitely pleasurable to feel the pain draining away from his chest. He clenched and unclenched his hands under the rug. They felt soft and pliable, strangely jointless. His breathing eased a little. He coughed up a little more blood. Peeb began to doze off. So that fellow Household had been flying the BF 109 all the time? Yet he could have sworn he said his name was von Greifswald or something. That was the Hun Peeb had shot down. Very odd. It was all very odd indeed. Brian and Susan arrived simultaneously with the ambulance.

'Daddy . . .', said Susan softly and bent down and kissed him on the forehead. The skin was clammy. Brian gently eased her away and looked at Peeb's pupils and then put his stethoscope on his chest. He saw the blood. He went over Peeb thoroughly, at the same time getting a story from Household.

'He was . . . completely out of breath, gasping for air.'

'Then when he got in the barn, he saw the Messerschmitt?'

'Yes. . . .'

'And you?'

'Of course. He coughed up some blood.'

'He'd been trying to find out where the plane was, and who the pilot was for a long time Mr Household', said Brian.

'I know,' said Willi. 'Everyone in the district knew about Peeb's problem.'

'Anyway, quite a series of shocks for him tonight in rapid succession,' Brian said quietly.

Willi decided not to mention the additional ones of his German name and the Luger.

The ambulance team put an oxygen mask over Peeb's face.

'Brian, is he . . . is he going to. . . ?' asked Susan.

'No. He must have fractured a rib. Punctured a lung. He's got a haemothorax. His colour's not bad now. He should be OK. He hasn't had a heart attack.'

Please . . . please,' whispered Susan to herself.

'I'm so sorry,' said Anna, 'that this should have happened. My husband never intended . . . he was only. . . .'

'Your husband has probably saved Peeb's life. The morphine injection was vital,' Brian smiled at Willi. 'I won't ask how you happened to have some lying about.'

'For a very special emergency,' Willi answered.

'Well we'd better get the Group Captain to hospital,' said Brian. 'I'll go with Peeb in the ambulance to keep an eye on him. Susan, you follow in my car.'

They put Peeb on a stretcher. He was still in a doped state from the morphine. He was carried out to the ambulance.

'I'll come with you my dear,' said Anna to Susan.

'There's no need, really. . . .'

'Perhaps not. But I'd like to . . . For various reasons.' She called over her shoulder to Willi. 'Food in the fridge Willi. Be back later.'

Willi nodded and closed the front door behind them. He had the impression that he was being excluded, that he was the uncharged suspect in a crime he had not committed. After all these years there was still no way he could entirely escape the feeling of being a foreigner. Thoughtfully he went back to the barn, put the tarpaulins over the Messerschmitt, switched off the lights and returned to the farm. Perhaps it had been a mistake to bring Anna back from the States even temporarily, once they had made the decision to stay over there.

Susan sighed and closed her eyes. She listened to her own heart beating in the pillow. She felt the regular movement of Brian's breathing. She concentrated on keeping absolutely still so as not to disturb him. Her unnatural immobility communicated itself. Brian switched on the bedside light.

'OK, Susan, what is it?'

'How did you know I was awake?'

'I can hear your thoughts. The air's stiff with them.'

'It's not about Daddy.'

'Good.'

'Something Anna told me.'

'Tonight?'

'Yes and once before; when I was in the shop before I bought it. She said she was once in love with a Battle of Britain pilot.'

'So were a lot of people.'

'But the Messerschmitt is the actual plane Daddy shot down in the war.' Susan gave the information slowly for emphasis.

'Fifty years ago? How could it be?'

'It came down in the sea . . . well, the Swale. Off Marsh Farm.'

'With the dead pilot inside?'

'The pilot wasn't dead.'

Brian was silent for some seconds. Then the lightning implication struck him.

'Willi. . . !'

'Yes.'

'Household?'

'Von Greifswald. *Oberleutnant Wilhelm von Greifswald.*'

'Peeb's Hun. . . !'

'Willi was a prisoner of war. Anna told me he was eventually repatriated, but decided to come back to England. He became naturalised, changed his name to Household, and married her.' Susan sighed. 'All that time. What a fantastic romance.'

Brian absorbed this information and tested it for plausibility.

'I suppose one of these Aircraft Archaeological clubs found the plane, and salvaged it?'

'No. Anna said Willi did. Not many days after it came down. Willi worked on it all through the war in the barn. It was years later that he at last got it to fly.'

'Quite incredible,' said Brian. 'An unbelievable achievement. Even for an engineer like Household.'

'Don't you believe it?'

Brian drew in his breath.

'I know what my dear departed father would say.'

'What?'

'Only a Hun could do it. *Would* do it.'

'The Messerschmitt has been a talisman – a kind of good luck charm for their marriage. You see, it brought them together.'

'Is that why they came back from America? To pick up the plane, and take it with them?'

'No, they came back to sell the farm and collect some family belongings.'

'I wonder if *Oberleutnant* Household . . .', said Brian following his own train of thought, 'is going to fly it again . . . Willi's crazy enough. Look at the way he flew over Bluff Cottage. If he's not more careful he'll crash the thing and kill himself.'

'Or someone else,' said Susan.

'Like for instance?'

'Daddy.'

'Peeb. . . ?'

'Of course. What about tonight? Daddy wouldn't have ditched the Lagonda like that, unless he thought something was going to hit him. There was no other car involved. Anna said so. Daddy wasn't drunk. I think Willi tried to kill Daddy tonight . . . frighten him to death.'

'Well he didn't succeed, darling . . .' Brian comforted her. 'Peeb hit his chest on something. And he'll make a rapid recovery.'

'I know Brian . . . thanks to you. Anna is furious with

Willi. She's a very sweet person. After what happened tonight she says she's going to "ground" him.'

'There'll be no after-effects on Peeb. He'll be OK for years.'

'Daddy'll do exactly as you say.'

'He'd better. And so had you. Now go to sleep.'

Brian switched off the light. Susan turned on her side and drew up her knees. Brian applied his body closely to hers and put his arm around her waist. Safe, protected, and loved was Susan's summing-up of her position. She was soon asleep.

But Brian remained awake. Susan's remarks suggesting a deliberately dangerous, even malicious dive by Willi on Peeb along the road to Marsh Farm, made Brian assess afresh the husband of his former patient Mrs Household.

The past history was not entirely favourable. World War II experiences. A limp. A hand-scar. War wounds? POW. Unfathomable previous Nazi influences. On the plus side was a loving warm-hearted wife. Yet the unbelievably meticulous repair of the Messerschmitt, and Willi's behaviour when flying it, keeping the whole procedure secret, all seemed tangibly abnormal. The suspect's personality was proud, withdrawn, on guard, as if protecting some much deeper emotion. Guilt? Resentment? Revenge? He had courage certainly. Early signs of endogenous depression? Did the *Oberleutnant* suffer from the classic German illness of the spirit, *Liebestodt*? The deathwish. It was lurking about all right. Brian recalled the neat labelling on the pack from which he had noticed the hypodermic syringe projecting. W.W.III in gothic characters. There was nothing ambiguous about that.

CHAPTER NINETEEN

In the Kent and Canterbury Hospital Peeb was all packed up and ready to go. Fully dressed in his best dog's tooth check suit, brought the previous day by Susan, he sat in the chair by his bed in the small side-ward which had been his home for the last four weeks. Apart from the first few days, when he was in intensive care, Peeb had enjoyed a return to the communal life, remembered through the rose-glass of time from the Plastic Unit at East Grinstead in 1940 and 1941. Strangely, he felt fitter than he had done for years. Indistinctly, he heard the voices of his son-in-law and the consultant physician talking at the Sister's desk in the corridor outside.

Dr Bruckshaw looked at the x-ray screen.

'These are yesterday's, Sister?'

'Yes, Doctor.'

'Excellent. Lung fully re-expanded. Rib uniting. ECG quite normal too.' He put the tracing back in the file. 'No need to keep him a moment longer, Sister.' He smiled at Brian. 'Safely back into your hands, Brian.' The Sister opened the door into the side-ward and they went in.

'No, don't get up, Group-Captain,' said Bruckshaw, and sat on the end of the bed. 'I see you're packed to go,' he smiled.

'All set,' replied Peeb. 'Feel very fit.'

'Good.'

'No snags?' Peeb asked.

'None at all,' replied Brian.

'Go away and do what you like,' said Bruckshaw.

'Anything?'

'More or less. *Me den agen*. Within reason.'

'Willco,' said Peeb as if responding to an order.

'You've lost one stone in weight. Don't put it on again.'

'Beer?' asked Peeb.

'One pint not two. And *no* smoking.'

'Never touch 'em sir,' grinned Peeb. Bruckshaw shot out his hand.

'Goodbye, Group-Captain. Look after him, Brian.'

'Thank you, Doctor,' said Peeb.

The consultant got up and left the room with the Sister.

'Susan's a bit late,' said Brian. 'We'll walk down to the entrance. Here, let me take your suitcase.'

'What about a porter?'

'They're working to rule,' said Brian.

Susan met them in the corridor. She kissed her father and when Brian had departed for his morning round in his old mini, she put Peeb in her car. Before she started the engine, she took a cream-coloured envelope out of the glove compartment and handed it to Peeb.

'This came for you this morning. Looks very official.'

Peeb surveyed the embossed crest on the back and then opened the envelope. He took out a gilt-edged card. It was an invitation to the Battle of Britain 50th Anniversary Memorial Dinner, to Group-Captain Michael Peebles-White, DFC to be held at the Savoy Hotel. The name of the Guest of Honour was the most prestigeous in England. The date was September 14th 1990 at 7.30 for 8.00.

In the upper right-hand corner was '*Top Table Number 5*' and at the lower left '*Black Tie. Decorations will be worn.*'

Peeb beamed and handed it to Susan.

'Daddy how wonderful . . .' she said.

'They've got the date wrong,' said Peeb.

'I think that's because they don't want it to clash with all the Air-Displays on the fifteenth, and your separate squadron dinners earlier.'

Peeb did not reply. He was looking at a personal letter to him which was in the same envelope. It was from the Air Chief Marshall and signed personally. Peeb's face fell and he handed it to Susan. She read,

'*Dear Peebles-White. I received your letter, and both I and my staff have given it long and careful consideration.*

Unhappily we are unable to accede to your request to pilot the Spitfire in the Memorial Flight at Manston on September 15th.

I am sure you will appreciate that in spite of your medical fitness, as you are over 70, the safety regulations must be strictly adhered to.

I shall personally be honoured to meet you at the dinner at the Savoy on the 14th. Yours sincerely. . . .'

'Daddy!' exclaimed Susan. 'You didn't think they'd let you . . .!'

'Why not?' said Peeb. 'I may not be able to fly a Harrier, but I bet I know more about Spits than any of these young bods. . . .'

'I bet you do . . .' Susan laughed for some time.

'Come on,' said Peeb irascibly. 'Let's get back to this love-nest of yours . . . Though I'm quite OK at Bluff Cottage with Mrs Figgins coming in.'

Susan started the car.

'Not for a week or two. Then we'll see.'

'Dammit, I'm not an invalid. Bruckshaw said. . . .'

'Has it occured to you, I might like to have you staying with us for a bit? To see what a good doctor's wife I'm making?'

'Well, if you put it like that, darling,' said Peeb, 'I shall enjoy every moment.'

'I know you'll enjoy the little surprise I've got for you,' said Susan.

'Oh. . . ., what's that?'

Susan didn't answer until she turned through the gate to the house where Doctor Page had once practised. Peeb had no need of an explanation. The maroon Lagonda, the body-work once again perfectly restored, was parked in the drive. Peeb got out wearing an expression of joy and affection. Then his face fell, and a scowl replaced the former look of pleasure. He jerked a thumb towards the car.

'Who repaired this?' he asked Susan, knowing full well the answer.

'Willi Household.'

'Household?' shouted Peeb. 'Greifswald, you mean.'

No, Household. He's been British now for years.'

'Once a Hun, always a Hun,' growled Peeb.

'Yes, Daddy.'

Susan sighed. So that's how it was going to be. She had been worried that Peeb had not mentioned the Messerschmitt and the circumstances of his chest injuries, where they had happened or why they had happened. But obviously the subject had been occupying his mind hugely. Her father said surprisingly,

'The bastard never even came and visited me once in hospital.'

'He wanted to . . .' said Susan.

'I'll bet. . . .'

'It's true. But Anna, Brian . . . all of us decided the meeting might excite you . . . upset you, delay your recovery, so he didn't come to see you.'

'Well then,' said Peeb. 'I shall have to go and see him, shan't I?'

Susan sighed again. It sounded very much like open warfare.

Willi heard the car when it was half a mile away. He knew one of the silencers was slightly defective and would soon have to be changed, but this only accentuated the deep throbbing sound which emanated from the exhaust manifold of the L.C.45. The Lagonda came into the garage forecourt after showering some of the chippings onto the road behind it, and slid to a standstill in front of the pumps. The engine revved right up and then died. It was a showy performance, setting the tone to the encounter which Willi knew would follow. Peeb honked the horn. Willi wiped his hands on a piece of cotton-waste and came out of the workshop into the sunlight. Peeb was wearing an old green cap, and polo-necked sweater to match, and leather and cotton driving gloves. Willi went over to the car. Peeb sat quite still. They looked at each other in silence for ten seconds.

'Good afternoon, Group-Captain,' Willi made the greeting formal.

'*Guten tag*,' replied Peeb.

Willi made a small movement of acknowledgement with his head. 'If you wish,' he said. 'Glad to see you're better. Can I do anything for you?'

'I think you've done enough one way and another,' said Peeb. Ignoring the implication Willi said,

'Apart from the panel-beating and other cosmetic jobs, the only replacements being a nearside front spring, tyre and headlight.'

'I noticed,' said Peeb. 'I came to collect the bill, squire.'

'No charge,' said Willi.

'I insist,' replied Peeb.

'What are we going to do, fight for it?'

Peeb got out of the car and took off his gloves.

'I thought we'd done all that fifty years ago.'

'It was an unfinished battle.'

'I shot you down!'

'You shot me. . . .' Willi gave a faint smile, 'in the arse. But you didn't shoot me down.'

'How can you say that? It's in the records, man.'

'The records are wrong. I tried to tell you once, remember?'

Peeb recalled the words of the man in the Three Crowns.

'You ruddy liar. I gave you a burst, my last burst. You flipped over and dived down out of control. . . .'

'I turned over and glided down under full control . . .'

'In flames. . . .'

'Only in your report. . . .'

'And disappeared in the drink. . . .'

'I did a belly-flop, and sank.' Willi pointed towards the causeway and the Swale. 'I was out of petrol. If I hadn't been, the combat might have had a different ending.'

'Meaning. . . .?'

'Well, you were out of ammo presumably, and I wasn't. . . .'

'I still shot you down.'

'No. Without fuel I would have gone down anyway whether you were there or not. With fuel I might well have demolished your Spitfire.'

'My dear fellow. . . .' Peeb was beginning to bluster. 'The "Emils" were no match for the Spits. . . .'

'On the contrary. Of the five I put away. . . .'

'Five?'

'And three Hurricanes.'

'Nonsense. . . .'

'It's in the records. . . .'

'The German records . . .' Peeb shrugged.

'Are quite as accurate as the British.'

The conversation came to a standstill. Then Peeb smiled.

'What a bloody silly thing to be arguing about.'

'I thought so for many years. It was always there with me, you know? A matter of honour as well as a matter of accuracy. Both are important. But I thought it might open old wounds, raise questions. . . .' Willi broke off knowing that the main reason he never made an attempt to publicise the correct version of that little piece of the Battle of Britain was because of Anna. He was always afraid of compromising her. But for a long time he had been sure there would be no repercussions of any sort. 'So I let the matter rest. Until you started to provoke me.'

'Me?' Peeb looked astonished. 'How did I provoke you?'

'You came to live in Bishop's Felix. . . .'

'So?'

'You were in the records too. I was on the point of making myself known to you, to talk over old times when you started to tell that story of how you shot down a Hun in flames in his Messerschmitt. Not once, but night after night in the Three Crowns. It wasn't that it couldn't have happened. But it didn't happen. It wasn't true. And gradually the tale of your superior combat skill, and your superior plane began to irritate me and then infuriate me. When I heard you blasting off about. . . .'

'You kept coming into the pub?'

'Only the once when I spoke to you. I'm not much of a pub-goer. I heard though. Anna heard. The whole damn village heard about Peeb the hero of the RAF.'

Peeb pondered the outburst from Willi. Things suddenly began to appear in a new light.

'I didn't . . . didn't intend to boast like that . . . but, look here! You were flying that plane all over the place long before that. Flying it at my house, flying it at me. . . .'

'I wanted to prove to you that you'd forgotten what ME's were like in 1940 . . . that perhaps your memory of the battle was not so accurate as you thought. I wanted to shake your damned confidence. . . .'

'You . . . you nearly sent me . . . bonkers, do you know that?'

Willi smiled.

'It had occurred to me.'

'I thought I was haunted. You disguised yourself. You . . . you spoke to me at the Air Display didn't you?'

'That was irresistible. So was the Luger. I knew you'd get on target in the end.'

Peeb looked into the pale blue eyes which stared back unflinchingly.

'You're mad,' he said.

Willi shook his head. 'Only in the sense of mad with anger . . . and regret.'

About what?'

'The whole damn war. And how you can never put things right again. You never get over it, you know. I mean those who were right in it, like you and me. The scars never completely heal, do they?'

Willi was thinking of Renate, and Giselle and now Klaus.

Peeb felt his mouth was very dry. Willi suddenly looked smaller, very old, as if the fight had gone out of him. He rubbed the chromium on the Lagonda headlight aimlessly with the piece of cotton-waste.

'Look. . . .' said Peeb. 'If you like . . . if you like I'll write to the Air Ministry . . . the Ministry of Defence, see the Record bods, and confirm your story; your account of the battle, shall I?'

Willi looked up at him.

'Would you?' he said. 'Would you really do that?'

'Yes,' said Peeb. 'If you'll do something for me, in exchange.'

Willi looked suspicious again.

'What's that?'

'Let me fly your ruddy Messerschmitt.'

There were three seconds of searching hesitation in Willi's eyes, in the taught indecision of his body and the sag of his lower lip. Then he started to laugh and the infection spread and a passing car driver observed two old men standing beside the petrol-pumps amid the marshes roaring at each other as if it were the best joke they had ever heard in their lives.

As August neared its end the days were warm and humid. A low mist lay over the marshes and the estuary in the early morning and descended again in the evening. Though the daytime was bright and sunny Willi insisted that flying then, during maximum air-traffic time would inevitably alert the authorities to track down his home-based unofficial airfield. As Peeb well knew the Messerschmitt had always appeared in the twilight and this had proved a successful period for avoiding detection so far.

'You'll have to wait till the weather changes, my friend,' said Willi.

'Absolutely right, old boy,' replied Peeb. 'Can't have anyone stopping the fun just as I'm airborne.'

The word 'fun' unnerved Willi. He half regretted his promise to let Peeb take up the BF 109. He knew enough about the antics in the air the RAF used to get up to and as he came to know Peeb better, if not intimately, he recognised his potential as a daredevil. A piece of that quality was needed to make a figher-ace, and he detected the same element of show-off in the Group Captain, as he did in himself. He was afraid once Peeb was up in the air quite outside anyone's control, he might try tricks and games which could lead to disaster. Both wearing their white overalls, they stood outside the large barn.

'Remember Peeb,' warned Willi, 'you haven't flown at all for over thirty years, let alone a Messerschmitt.'

'No problem. You'll see. Once I'm off the runway. . . .'

'There isn't a runaway. Look, just a field. On a farm.'

'Piece of cake,' said Peeb. 'I've taken off and landed from places that make this look like a putting-green . . .'

'Not in a Messerschmitt.'

'No,' laughed Peeb. 'In a Spit, naturally.'

'On rough ground the 109 can be a "sonofabitch" as the Yanks say. She's so light, and the undercarriage entirely supports the fuselage so the wheels are much closer together than in a Spitfire or Hurricane. She can hop about like a pea on a drum. She comes off the ground quickly and has a much shorter run than a Spit, but she lurches as badly if not worse. Remember you have to keep your foot on the rudder-bar all the time.'

'Willi . . .' said Peeb putting an arm round the other's shoulder. 'You're talking to a veteran pilot. . . .'

'And you're talking to an aircraft engineer as well as a pilot. All I want to make sure is that with your first solo in the 109 you don't touch a wing tip on the ground and end up in the ditch over there by that dead elm tree.'

'Of course I shan't old boy. Not fond of ditches.'

'Except in the Lagonda.'

'Stop worrying about me.'

'I'm not,' grinned Willi. 'But I am about my Messerschmitt.'

'I'll treat her like a baby, old boy. Circuits and humps. That's all I'll do. Till you give the word. . . .'

'*Gott hilf mich*! sighed Willi.

Two Jaguar aircraft about a hundred yards apart screamed over the barn.

'And don't get in the way of one of those.'

Peeb felt an exquisite shiver of excitement as he watched the jets tear away into the distant blue somewhere beyond the north Kent coast.

'Bloody marvellous,' he said. 'Nato exercise.'

'They need it,' said Willi. 'Much much more exercise. And bloody quick too. Now come on, Group Captain. Let's go through your static cockpit drill. You have to get things absolutely right, you know.'

'*Jawohl, Herr Oberleutnant*,' Peeb saluted, and the two men went inside the Dutch barn.

* * *

The old doctor's house had no distant view of the estuary like Bluff Cottage, but the Georgian symmetry of its windows, its fine old lawn and the ancient cedar tree made it almost a twin of the vicarage with which it shared a common high wall. Earlier in the year, a profusion of Wistaria had tumbled along its near side. Now in the early evening the horizontal sunlight silhouetted the church tower and caught the tops of the Buddleia. Butterflies were still feeding on the purple blossoms, Peacocks and Red Admirals and Painted Ladies.

Susan carried a tray of drinks out to a slatted table through the very English French windows. Anna followed her and they sat down in adjacent chairs. The older woman had a gin and tonic; the younger a Campari soda.

'Willi will be along shortly. He said he just had a final job to do in the garage,' said Anna.

'Don't apologise. Brian is bound to be late. Wednesday's a big surgery – early closing day,' replied Susan. 'Which includes the solicitor's office.'

'How's it going?'

'Slowly. But it's coming along.' Susan added some more soda to her Campari. 'I don't know where Daddy's got to. He assured me he wouldn't be late.'

'Your father's looking marvellous. You must be relieved.'

'I am. It's much easier making him stick to rules now Brian's in the family.'

Anna took a sip at her drink and coughed, then took some deep breaths.

'Your husband was quite right about this climate for me,' she said. 'Since I've been back in Bishop's Felix even for a short time I've been getting some of the old chest symptoms again.'

'You were fine in California?'

'Palm Springs is perfect for me.'

'Willi'll miss his Messerschmitt won't he?'

'I've finally got him to stop flying. It's too dangerous. He's getting far too old for these games.'

'What will you do with the plane?'

'Donate it to a museum – where it. . . .' Anna's voice broke off.

The unmistakable sound of the BF 109 came from the direction of the church. Just as Brian joined them on the terrace the Messerschmitt appeared in the sky above and beyond the tower at about five thousand feet. Suddenly the engine cut out and the plane went into a spin. It spiralled down for about three thousand then the engine came in as the dive was checked. For a brief second the church tower obscured the machine and then with full throttle it roared over the cedar trees and soared upwards in a tight climbing turn before it disappeared southwards towards the marshes. As the sound died away the telephone extension began ringing in the room behind them.

Anna's face was pale with anxiety.

'Obviously I spoke too soon,' she said.

Susan got up.

'Never mind, I'll get it.' Brian went inside and picked up the phone.

'Doctor Bayliss . . . oh yes . . . Good. We'll expect you then in about half an hour. . . . Bye.'

Brian went back to the terrace and mixed himself a large gin and tonic.

Emergency?' asked Susan.

'I hope not.'

'Who was it?'

'Willi. He won't be long now.'

'Willi . . .?' exclaimed Anna. 'Then. . . .?'

Brian put his arm round Susan.

'Not to worry, darling', he said, 'obviously from that performance Peeb knows exactly what he's doing.'

Peeb indeed had no difficulty making his landing approach to the home field. The landmarks of the twin barns on the left and the causeway to the Swale beyond the farm on the right were easy markers. He noticed that Willi had put out two lights on the ground just to make sure. Peeb had found the 109 cockpit small compared to his old Spitfire and the thick bars on the hinged hood reduced the visibility he was used to with the sliding roof. But it had been a wonderful experience, flying a plane again. He wished he'd never given up when he came out of the RAF.

Peeb eased back the stick, throttled down and then the wheels were bumping along the field up to the barn. Willi had opened the large side doors and Peeb taxied the plane round and into its hangar. He switched off, climbed out of the cockpit and jumped down off the wing, removing the flying helmet he'd brought with him.

'Thanks, Willi,' he said. 'I've enjoyed that more than anything since our little argument together all those years ago. How you've got it in such perfect shape I shall never know. Congratulations. She's a lovely job.'

'I noticed your demonstration over the village. That wasn't in the bargain,' complained Willi.

'No harm done,' said Peeb.

'I'm not so sure. It's just the sort of thing people complain about.'

Peeb chuckled. 'I spotted the three of our dear ones looking up from the garden. They seemed to care for the old aerobatics.'

'Well, as a precaution I phoned them just to prove it was you and not me. So you'd better get ready to face the music. Come on, we're late.'

With strict reciprocity Peeb let Willi drive the Lagonda. When they came down the High Street Peeb said,

'Pull in at the Three Crowns. We'll just have a quick one to celebrate. Won't take a minute.'

Willi shook his head sadly. But he was enjoying himself enormously and he parked the Lagonda in its usual place.

In the bar Peeb's magnanimity and infectious bonhomie soon drew an appreciative group round them. Unnecessarily he introduced Bill Mitcham the landlord to his companion.

'Bill, want you to meet a very very old chum of mine, Willi Household.'

'We have met,' said Willi.

'Indeed, sir,' replied Bill. 'Marsh Farm isn't it? Wife used to have the antique shop?'

'That's right,' said Willi. 'Don't often get the time to come into the Three Crowns though.'

'But we're going to change all that,' said Peeb. 'Two pints of the best, Bill. . . .' Peeb turned round to the half a dozen young folk in the bar. He recognised two of them. 'Hello, Sal . . . Reg. What's your tipple?' Before they could answer he got back to Mitcham. 'Anyway whatever it is, fill them up, Bill. And their friends. It's all on me.'

'Celebrating something, Group?' asked Bill.

'I certainly am. Tonight for the first time. . . .'

Peeb felt a kick on his shin.

'For the first time, he's taking me to dinner with his daughter and son-in-law,' Willi interrupted and gave Peeb a warning glance. 'Right, Peeb?'

'Right,' agreed Peeb, grinning. 'Just what I was going to say.'

The drinks came across the bar and were suitably distributed. Peeb raised his tankard.

'Cheers, everyone,' he said.

The response was general. Reg nudged close to him.

'Shot any more Huns down, lately Group?' he asked cheekily.

Peeb threw a glance at Willi.

'Me? Shooting down Huns? Whatever gave you that idea?'

'You know,' said Sally. 'Like you told us. In the sky – over here. Years and years ago.'

'My dear little lady,' said Peeb. 'You must be mixing me up with someone else. I was in the Navy. Isn't that right, Bill?' He turned to the landlord and winked.

'Could well be,' replied Mitcham.

Willi faced Sally and Reg.

'Captain Peebles-White', he said seriously, 'may not have shot down a Hun, but I know for a fact, he sank at least two U-boats! Isn't that right, my friend?'

Peeb held Willi's glance a second.

'Bang on!' said Peeb, and then they both laughed in the conspiratorial way schoolboys sometimes do.

CHAPTER TWENTY

'Is that you, Susan?' called Peeb from upstairs.

'Yes, Daddy.'

She had called in at Bluff Cottage to see him off.

'Down in a minute.'

Peeb set his black bow-tie straight, put on his dinner-jacket and clipped his medal ribbon-strip to his left breast pocket. Remembering the same occasion of the Squadron Dinner a year ago, Susan refrained from asking if she could help him tie his tie. She still felt a responsibility for her father even though she was now married, and Peeb was back living on his own at Bluff Cottage. He trotted down the stairs beaming at his daughter.

'Kit inspection and final briefing. Sah!' he said.

Peeb sprang to attention and Susan walked round him, picking a small feather off the back of his left shoulder.

'All right, stand easy,' she said. 'You look very nice.'

Peeb winced at the word.

'It's a rather special "do" this year. 50th anniversary and all that. So everything's got to be bang-on!'

'Well don't get too excited. You know you've been ill. . . .'

'I'm in cracking form,' he retorted. 'Brian says so.'

'Well remember . . . only two drinks. . . .'

'Absolutely.'

Peeb put on his light raincoat, wound his silk scarf round his neck and kissed her again. Then he picked up his driving gloves from the hall-stand as the clock chimed five.

'Aren't you going rather early?' asked Susan suspiciously.

'No, I've got to pick up Willi, you see?'

'Willi. . . .?'

'I'm taking him as a guest. It'll create quite a stir, when I tell the chaps I shot him down, and he's officially dead.'

‘Do they know you’re taking a Luftwaffe pilot to an RAF. . . .?’

‘Of course not. That’d spoil the fun. Put them in a bit of a flap I shouldn’t wonder . . . No, they’ll love it.’

‘What does Willi say?’

‘Can’t wait. Tickled pink. You know he’s an awfully nice chap.’ Peeb opened the front door. ‘Especially for a Hun.’

Susan laughed at the indelible prejudices.

‘You’d better not make remarks like that in front of Anna. Goodbye, Daddy. And do be careful,’ she said, and watched him go to the garage, back out the Lagonda and with a celebration burst from the exhaust, tear away down to the village.

Peeb stopped outside Marsh Farm, switched off and sounded the horn. It was still warm for early September, and the mist had not yet materialised. The colour of the water down the estuary was beautiful – a mixture of Rose Madder and Cobalt. There was very little breeze. Along the marshes past the old salt-workings at the eastern tip of the island, he could just see near the horizon the tiny sails of the straggling competitors in the Margate regatta. He sounded the horn again. A bedroom window shot up and Willi leaned out.

‘Sorry to hold things up,’ he shouted. ‘Be with you in one minute, Group Captain.’

‘That’s OK, *Oberleutnant*,’ Peeb called back. ‘Bags of time.’

But to save a few seconds Peeb turned the Lagonda round and kept the engine ticking over. He heard the front door bang. Through the open car-door window he watched the figure striding towards him. In spite of the just detectable limp, the carriage was erect, the gait smart and the footfalls percussive. Peeb’s eyes opened wide. Willi came up to the car, clicked his heels and saluted. He bestowed on Peeb a proud smile. In return Peeb’s expression remained blank and incredulous.

‘What. . . . on earth . . . are you wearing?’ Peeb’s voice emerged as a croak.

‘The dress uniform of an *Oberleutnant* of the Luftwaffe, 1940’, Willi smiled proudly.

'My God. . . .' said Peeb.

'Since your invitation, I have had quite some difficulty obtaining it,' laughed Willi. 'In the end I found a theatrical costumiers in Covent Garden.' Willi moved his arms and shoulders, and revolved for Peeb's inspection. 'Not a bad fit, yes?'

Peeb observed with fascination the grey-blue leather-belted tunic, the breeches and the shining-black knee-length boots. On the peaked cap and above the right breast were repeated the Luftwaffe eagle and Swastika. On the hat-band the oak-wreath and wing were woven in silver wire. Above the left breast was the fighter-pilot's mission clasp in gold. Willi pointed to it.

'This is known as a *Frontflugspange*,' he explained with satisfaction. 'Awarded after a hundred and ten missions over the front. And here are the medals – "gongs" as you call them.' With an immaculate white-gloved hand Willi touched first the Iron Cross on his left breast pocket, and then at his throat the red white and blue ribbon with the distinguished Knight's Cross of the Iron Cross with Oak Leaves. 'It is a pity I could not obtain a cuff band with the honour title of my old unit,' he apologised.

'What . . . what was that?' asked Peeb, totally bemused.

'I told you, remember? *Jadgeschwader Schlageter*,' said Willi. 'The insignia is on the side of the Messerschmitt fuselage – a white crest with a black "S" in it. You must have noticed that.'

Willi walked round the front of the Lagonda and opened the nearside door. Peeb switched off the engine and got out. The two men faced each other across the shining maroon bonnet of the car.

'What is the matter?' asked Willi. 'Are you out of petrol? We will push it to the pump. I have the key. . . .'

'Willi. . . .', said Peeb. His face was flushed, but his voice had regained its normal strength.

'Yes. . . .?'

'You'll have to go and take all that gear off.'

'Gear . . .?'

'Uniform . . . clothes . . . all that Luftwaffe stuff . . .'

'Why . . .?' asked Willi, genuinely astonished. 'What is wrong with it?'

'Nothing, nothing. . . .' said Peeb. 'But go and put on a dinner-jacket.'

'What for?' asked Willi sharply.

'Because you can't wear it . . . it's . . .' Peeb dried up as he realised how impossible it was going to be not to offend Willi.

'It's an official formal dinner, is it not? You said. . . .'

'I know,' said Peeb. 'But. . . .'

'Then it must be *korrekt* to wear official uniform.'

'Not at an RAF dinner. Not in our group anyway. . . .'

'Why should anyone object?'

'Object?' Peeb laughed. 'Look, old boy, when the chaps see that, they'll have your bags off – breeches, boots, everything – in no time at all. . . .'

'But I am your guest. . . .'

'Exactly. And I shall end up in the nearest spot of water too,' said Peeb. 'I'm sorry, Willi. You'll have to change into the right togs.'

'And what are those?'

Peeb opened his raincoat.

'DJ. Black tie.'

'DJ'

'Dinner-jacket.'

Willi's mouth set hard, and he controlled his deepened breathing.

'Why did you not tell me about the dinner-jacket?'

'It just didn't occur to me, old boy.' Peeb looked at his watch. 'Christ it's getting late. Now press on and pop into the old DJ, there's a good chap. You can still wear your "gongs" of course.'

Willi seemed to be seething with rage.

'I haven't got a DJ,' he snapped.

'Oh. . . .' said Peeb. 'That *is* a bit awkward. Still, can't be helped. A lounge suit will have to do. Not to worry. Now come on. Scramble! I'll make appropriate excuses for you.'

'Excuses. . . .' shouted Willi. 'Group Captain Peebles-White. I do not need to have any excuses made for me. As a German officer. . . .'

'You're *not* a German officer now. . . .'

'Very well. As a British subject. . . .'

'That's better. . . .'

'Who *was* a German officer,' continued Willi obsessionally. 'And who fought in the Battle of Britain. . . .'

'Who's arguing?'

'As much as you did. . . .'

'I know all that Willi,' said Peeb with exasperation. 'Why do you think I'm taking you to the "do"?'

'As your friend who is also an ex-officer of the Luftwaffe. Therefore why am I not entitled to wear the dress-uniform of an ex-officer of the Luftwaffe?'

'Because it's an RAF dinner and not a dinner for the Luftwaffe. . . .!'

'To which the RAF feels superior.'

Peeb's patience snapped.

'Well, we won the ruddy Battle, didn't we?'

'Only because of a strategic error by Goering. If we had continued to attack and destroy your airfields, instead of switching to London. . . .'

'That old myth,' Peeb snorted. 'You'll be telling me next the BF 109's were better planes than the Spits.'

'Of course they were!' shouted Willi.

'Balls!' responded Peeb.

'And what is more, we in the Luftwaffe had far superior fighting skill to the RAF.'

Peeb jumped into the driving seat of the Lagonda. 'What do you want to do? Fight it all over again? Why the ruddy hell do you think we shot you all down?'

'You did not. At least not you, Group Captain.'

'I thought we'd settled all that,' said Peeb. 'And I resent your bringing it up. I'm getting the records changed.'

Peeb switched on the engine. Willi gripped the other door, holding it open.

'Where do you think you're going?'

'To my squadron dinner, of course.'

'Without me?'

'Yes, unless you change your clothes. Now stop all this poppycock, Willi. I'll give you five minutes. And for God's sake when we get there don't start spouting all that rot about the Luftwaffe being superior . . . For Christ's sake hurry up, will you?'

Willi became icily calm.

'If I come to the dinner,' he said. 'I come with honour as an ex-German officer. And I come dressed as a German officer.'

'Then the deal's off,' said Peeb. 'Let's forget the whole thing!'

'*Sheisse*!' blazed Willi. 'It is right! It has always been right. It always will be right. England cannot be trusted. She will always break her word. And if ever the Russians invade Germany, we shall not be able to rely on the English.'

'Don't be such a silly bugger. . . .' said Peeb.

'You will regret that remark, my friend . . .'

'Why?'

'Because we are friends no longer.'

'Suit yourself,' said Peeb. 'Perhaps it's better that way. Now shut the door and shove off.'

Willi slammed the door and the car jerked forwards.

'Perhaps,' shouted Willi. 'Germany and England are always better enemies than friends.'

'Up the Fourth Reich!,' flung back Peeb making a sign with his fingers.

As he shot along the road past the garage, Peeb watched the erect uniformed figure in the driving-mirror growing slowly smaller.

'Stupid bloody Hun!' muttered Peeb as he gunned the car savagely past the old asylum building. He said it again as he turned onto the motorway, and once more when he crossed Lambeth Bridge and roared up Millbank. Finally he mouthed the vulgar phrase as he parked in St James's Square where the dinner was being held. But by then he added, 'Stupid bloody childish argument.'

As always, he listened with slight embarrassment to the official announcement of his arrival 'Group Captain Michael Peebles-White, DFC and Bar, number 0-six-three squadron'. The cheers rose up and the cries of 'Good old Peeb' came from the bar at the other end of the room. As he raised his arm in acknowledgement he realised he was relieved not to have the much greater embarrassment of introducing Willi. By the end of the first gin and tonic, he was convinced inviting Willi had been a bloody silly idea anyway.

Peeb did not set eyes on Willi again until the Memorial Dinner at the Savoy on September 14th. The surviving Luftwaffe pilots of the battle were guests at the other end of the top table. Peeb noticed Willi had found a dinner jacket for this occasion. Their eyes met for one brief second and then flicked away. Neither seemed to seek any further contact. The battle was over, finished, settled, and in its place, out of place there seemed an enmity, never to be resolved now.

The speeches droned on and perhaps Peeb and Willi were the only two present who were sunk in apathy at the secrets they shared, amongst the otherwise convivial atmosphere exhibited by all the others present.

The final speech, as it drew to its conclusion failed to raise their spirits.

'. . . . and so I come, ladies and gentlemen, to the end of my speech. We are not here tonight just to commemorate the fiftieth anniversary of the Battle of Britain in 1940, but something more important; the beginning of a free Democratic Europe. No curtains. No walls. Just an open carpet.

'Fifty years ago all the countries from France in the West to Russia in the East were enslaved and living under cruel tyrannies. Hitler and Stalin had seen to that.

'Except for the 'Few' in the skies above our island, we too – indeed the whole world – yes including the mighty United States of America which, if we had failed, would have suffered their Pearl Harbour at the hands of the Japanese in December 1940 instead of 1941. A new Dark Age would have begun and could have lasted a hundred or more years, long past this September 1990.

'Instead, the dawn of freedom and democracy has risen dramatically on our planet, so that we can all look forward to the high noon of universal concord. I salute again not only the

British 'Few' who are here, but also the remaining German airmen who are now our guests.

'I ask you to raise your glasses therefore in a toast for mankind; not in Neville Chamberlain's words 'Peace in our Time' but 'Peace for all time.'

The guests rose and raised their glasses, and to all intents and purposes the celebration was over. Shortly afterwards, Willi and Peeb left separately and returned to their homes. Instead of feelings of triumph and friendship and hope, they both went to bed saddened disillusioned men.

At eleven o'clock on Saturday September 15th 1990 Susan came out of her office in the High Street and locked it behind her. In her hand was a manilla brief-sized envelope and a white foolscap envelope. Brian was at the wheel of his parked new Peugeot. He opened the nearside door and she got in.

'Thanks, darling, for picking me up.'

'Super day for it all,' said Brian.

'I have to drop these into the postbox on our way.'

'Important?'

'Naturally,' she said. 'This is my formal acceptance of appointment to the Bishop's Felix Parish Council, and in here,' she indicated the buff envelope, 'are the Deeds of Marsh Farm including the garage, for Anna to sign.'

Brian stopped the car by the Post Office near the church. Susan disposed of the letters. Brian got out and climbed into a rear seat.

'You drive.'

'You needn't do that. . . .' Susan said.

'Easier for Peeb,' said Brian. 'He'll prefer to be in front with you. It's his special outing.'

'I'm surprised he's not taking the Lagonda. He always does for an Air Show.'

Susan chose the left fork past the War Memorial and drove up Barrow Lane.

'There's a small dent or scratch in the Lagonda bodywork somewhere,' she said. 'That'd spoil Peeb's day if someone noticed it.'

'Your father's an obsessional, you know.'

Susan slowed up as they neared the cottage.

'Ever since the memorial Dinner last night he's been very withdrawn and subdued.'

'Know the reason?'

'He hasn't told me. Anyway our veteran pilots haven't seen each other for some time.'

Peeb was waiting at the gate when they reached Bluff Cottage. Brian and Susan stared at him. Peeb was wearing white overalls which just showed where the top buttons were open reveres of his faded RAF tunic into which was tucked an old polka-dot silk scarf. He had on his old fleece-lined Irvin jacket. In one hand he carried a leather flying-helmet with ear-phones and dangling mike connecting leads. In the other were a pair of goggles.

'Come on you two,' he greeted them. 'Must get a good place in the car park.'

Susan opened the front door and Peeb got in.

'Daddy! What *is* all this?'

'Well. . . .' he said, his eyes smiling brightly. 'Never know. They might need a replacement at the last minute. And I'd be ready. Couldn't hold the flight up.'

Susan gave a wide-eyed stare at Brian in the back. He raised his eyebrows at her. Peeb caught the glances.

'Never mind what I look like. Keep your eyes on the ruddy road and get a move on. Morning, Brian.'

'Morning, sir,' said Brian tactfully.

They drove in silence for a mile or two. Peeb's humour seemed to improve. He took some deep breaths.

'Marvellous visibility,' he said craning his neck and looking up through the windscreen. 'If they're flying over twenty-thousand, there'll be vapour trails everywhere. Bloody useful vapour-trails. Makes it easier to pick out the ruddy Huns. Do you know?' he chuckled. 'We're going to get a hundred and seventy-five of the bastards today.'

Susan again caught Brian's expression in the driving mirror. There was the faintest contraction between the inner ends of his eyebrows. Then he saw her reflection and relaxed his frown.

'Not today, Daddy,' she said. 'Fifty years ago.'

'Of course,' replied Peeb irritably. 'I know that!' He put his hand up to the scarred area on the left side of his forehead. 'Never forget a thing like that you know.'

They covered the twenty odd miles to Manston in under an hour. Though now only an Emergency Airfield, Manston had been chosen as the main Battle of Britain air display site because of its long runways, and also because it was no longer a Nato base. Susan found a good place for the Peugeot in the second row of cars.

They got out to stretch their legs. Although it was only twelve-thirty they decided to eat Susan's smoked salmon sandwiches and drink Peeb's Veuve Clicquot immediately. Over the tannoy came the strains of the military band playing near the hangars where the static displays of some of the new missiles were housed. The freshness of the air off the sea by the North Foreland only a short distance away combined with the indefinable smell of newly trampled grass completed the setting for the unique spectacle they had come to watch.

Brian was reading one of the programmes they'd bought at the entrance to the airfield.

'Flying events don't start till one twenty-five. There's nearly an hour to fill in,' he said.

'When's the Battle of Britain Memorial Flight?' asked Peeb.

'Two thirty-three. Spitfire, Hurricane and Lancaster Bomber.'

Then I suggest we wander along to the spectator-barrier and look at the Jaguar static,' said Peeb.

'After the Memorial Flight,' Brian continued, 'there's a special flight of three privately-owned Spitfires. Squadron Leader James Arkle, Flight Lieutenant Billy King, and. . . .'

'Here let me see that,' said Peeb snatching the programme. 'Led by Wing Commander Sir Cyril Bunton. . . .' he read. 'Shorty Bunton!' Peeb exclaimed. 'Wasn't at the dinner last night. I didn't know he had a Spit! Fantastic! Good old Shorty. . . .! I've got to see this.'

Peeb forged away across the rough grass of the car park, at a brisk pace. Brian and Susan shrugged and followed him with dutifully large strides. It took Peeb a long while to find what he was looking for.

The three planes were lined up only thirty yards from the far end of the roped barrier, which was guarded from the growing crowds by sparsely separated RAF corporals and one or two civilian policemen. On the main runway, a bowser had finished its job and was moving away downfield. A trolley accumulator moved from engine to engine of the three fighters checking that all engines were behaving correctly. The sound of the old Rolls Royce Merlins bursting into life made Peeb's hair stand up on the back of his neck. After the warm-up, the aircrews one by one came to rest. The pilots climbed out of the cockpits. Peeb exclaimed joyfully.

'There he is. That's Shorty all right.' He cupped his hands and shouted 'Shorty! Shorty you old sod. . . .!'

But his voice was drowned by the jet-scream of a Buccaneer as it rose from the runway beyond. The air display had begun. Peeb ducked under the barrier and immediately a hand of one of the young RAF guards gripped Peeb's arm.

'No spectators allowed beyond the barrier, sir.'

'I'm not a spectator,' said Peeb freeing his arm.

'Daddy . . . where are you going?' Susan's voice came from behind him.

'It's dangerous, sir,' said the uniformed young lad.

'What do you know about danger?' smiled Peeb.

'Not much, but I know my orders,' was the spirited reply and this time he gripped Peeb's arm firmly with both hands.

'Daddy, come back. . . .' said Susan.

'That's right, sir. Pleased go back behind the barrier.'

This time Peeb wrenched himself free from the airman's grasp forcefully.

'Do something, Brian. . . .' pleaded Susan.

'Do you know who I am, Corporal? I'm Group Captain Peebles-White, and I'm just going across to speak to Wing Commander Bunton. . . .'

'Oh. . . .?' said the corporal doubtfully.

'Thank you,' said Peeb. 'And stand to attention when you're speaking to an officer!'

The voice of authority set up its ingrained chain of conditioned reflexes and to his own surprise the corporal came to attention and saluted.

'Yes, sir!'

Peeb saluted back.

'Good lad,' he said, and before the policeman who had been moving ponderously towards the site of the argument reached it, Peeb was halfway to the Spitfires waiting as patiently for their scramble as they had outside a dispersal hut fifty years earlier. The pilots and the 'Erks' or ground crew were even sitting in canvas chairs or lying on the grass as they had done in that summer when England's fate lay nonchalantly in the pale blue sky.

That same sky was now decorated with the smoke trails of the Falcons parachute team as they drifted down in graceful twisted skeins of colour to land on their drop target over to the west. Anxiously Susan and Brian watched Peeb reach the private Spitfires. He embraced one of the pilots and the two men rocked together in a greeting, over-exuberant for the ordinary English encounter, but then clearly this one had everything unusual about it. When the demonstration was over, Peeb took the canvas chair, and what must undoubtedly have been the Wing Commander squatted on the grass beside him as befitted a junior rank. After a moment the two figures looked towards the barrier and Peeb waved. Susan and Brian waved back.

'He'll be happy for a whole year after this,' said Susan.

Brian detected the slight thickness in her voice and took her hand in his.

The tannoy announced in succession the names of the various aircraft – Lightning F3, Hunter F5, Harrier GR3 – as they streaked past the mass of spectators who turned their faces in unison skywards like pink magnetic particles at the passage of a lodestone, when the planes soared through to their cruising heights. There was no break in the pattern of take-offs and landings, as the organisation of the display proceeded with its precise sequences.

The clear unemotional well-spoken voice of the announcer came from the loudspeakers.

'And now ladies and gentlemen, the Battle of Britain Memorial Flight – a Lancaster bomber with its two escorts, a Hurricane and a Spitfire, will take off from the north end of the runway – that is from your right – and will fly past to your left at two hundred feet. As they return the three additional Spitfires of the next item on your programme, ladies and gentlemen, will scramble and then perform a mock attack in formation on the Lancaster and its defenders.'

The crowd craned their heads to the right to get the first view of the old four-engined bomber as it lumbered off the ground. It soon came into view with the Spitfire and Hurricane behind and above it. The crowd gave first a cheer of affection and then continued with applause for the old guardians of freedom.

The Messerschmitt came in from the East at full throttle at a hundred feet.

The crowd ducked instinctively and then looked up to see the black and white German crosses under the wings and glimpse the Swastika on the tail of the BF 109. The applause died away and a collective gasp rose up as the German fighter banked steeply round the control tower and then made for the crowd again from the other end, this time at barely fifty feet. As people started to stampede and throw themselves on the grass, the Klaxon alarms sounded all over the airfield.

'Ladies and gentlemen', came the voice over the tannoy, 'please stay exactly where you are. This is an unscheduled event on our programme, and we shall have it sorted out in a few seconds. There is no danger if you keep quite still. I repeat, no danger at all.'

The voice clicked off and for a second or two there was an unnatural silence. Then the people got to their feet, some laughing with relief, some children crying. Excited talking broke out. The observant would have seen the movement of the ambulances and fire-engines round the perimeter and in front of the car park. The low-flying plane was the subject of amused, heated argument, but older faces wore expressions of doubt and puzzlement.

From the left the slow-flying Lancaster was making its approach, the Spitfire and Hurricane behind it. Suddenly the Messerschmitt was diving at them. It shot between the two fighters and under the Lancaster's tail. It levelled out breathtakingly at virtually zero feet and then climbed up in a tight spiral, and rounded the whole thing off with an Immelmann turn.

Bewildered, it seemed, the Lancaster and escort continued to fly on course but way off beyond the airfield in the direction of Margate.

Whatever he said was never known, what words he used were not recorded, but Susan and Brian saw that the persuasion Peeb employed, succeeded. Wing Commander Bunton seemed to surrender without argument. Perhaps Peeb had just pulled rank and a Wing Commander had merely deferred to a Group Captain, but already Peeb was running to the nearest Spitfire of the three, putting on his helmet and goggles. He climbed up into the cockpit and gave a signal to the 'Erk'. The Merlin fired and roared. The chocks were pulled away. The plane taxied forward and rapidly gathered speed down the runway.

A crisp announcement came from the public address system.

'Ladies and gentlemen. We apologise for an unavoidable break in the display, but in the interests of safety, for the time being, all planes will remain grounded.'

Peeb heard a different voice through his head-set which he had plugged in. He glanced at the flickering dials in the familiar cockpit. He jerked the sliding canopy forward and felt and tail-wheel come off the tarmac. He increased throttle, eased back the stick and the nose tilted up. When he had been airborne five seconds he pumped the undercarriage handle and felt the 'junk' as the wheels came up into their beds under the wings.

'This is control . . . control calling Spitfire Blue Leader. Do you read me?'

'Spitfire Blue Leader. Read you Control. Over,' said Peeb.

'Spitfire Blue Leader. Return to base, land and stay grounded. Over.'

'Like hell, old boy. . . .' replied Peeb.

'Spitfire Blue Leder. Return to base. That's an order.'

'Blue Leader to Control. Request vector on Bandit,' was Peeb's response.

Peeb was climbing now at about five thousand feet and began turning back along the reciprocal. It was all an astonishing exhilarating sensation like swimming in champagne.

'Spitfire Blue Leader,' barked Control. 'Bandit was freak unscheduled flight. Spitfire Blue Leader return to base immediately. Repeat Bandit unscheduled. . . .'

'Balls,' said Peeb. 'Bandit's a ruddy Hun. I know the bastard! And there he is. . . .!' Peeb shouted into his mike 'I've got him. I've got him! Blue Leader to Control, Bandit at Angels ten five eight miles due west. . . . I'm going in. Tally Ho!'

Peeb unplugged his communications lead. He needed no help and wanted no interference now.'

'Spitfire Blue Leader . . . Spitfire Blue Leader. . . .' bleated the voice in the Control Room. 'Come in Spitfire Blue Leader. Over. . . .'

But answer came there none.

The Battle of Britain Memorial Flight was over. The Battle of Bishop's Felix was about to begin.

Willi took the Messerschmitt up to over ten thousand feet banking gently all the time to make a wide circuit over Manston so that he could see what was happening on the airfield. To his gratification he saw one of the three Spitfires take off and start climbing. He was not absolutely certain that the pilot was Peeb, but he could not imagine that it could be anyone else.

Ever since the insults of the night of the Squadron dinner, Willi had felt an implacable rage. It seemed that all that had happened to him in the years after the war, including his rationalisation of the follies of Germany which had preceded it, the realisation of grim menace of the Communist Empire, his new allegiance to Britain which had become his home had been an emotional pact with himself which in the end he had seen as sterile and false. In simple terms, since the row with

Peeb, he had felt a traitor. But the feeling excluded Anna. He saw Anna as the only abiding truth of his life. Anna was no part of his present conflict. He refused to mix Anna up with patriotism, hers or his.

But Willi himself could not escape from his intense sense of honour and pride. Those old-fashioned derided principles finally decided how, in spite of the friendship which for a while had grown up between them, he would respond to Peeb's behaviour. Their relationship now had the antique stuff of which duels are made. It took Willi no time at all to pick up the gauntlet.

Peeb could not possibly miss the air-show. From the Land Rover parked unobtrusively by the vicarage, he saw Brian's new Peugeot swing up the High Street with the doctor and Peeb as passengers. His surmise had been correct. The programme and times of the day's events at Manston was well advertised in the local paper. Willi took off from Marsh Farm and timed his spectacular arrival for the Battle of Britain Memorial Flight with satisfying accuracy. As the Messerschmitt had '*strafed*' the runway and the crowd, Willi remembered all the exhilaration of the power of unopposed aircraft over lines of refugees in Poland and Belgium and France. Willi accepted as a good German that morally the action then was defenceless; as a bad German it was strategically and tactically necessary. Wars were not about morals, even holy wars. Wars were about power, aggression, greed, but ultimately survival. Wars had to be won and lost. Battles had to be fought. Peace was a nice idea, like freedom. And for both, wars were fought. Again and again and again.

Willi saw the old Lancaster bomber and its two fighters returning to the airfield below him. The crowd was a mottled wodge of grey-pink along the whole length of the runway. Well, at least he'd given the 'damned Englanders' a thrill today most of them would remember far longer than the other events in the programme.

It was clear the Spitfire had spotted him and was coming up in a straight climb from the east. Time to have a recce to see if it was Peeb. Willi rolled over and went into a steep dive, the sun behind him. The Spit went through his gunsights at three hundred yards. He kicked the rudder bar and pulled back the stick and came up close behind the tail of the other plane. Then he drew level and looked across at the pilot in the cockpit. It was Peeb all right. Willi raised his hand in salute but Peeb squeezed another few miles per hour out of the Merlin, rolled over, dived, flattened out and came up, up, up to the top of his loop way above the Messerschmitt. Peeb emerged from the blackout of the extra 'G'. He felt a flick of pain across his chest. His pulse was doing a hundred and fifty. God, nothing like that must happen. He switched on his oxygen and felt better in less than a minute.

Peeb looked in his mirror and Willi was still there. He cursed vehemently. If they'd been armed Peeb knew he'd have been a dead duck twice over. But Willi wasn't armed and so the score was going to be added up in different ways. For a couple of moments Peeb's heart missed several beats. He heard Willi's voice 'I have put the guns back. . . . I have put the guns back'. The thought came out of the blue like a cannon shell. Against all probability had Willi after all managed to get some ammo in spite of his denials? His immediate reaction was 'Could Shorty Bunton's eight Browning machine-guns, the muzzles hidden in the wing-edges, be fully operative too?' Peeb put the button on 'Fire' and squeezed it. Nothing. No familiar rattle of the stream of bullets speeding off ahead. 'Oh my God,' he muttered. 'Could Willi actually shoot me down?'

The 109 went down into a screaming dive, disappearing from view in Peeb's mirror. Willi was jinking away heading east and only flattened out at three hundred feet.

Peeb followed Willi down interpreting the evasive manoeuvre correctly. He broke out in a cold sweat. He checked the fuel gauge. A good twenty minutes left. As he came in again right behind the 109 his brain grappled with a simple question. If fifty years ago to the day it was right for him to shoot Willi down, why was it wrong now for Willi to shoot him? It *was* wrong, of course. He knew it perfectly well but he hadn't the time to formulate the argument.

The estuary was in high tide and the Thames and Swale reflected the sun dazzlingly. The two aircraft followed each other over the eastern tip of the Isle of Sheppey, their T-shaped shadows rippling over the reeds and marsh grass. Willi came down to a hundred feet. Peeb thought Willi was going to land at the farm but the two barns flashed below them. Willi banked and turned sharply making for the village. Peeb kept close on his tail.

Though virtually immune to the sight and sound of aircraft in their area the inhabitants of Bishop's Felix, and particularly the vicar and his wife who were showing some old friends round the vicarage garden, looked up as the Messerschmitt and the pursuing Spitfire seared down the High Street skimming the TV aerials. As if it were a display the two fighters banked and climbed to the right and left respectively past the church tower like two swallows on a summer's evening. The manoeuvre had soon separated the planes by half a mile. The respite gave Willi time to decide on his tactics for the battle; for battle for real now, he was convinced it was.

If Willi landed, on his own field or anywhere else, Peeb would have no difficulty skimming over him and later claiming he'd again brought him to earth. Group Captain Peebles-White would then have another certain 'kill' in his flying record. But Oberleutnant von Greifswald had no more intention of suffering total defeat in 1990 than he had in 1940. Perhaps it was still 1940, and all his old comrades were in the sky with him.

Willi saw Peeb closing up again behind him. As they came back over the farm, Willi glimpsed Anna standing in the field and watching them go over. Poor Anna. Poor darling Anna. '*Auf wiedersehen, liebchen*!' Without warning Willi pulled the stick back and went into a steep climbing turn. Peeb overshot, banked and then started to come up after him. To Willi there was never any doubt that he would do so. Willi reached about ten thousand feet, then holding his breath he rolled over and went into a vertical dive.

The Messerschmitt hit the Spitfire in front of the cockpit. There was an immediate explosion and small pieces from each aircraft were flung into the surrounding space like parts of a firework display. Then the two planes, locked in a bundle of flaming metal, snaked down to the earth leaving a black smoke trail with white glycol streamers stretching up above them into the heavens.

Anna did not move. It all happened as if she had watched it in a dream long long ago. The mass of fiery debris fell onto the two barns and the conflagration consumed both of them. After five minutes she could hear the urgent alternate notes of the fire engine approaching from the distance.

CHAPTER TWENTY-ONE

The Reverend John Siddons, vicar of the Parish Church of Bishop's Felix, conducted a combined funeral service for Peeb and Willi five days after the crash. The charred remains of their bodies were interred in two graves side by side in a corner of the churchyard. Because of the mass media coverage of what had been dubbed as the Battle of Bishop's Felix, a massive crowd attended the occasion. Susan, Anna and Brian were the only close relatives. Rodney, old Arthur's son, and his wife came from the farm cottage. The landlord of the Three Crowns, and his wife Muriel were there. Surprisingly two young people arrived on a motor-cycle and remained respectfully silent throughout the service and the burial. As they went to the Honda parked outside the Lych-gate, Susan asked them who they were.

'Just friends of Group's,' the boy said.

'My name's Sal. And he's Reg,' explained the girl, shyly, climbing onto the pillion seat.

'Where did you meet . . .?'

'In the pub,' said Reg.

'Are you his daughter then?' Sally enquired.

Susan nodded. 'It was kind of you to come.'

'You'll miss 'im,' said Sally.

Reg let in the clutch and the motor-cycle split the air around it as it sped away up the High Street. Ex-Flight Lieutenant Pip Arrowsmith and ex-Squadron Leader Dickie Oldfield from the Squadron made discreet condolences to the relatives and then melted away. Wing Commander Shorty Bunton sent his sincere respects but was at pains to let Susan know in a letter that he had the burnt-out Spitfire fully insured.

As the mourners dispersed Anna looked up the now deserted street.

'Will you stay now?' Susan asked Anna.

'Oh no,' she replied. 'I shall go to California as arranged. Sell the farm for me, Susan.'

At a meeting of the Parish Council which Susan regularly attended, it was agreed that what had happened in the village on Battle of Britain day 1990 to two members of the parish was in fact a continuation of what happened during World War II fifty years earlier.

It was accordingly proposed, seconded and carried that a Peebles-White – Greifswald Memorial Fund should be endowed to open up the closed wing of the former asylum to increase the amenities of the Old People of the village. The fund was to be started by a donation from Mrs Susan Bayliss with part of the proceeds of the sale of Bluff Cottage and one from Mrs Anna Household, from the insurance payment on the fire of the barns. It was further agreed that the occasion should be marked by having the names of the two pilots killed in action, so to speak, added appropriately to the list of names on the War Memorial. The engraving was in due course carried out and there was a small unveiling ceremony on Armistice Day 1991. As nearly always on the 11th November it was a damp grey day with sodden horse-chestnut leaves trampled underfoot like used tickets to a forgotten summer.

Anna had flown back from LA once more for the ceremony. Susan of course was present amongst the gathering of about fifty persons. The chairman of the Council drew aside the little curtain which hid the new names on the memorial and the vicar said a prayer and called for two minutes silence. Two lorries which had been held up by the proceedings lumbered past the church.

Anna and Susan stood together looking at the freshly cut letters in the granite of the rectangular memorial.

'They just fill up the space at the bottom,' observed Susan sadly. 'It looks somehow complete now.'

'There's plenty of room round the other three sides,' murmured Anna.

EPILOGUE

The following names appear on the War Memorial in the village of Bishop's Felix on the Isle of Sheppey in the County of Kent, England.

THE GREAT WAR
1914–1918

T.B. Adams
R.B. Agnew
R.C. Barber
J.S. Barber
Carter
E. Collis
M. Davies
P. Elson
O.J. Faulkner
T.F. Gibbons
R.S. Henley
E.J. Juggins
A. Kenlock
F. Kenlock
P. Kenlock
W.R. Monk
R. Nordon
G. Nordyke
B.K. Nicholls
F. O'Brien
J.G. Pasmore
D. Paxton
J. Rattray
P. Rattray
M. Stevens
B. Taylor
F. Taylor
W. Wickers
J. Williams
J.A. Young

WORLD WAR II
1939–1945

P. Agnew
L. Anstey
J. Cox
J. Douglas
P. Juggins
T. Kenlock
F. Osborn
W.S. Potter
F.J. Wickers

1989–1990

W. Household
M. Peebles-White